I0757258

A
FUTURE
AND A *HOPE*

ENDORSEMENTS

Caroline Powers is a wonderful storyteller. Her captivating characters pulled me in right from the start. I didn't want to stop reading.

—Anneliese Dalaba, author, *The Arranged Marriage Series*, Historical Christian Romances

This story is compelling and filled with healing for those who have suffered losses. Woven artfully into the romance is the redemptive message of forgiveness and reliance upon God. It is my pleasure to recommend *A Future and a Hope* by Caroline Powers.

—Diane Virginia (Cunio), author of the Selah Award finalist, *The Kiss of Peace: A Contemporary Exploration into Song of Solomon*, Executive Director/Founder of Song of Solomon Expeditions

Caroline Powers' book, *A Future and a Hope,* is an inspirational read. Larkyn and Gabe navigate the chilling waters of acute loss and disappointment to find that beyond the pain there is a future. If you've ever walked the road of grief and would like to find encouragement and truth within the pages of a great story, I recommend this book. Add a sprinkle of mystery and a dash of romance and you have an entertaining read. I particularly love the spunky, humorous writing gift of this author and the way she paints a picture and draws me into each scene with her descriptive writing. I look forward to reading many more books from this author.

—Blossom Turner, author of the award-winning *Shenandoah Brides Series* and *Anna's Secret.*

A FUTURE AND A *HOPE*

CAROLINE POWERS

A Christian Company
ElkLakePublishingInc.com

COPYRIGHT NOTICE

A Future and a Hope

First edition. Copyright © 2022 by Caroline Powers. The information contained in this book is the intellectual property of Caroline Powers and is governed by United States and International copyright laws. All rights reserved. No part of this publication, either text or image, may be used for any purpose other than personal use. Therefore, reproduction, modification, storage in a retrieval system, or retransmission, in any form or by any means, electronic, mechanical, or otherwise, for reasons other than personal use, except for brief quotations for reviews or articles and promotions, is strictly prohibited without prior written permission by the publisher.

This is a work of fiction. Names, characters, businesses, places, events, locales, and incidents are either the products of the author's imagination or used in a fictitious manner. Any resemblance to actual persons, living or dead, or actual events is purely coincidental.

Scripture taken from THE HOLY BIBLE, NEW INTERNATIONAL VERSION ® (NIV). Copyright© 1973, 1978, 1984, 2011 by Biblica, Inc.™. Used by permission of Zondervan

Cover and Interior Design: Lana Ziegler, Dorinda Babcock, Deb Haggerty

Editor(s): Cristel Phelps, Deb Haggerty

PUBLISHED BY: Elk Lake Publishing, Inc., 35 Dogwood Drive, Plymouth, MA 02360, 2023

Library Cataloging Data

Names: Powers, Caroline (Caroline Powers)

A Future and a Hope / Caroline, Powers

362 p. 23cm × 15cm (9in × 6 in.)

ISBN-13: 978-1-64949-792-5 (paperback) | 978-1-64949-793-2 (trade hardcover) | 978-1-64949-794-9 (trade paperback) | 978-1-64949-795-6 (e-book)

Key Words: Christian romance books; Christian romance books for women; Christian romance fiction books; Inspirational romance; Christian romance fiction books for women; Christian romance; Christian romance novels for women

Library of Congress Control Number: 2022952423 Fiction

DEDICATION

I dedicate this book to my husband, Dan Powers, whose vision of my writing always exceeded my own, and to Jesus Christ the true author of our future and our hope.

ACKNOWLEDGMENTS

I have found that writers are generous people. The work may be solitary, but being part of a writing community is essential.

My many thanks to the Scribes at ACFW who faithfully critiqued my work, and to Word Weavers International of Winston-Salem, whose embrace brought me to the finish line.

Special thanks to Cristel Phelps of Elk Lake Publishing for her time and encouragement before she saw my manuscript and for making sure the editing process was finished on time.

High praise and thanks to the Holy Spirit of Jesus Christ who gave me joy and practical help at every step.

For I know the plans I have for you," declares the Lord,
"plans to prosper you and not to harm you, plans to give
you a hope and a future." Jeremiah 29:11

CHAPTER ONE

Seven-hundred and fifty-two days, but what was the point of counting? Larkyn Wagner merged with the afternoon surge of traffic leaving downtown Raleigh. She could ignore her exit. Drive until she reached the Atlantic Ocean.

Like a motorized Forrest Gump, she would come to the end of the highway and face the vast expanse of water. A barefoot tromp across the beach would take her to firm, wet sand.

What if she fought beyond the breakers to reach the neck-deep swells? If she dared to leave the bottom, her head would go under. Her hair would float in a fan, suspended, until the ocean took her.

A sleek speeding sedan cut in, forcing her to hit the brakes and a zing to shoot through her belly. *Yikes*. She might die right here in the car if she didn't pay attention.

Her morbid fantasy dissolved as duty geared up. She was a bridesmaid now and had a job to do. Not to mention that such thoughts were wrong, and she'd never have the nerve.

Larkyn eased right into the slower lane and aimed for the looping exit. Her best friend, Sara Kelly, had been her loyal supporter through the week of Matthew's coma, his funeral, and for the past two years—and twenty-two days.

Her little Jeep Patriot hunkered down and held its line as Larkyn hugged the boundary stripe. It was already five-thirty but only two blocks to go. The mall had been a dumb idea. Completely wrong for something Sara would like. Now, with forty-eight hours left to produce the perfect gift, she came face to face with the reason behind her procrastination.

Jealousy. Of Sara's new life with Cisco.

Her shoulders slumped. The first time Sara needed something from her, she could only think of herself.

Vi's varicolored sign stood out in the quaint row of run-down storefronts. Steps toward gentrification stood out in fresh paint and new awnings. Hopefully, most of the shops would make it, especially the Tea Boutique. But never mind the tea. Vi's Antiques invited the discriminating shopper to explore the crafts, gifts, and certain-to-become heirlooms within.

Larkyn parked under a tree and stepped into the mid-September heat. Surely among Vi's treasures, she'd find the perfect gift for a bride who leaned toward the quirky and eclectic—along with superfoods, sustainable energy, and organic cotton underwear.

The door creaked as Larkyn pushed in and set off a tinkling bell. Her entrance loosed a flurry of dust motes into air scented with furniture polish and lavender. Venturing deeper into the hush, she passed by a kitty the size of a sumo wrestler who slept undisturbed by her presence.

"My stars." A white-haired matron appeared from behind a dresser patting her flat bosom with her wrinkled hand. "I didn't hear the bell. I'm Vi. How can I help you, dearie?"

Larkyn smiled at the proprietress whose vintage dress came straight from *Driving Miss Daisy*. "I need to buy an engagement present for a special friend. Her party's Saturday. I wanted to find something unique."

"Something befitting the nature of your deep friendship." She nodded as if Larkyn's mind were an open book to her discerning watery-blue eyes. "How about a picture frame? It's a timeless gift made only more valuable by the photograph inside."

Yes, what a great idea, since photographs were Larkyn's thing. Thank goodness she had dozens because pictures were all she had left of her marriage and the love of her life.

She picked up an elegant silver frame encrusted with tiny seed pearls. Heavy. Practically a piece of art.

Fruitless hours spent shopping at the mall made the decision easy. With a smile of relief, Larkyn handed the frame to Vi. Now Sara could start a collection of her own.

"This one is perfect. Can you wrap it for me?"

Miss Daisy nodded her approval and led the way up front where she used her bony arthritic fingers to pad the frame until nothing short of a drop from space could cause damage. She wrapped the box and topped it with a lacy silver bow.

Larkyn left the shop with a lighter step. The weight of the package in her hands lifted the burden of this mission from her shoulders. Skirting the cracks in the buckled sidewalk caused by the roots of an ancient sweetgum tree, she reached her car. Sara's engagement shouldn't have hit her so hard. Just because Matthew died didn't mean her friends couldn't be happy even if their marriage left her dangling like an extra buttonhole.

With the window lowered, the breeze lifted her hair from her shoulders. The freeway with its rush hour snarls would take forever. Instead, she cruised a back road where rambling fences bordered fields dotted with modest country homes.

A glance in her rearview mirror revealed the chrome of a monstrous grill. When the aggressive driver didn't back off, she tightened her grip on the steering wheel. Why didn't he go around?

Larkyn waited for a way to escape. Looking more backward than forward, she took a sharp turn at the first available corner. Go, Mr. Bully, move on.

Returning her eyes to the road in front of her, she jerked. A man on a bike filled her view. She stabbed the brake with a shriek. The Jeep swerved and came to rest in a shuddering skid. Her stomach curled.

Open, open—she yanked at the door. No, no, no. She hadn't done this. Her heart thudded as she lurched from the car. Her flats dug into the gravel.

"I'm sorry." She rushed toward the man on the ground. "Are you okay? Did I hit you?"

The rider in Lycra biking gear struggled to his elbows and managed to sit up. His arm was bleeding, but the bike appeared to be undamaged as he pushed it off his body.

Larkyn dropped to her knees. Her breath caught. An artificial leg? She'd run down an amputee?

The man removed his helmet to reveal sweaty, closely cropped hair and ran his shaking hand along the top of his head. His eyes narrowed.

"What was that? Oh, let me guess. You were on your phone."

Tears that came so easily to Larkyn welled up. "No; not at all. That truck kept tailgating me." A weak gesture over her shoulder proved useless. Naturally, the truck was long gone. "I was looking back. I never saw you until ..." She moaned. "Oh, this is terrible. I can't believe I did this."

"Well, take heart." He patted his different body parts and frowned at the scrape on his forearm. "I appear to be in one piece, such as it is."

She watched the cyclist maneuver himself awkwardly into position on his knees. The tight fit of his synthetic riding shirt revealed the muscular definition of someone familiar with the weight room. Okay, he was hardly feeble, but a metal rod emerged from his shorts to form a joint at the knee, then extended into his shoe. His expression, stiff with the stress of being run down, couldn't hide his striking features.

Whoa.

"Well, here goes nothing." He grimaced.

Larkyn cringed and placed her hand over her quivering heart as he used his handlebars for balance. From a humble position on both knees, he rose to a half-kneel and slowly stood. She wanted to cheer. She wanted to weep. But nothing made it past the knot of guilt in her throat.

He bent over to right the bike and flinched.

What was wrong with her? "Wait. Let me help."

"Just get it up here where I can lift it the rest of the way."

The bike felt amazingly light. It had the same TREK logo as Matthew's. His clothing too—like Matthew's gear. How totally bizarre.

"Thank you." Her heart squeezed at his simple words.

When she dared to look into his warm brown eyes, her knees went weak. Trance-like, she observed the rider's slight limp as he walked his bike to the curb.

"Hey, I'm fine. Honestly. Just shook me up a little bit there." The corners of his mouth pulled upward with a trace of humor. "No tire marks, see?"

Larkyn shook her head. "Are you sure you're all right? I'm sorry. I can't tell you how much."

"Well, I forgive you, okay? You can move on with your life." He straddled the bike and hunted for the pedal with his normal foot. "I'm almost home. I can soak out the soreness in the tub."

"A hit-and-run driver killed my husband while he was riding his bike." What? She'd spoken that aloud? A gulp of air couldn't stop the flow of words. "I can't believe it. I've hated that person for two years. And now it's me." Like the person who took Matthew's life, she could have killed this man.

"Hey, hey. I'm sorry about what happened to your husband, ma'am. But you missed me. An honest mistake, I'm sure. You can see I'm fine." He hesitated as if he might need to put down his bike to reassure her.

No. He was the victim here, not her. Time to get away now, before she started sobbing. What a spectacle that would be.

Instead, she made a rude about-face and fled to her Jeep. Taking jerky breaths, she turned the keys. Her foot caused the engine to rev. Too loud.

A quick look both ways showed the road was clear. Her tires bit the pavement with a squeal as she pressed the gas and drove away.

CHAPTER TWO

Gabriel DeSantis twisted his torso to examine the golf ball-sized bruise on his hip. A souvenir from his near-miss with one of the nation's reckless drivers.

He'd been plenty ticked at first. As in, why does this woman have a driver's license? But her obvious distress and those luminous blue-green eyes had tempered his outrage. The way she trembled over her almost disastrous lapse cut right through the lecture he could have delivered.

Wouldn't it have been ironic? Soldier survives bomb blast and returns home only to be run down by a distracted driver. Not funny, but hopefully she'd learned a lesson.

He pressed the swollen bump and winced. Never a weakling, never one to slow down for things like stitches, Gabe had been forced by a roadside bomb to become a different man.

His cousin leaned through the door to his bedroom, shoulder-length, dark hair swinging. Brown eyes like Gabe's own gleamed in anticipation. "Hey, bud. Ya wanna play some HORSE?"

One-on-one basketball? Oh, why not? Wasn't humiliation good for the soul? "Give me a minute."

"See ya outside." His cousin vanished, and a moment later, the back door slammed.

Gabe tugged a faded ARMY T-shirt over his head and tucked it loosely into the elastic waistband of his regulation running shorts with a snort at himself. Flapping shirttails felt slovenly after five years of dressing for Uncle Sam. Years which now meant virtually zip because the Evaluation Board had lied.

Could he return to his unit? No problem. Work hard. No one can stop you but yourself. And his favorite—the enemy might set you back, but he can't destroy your dream.

Every promise, baloney.

Ironically, the Army's Integrated Disability Evaluation System (IDES) had sealed his fate with their generous offer to let him continue serving his country—in a less physically demanding role. How could he say yes to that? He was an infantry soldier, and soldiers went to combat.

Gabe bounced a little to check the vacuum seal that made his artificial leg feel and function like part of his body. MyoPro, his cousin's employer, had created the military-grade technology he now wore, and helped him to obtain it.

The sound of dribbling on concrete and the jangle of the ball on the backboard warned Gabe his opponent was warming up. He should probably start slow and work out the soreness from his fall, but doubted his cousin would give him the chance.

"Hey, old man. You ready?" His almost-brother grinned as he palmed the ball.

"Who's old? If I remember, your birthday precedes mine."

"Guess it's all in the mileage then." With a short jump, his host let another shot fly. The ball rimmed the basket and flew off.

Gabe lunged on his real leg to snatch the rebound. "Let's talk about that." He bounced the basketball a few times to get the feel again. "You sit behind a desk with your computer screen while I hike all over creation, live in a tent, and get shot at. Only to come home to your abuse?" He bent with a familiar motion, and both legs worked. The ball left his fingertips and arced. Swish. "Ha. I don't think so."

"Okay, you're warmed up. Let's go."

Gabe held his own for a while, but in the end his game stank. Sweat stained his shirt, and his short hair dripped. He thrust the ball at his cousin's mid-section hard enough to sting.

"Yow. Okay. So, you're strong."

Yes, indeed. Nine months of rehab did that.

The winner used his shirttail to wipe his face as they retired to the back step. "Seriously, I'm glad you're here, man."

Gabe let his head sag, forearms resting on his thighs. Feeling plastic instead of flesh had taken some getting used to. "I know I fought you on coming here, but thanks for not giving up. I love this leg. Now all I gotta do is find a new career."

"So glad you came to your senses, little buddy. You'll figure it out."

Gabe ignored the false and demeaning reference to his size and sat up straight. He arched to stretch his back. "God's got a plan, right? I just hope he shows me soon."

"You got any ideas?"

"Next week, I'll be talkin' to the Forestry Service about their fire suppression teams. Firefighter qualifications are coming up. I think I stand a chance if I could train with the group up in Asheville." He shot a glance at Cisco, but his cousin avoided his gaze.

"Or you could go back to school. You've got benefits."

Gabe made a sour face. "Been there. Tried that. I'm not a student." Two years in junior college, completed for his mother, had turned out as he expected. After that, he'd finally followed his childhood dream and joined the war against terror. "I can't imagine a single desk job I'd want for the rest of my life."

"Who said anything about desks or the rest of your life?"

Cisco didn't get how it felt to spend ten months of your life in a hospital. While the folks at Walter Reed had tried to help him find new purpose and direction, he'd been discharged without a mission, a map, or a compass.

"What about a paramedic? That heroic enough for you?"

Gabe deflected the jab. Insults, always insults. Some things never changed—except that Brooklyn's Romeo was getting married. Gabe had met the fiancée, a cute little Irish fireball, red hair and all. Italian and Irish? What a combination.

Apparently, they'd found true love. Enough for Cisco to give up his womanizing ways. Now, they were having a party and Gabe, the best man, was obligated to attend. "Tell me about tomorrow night. What's the proper protocol?"

"Casual, man. Sara has everything under control. She'll probably come around later to set things up."

Gabe could manage casual. Not an extrovert to start with, he'd been out of commission on every front. But with hospitals and active duty in the past, he had a new motto—watch and learn.

CHAPTER THREE

Larkyn pulled to the curb and checked the scene ahead. Cisco's house lit the street like Christmas with every window ablaze.

One last look in the mirror on her sunshade confirmed her lipstick was fresh and her eye makeup hadn't smeared. Who was this woman with her hair done up in a twist? Certainly not the Larkyn she'd seen for the past two years.

From the look of the parking situation, the party was underway. Her plan had been to come early but getting ready had taken longer than expected. Thankfully, her current outfit had come together in basic black. Shiny threads in her tunic top and a long silver chain around her neck reflected her mood to the waiting world. Black for sad and sparkly for Sara's happiness.

Larkyn closed the mirror and gathered her purse and gift from the passenger seat with shaky hands. No more delay. Time to make her social debut as a single.

Through the glass storm door, she spied a crowd of assorted ages and styles of dress—none of whom she knew. Slipping inside unnoticed, she placed her white package on the foyer table alongside some lovely bags erupting with tissue paper. Laughter spilled in the buzz of conversation.

Where was Sara?

The fake ficus tree in the corner offered an excellent place to hide, but instead, she piloted through the bodies to the kitchen. Without her husband at her elbow, a job might help with this solo plunge. *Matthew, why aren't you here?*

Ah. Half of the couple of honor had her hands elbow-deep in the sink.

"Sara. What are you doing here? Go chat with your guests."

Sara turned. Her normally ivory complexion, set off by a cloud of coppery curls, glistened pink. She held an ice pick at a dangerous angle. "We need a lot more ice, but it's all stuck together."

One quick look confirmed—the ice had probably softened just enough to re-freeze in an unusable clump.

"You go. I'll figure it out." Larkyn took the weapon from Sara's hands as if disarming a sleepwalker. "Leave it to me."

"Thank you," Sara gushed. Her leopard-print palazzo pants and black halter top made a daring combination. "I've barely said hello." She paused at the threshold and grimaced. "Can you pour another ginger ale into the dispenser in the dining room?"

"Go," Larkyn nodded with shooing gestures.

Now for the ice. A tentative stab at her target did nothing useful. In a frenzy of chopping, she attacked again and produced a few chips and puncture wounds.

A poke around under the sink yielded trash bags. Perfect. She chased the slippery clump into one and sealed it with a twist tie. A drop to the cement would crack open this ice. Matthew had done it before.

She gathered her bundle into a frigid hug and carried it to the door. Pushing through backward, she stumbled down a step she forgot existed—and collided with sold flesh. Muscular arms kept her upright.

"Whoa, there." Her rescuer released her once her balance had been restored.

"Oops, sorry." She turned, and the stinging cold forced her to drop the ice. The bag struck the concrete, and she shook her arms. The two regarded each other warily as Larkyn took in the unusually short dark hair, tanned complexion, and intense brown eyes.

She pulled her gaze away. Grieving widows didn't stare at gorgeous men. "Excuse me. I need to break this ice up."

"A likely story." His lopsided grin brightened his striking eyes.

Heat set her cheeks on fire. This could not be happening. An entire pint of mint chocolate ice cream had finally put the incident on the road behind her. Relax. The biker survived. Be more careful. Let it go.

What was he doing here?

She uttered the only words her brain could form. "Excuse me." Never mind Sara's ice or Sara's party. She took off on feet with a mind of their own, leaving the bag behind.

In the safety of the foyer, she stopped to breathe and take stock. Running home was not an option. Bridesmaids had responsibilities. Explanations would be expected.

Her friends had been patient with her crazy flashbacks—which had to stop. Now would be a good time.

Gripping her courage by the neck, she slunk back to the empty kitchen and found the chilled liter of ginger ale. With a tight grip on the bottle, she edged between the grazing guests. Orange, lemon, and lime slices floated in something pink. The punch looked delicious. Now it fizzed anew.

Next? She spotted two coolers. One chest held ice-smothered cans, but the second, the one she'd promised to fill, contained only a lonely scoop.

"Coming through."

Larkyn turned as the crowd parted for the person she least wanted to see advancing with her trash bag in his arms. He directed a nod at the ice chest and raised his brows at her.

"Could you open it, please?"

Larkyn blinked. With a mental shake, she complied.

Assorted broken chunks of ice poured from the mouth of the bag. When it had emptied, he winked.

She followed him to the kitchen. "How did you do that?"

"Make ice cubes?" His grin turned unmistakably cocky. "Your drop did some damage, but I found a hammer in the garage."

"How amazing of you." She jutted her jaw. "I suppose I need to thank you."

He offered her the ice pick which she refused. "You needed blunt force—and you're welcome."

"I see you met Gabe." Cisco strolled into the kitchen, an easy grin on his face. His black jeans, white dress shirt rolled to the elbows and unbuttoned pinstriped vest spoke vintage Cisco. Despite dark hair slicked back behind his ears, the family resemblance was clear.

"We've run into each other a couple of times." Gabe lay the ice pick down and extended his hand. "Gabriel DeSantis. Cisco's cousin."

Good manners placed her hand in his, cold from handling ice. Gabriel? Like the angel? Not hardly. Unless angels looked like Bradley Cooper.

His full-on smile soared off the charts. Dangerous with a capital D.

"Can I get you a cup of that punch? You look a bit frazzled."

Frazzled? *Great.* She stifled a cheeky retort. Rudeness wasn't her normal nature and she represented Sara as a bridesmaid now.

"Thank you, I guess I could use some."

Gabe led the way to the dining table where he filled two cups with the fizzy punch and handed her a plastic plate. "I recommend the little sausages here. And I think this green stuff's good."

"You mean the guacamole?" She took the cup and the plate.

"Okay, right. And this?"

"That's Greek olive tapenade."

He passed it by.

Larkyn followed him around the table, avoiding the smoky jalapenos. She added a bite-sized crab cake, crackers for the tapenade, and tiny puff pastries filled with Brie and cherry. How had her friend done all this? When they reached the end of the buffet, Gabe's plate held only the basics.

"Grab us a couple of napkins, will you?" He beelined toward Cisco's saggy, vacant sofa seemingly immune to any awkwardness.

The request demanded a decision. Join this man she barely knew or take her chances with strangers. Put in those terms? No contest. Discarding caution, she made one last addition of a pineapple-mango kabob and picked up the napkins to trail him.

With the skill of a gymnast, the former soldier balanced his plate and held the cup of punch as he lowered himself to the sofa seat. Precision grace. Like his efforts to stand beside the road. On a mechanical leg.

Which leg was it? Pressed khaki slacks and matching loafers hid both. Her admiration strayed to his crisp, blue, oxford cloth shirt with sleeves rolled up like his cousin's.

No, the shirt wasn't the problem. The problem was the exposed, tanned forearms that had caught her stumbling out the door. Arms that felt capable of carrying twice her weight. Attached to broad shoulders, straight and even ... though he didn't come across stiff at all.

Are you kidding, Larkyn? Stop it.

With a settling breath, she gauged the space between them before sitting down. Best to not give the wrong impression. Yet all her careful calculations didn't dispel a fearful thought—that by the choice to join him she'd lost control of her prudent, predictable life.

Gabe had never been good with girls, but the Army covered for that. He'd been quite content to hide behind his uniform and the mission while Cisco sampled the world of the opposite sex. Not that he didn't like women. He liked them fine, but he'd watched good men make crazy decisions and had vowed to keep his head. Even the married guys suffered because their loyalties were split.

Life had changed, however, since those logical days. He'd lost his place in the world he understood, left with nothing but a failed career to stand behind. Yet somehow, here he sat, eating with the classiest woman in the room. Who happened, he now noticed, to wear wedding rings.

Just get through it, buddy. "Tell me your name again?"

She steadied the plate on her knees as if it might leap off of its own accord. Considering her record, however, the possibility loomed.

"It's Larkyn. Larkyn Wagner."

Oh yeah, the unusual name. Sara had mentioned her. A bridesmaid.

"I'm Gabe, in case you don't remember." *Oh, brilliant.* Hadn't he just told her in the kitchen?

"Yes. You're Cisco's cousin, right?"

"That's me." He tried not to groan aloud.

In the blessed silence that followed, he seized a basic carrot stick and discretely watched her decide which fancy hors d'oeuvre to tackle first—and how. He had to give her credit, though, as she bit into some flaky thing without spilling crumbs or the oozing filling.

"Do you work at MyoPro too?" He made another dazzling attempt at conversation.

She shook her head and swallowed behind her napkin. "I work for a law firm. Accountant." She took a sip of punch. "My husband did, though. That's how I met Cisco and Sara. They worked together in the simulation lab. Cisco and Matthew, not Sara."

Right. Another computer geek. The light went on. "I believe you said he was killed on his bike?"

Silence. Judging by the panicked look in her eyes, he'd just dumped the contents of his own plate, metaphorically speaking.

Her posture collapsed. "I guess I did mention my husband's death. I'm sorry, I don't know why I brought that up."

"You mean after you almost ran me down? Before you ran away?"

The words were out, and he grimaced. If he'd spilled his plate before, now he'd thrown it at the wall.

"As you well know," she glared. "I did not leave the scene. I stopped. And when I saw that you were okay, I left."

"Yes, ma'am." He rushed to backpedal, offering his palms in surrender. "You're right. You absolutely stopped. I only meant you left rather ... abruptly."

The fire in her eyes subsided. Luckily, she didn't have that ice pick. He dared to smile, but her scowl didn't crack.

Taking a risk, he opened his mouth again. How could this get any worse? "I imagine you mentioned it because of the whole situation." Blank expression. "So, uh, my bike and I made you think about what happened to your husband. Naturally." *Keep digging, Gabe.* "But, ah, fortunately, I was fine. I'm fine now. And so are you, I hope."

Sometime during his ridiculous analysis, she'd loosened her grip on the plastic cup. Gabe's breaths came easier as the lines in her forehead smoothed out.

"You're right about the connection to my husband's wreck. I spent the rest of the night trying to forget what happened." She shuddered. "When I realized you were here, all I could think was, get away."

"Which you did." Couldn't she see the humor?

The hint of a smile gave him hope there was more than sadness inside her. The spark went out again.

"My husband died because the driver who hit him *didn't* stop. He's never been caught. That was two years ago. I know I should be moving on."

Her voice trailed off, and Gabe suspected she was far from "moving on."

As if to affirm his observation, she explained. "We were married five years. And I can see the day coming when he'll have been gone longer than our time together." He barely caught her next words. "I don't think I can handle that."

What could he say? A burst of laughter reminded him of the party going on, but he couldn't ignore this woman's pain.

"I lost someone too," he blurted.

The worry lines came back as she lifted her head. "You did?"

"Josh. My best friend." *Oh, boy*. Nothing to do but keep going. "We met in our advanced infantry training group and were assigned to the same Company. We deployed together twice and served in the same squad."

"I guess that made you very close. I've heard that happens in war."

"Oh, yeah." People had no idea. "Closer than brothers sometimes."

"Do you have a brother?"

He answered easily. "Not by blood. Cisco's my cousin but our families lived together for a while." After Leo, his father, deserted the family to pursue his love of gambling. Too much information? Yes.

"How did Josh die?" He almost missed her whisper.

Gabe cleared his throat. "A roadside bomb. The same one that took my leg. Josh didn't make it."

"I'm sorry." Her fingers twisted the rings on her left hand. "I know sorry's not enough."

He shifted in his seat and stared at the crackers left on his plate. "I've learned 'what ifs' are poison. Since you can't go back, you might as well go forward."

"I'm sure you're right." She left the rings alone to pick up her cup of punch. "I get obsessed with what might've happened if Matthew had arrived at the hospital sooner." Her narrow shoulders barely lifted, as if she wished she could stop such thoughts.

Gabe nodded. Timing meant everything. "Believe me, I understand."

"Hey, you two," Cisco plopped between them, jarring the cushions, and jostling the lady's drink.

"Watch it. You're making Larkyn spill her punch." Her name on his lips felt presumptuous. As if he knew her. Maybe, in a way, he did. Either way, the words were out and he couldn't take them back.

"Oops." Cisco leaned back, making himself comfortable. "Mind if I sit for a spell? You enjoyin' yourself, Larkyn? My cousin isn't known for his charm."

Gabe frowned. What an oaf. What was she supposed to say? But the lady didn't hesitate.

"He's perfectly fine. We were just discussing Josh and Matthew. How are your other guests doing?"

Cisco looked from one to the other wagging his head at their pathetic condition. "I hope they're having more fun than you guys."

"Get up from there, Cisco." Sara advanced upon them. "I need you in the kitchen." She pulled him by the wrist.

"Saved." Gabe sighed. "My cousin can be a real boob if you haven't noticed."

Cisco looked over his shoulder as Sara led him away. His lips parted.

"Don't answer," his fiancée commanded.

Larkyn giggled and Gabe drank in the sound. Her unusual eye color struck him again, as if they couldn't decide to be blue or green.

"Sara has a way with him, don't you think?" Her light tone brightened the room.

He leaned back and enjoyed the moment, hoping her peace would last.

CHAPTER FOUR

The sound always reached Gabe first. Tramp, tramp, tramp. Dozens of boots on gritty sand. The familiar weight of his rifle rested secure, cradled across his chest. A convoy of armored vehicles, their huge treads powdered white with the desert rolled by, gaining on their column yard by yard.

He flinched as pain struck his eye and blinded him with tears. Probably, a grain of sand suspended in the ever-present breezes. Or a cinder from one of the village's cook fires. He stepped aside and blinked to dislodge the speck that felt like a rock.

A concussion wave flung him to the ground. Bursts of automatic weapons fire punched the air and exploded like a jackhammer inside his skull. Silence. His scrambled senses roared back online. Rough hands dragged him. Choking dust. Muffled shouts faded, then blasted his ears.

"Chopper's coming. Hang on, buddy."

Fire tore through his knee as rough hands dragged his body and hoisted him off the ground. His throat burned. He cried out but produced no sound.

Thrashing, gasping, he clawed at the twisted sheets. Josh? Where was Josh?

Gabe forced deep breaths to slow his heart. Shapes emerged from the darkness. A chair, his duffel. Luminous green hands on his travel clock pointed to four and five.

Precise, short jerks brought the second hand past the top of the minute. He rubbed his face with both hands, up over his head, and closed his eyes. Then prayed.

He'd gone weeks without a nightmare.

Gabe punched up his pillow, tucking it under his jaw. Just two more hours—please. His mind had latched onto remembered events that had to play out to the end.

The surgeon's face hovered with questions. No sense of passing time. Then, evacuation on a stretcher. Placed with other injured troops on a flight to Landstuhl, Germany, in the belly of a C-17.

During weeks of recuperation, he accepted the loss of his leg but not what he'd done to his friend. Josh tripped the bomb and died because Gabe left his place in line. End of story.

Enough wallowing in the past. Gabe flipped the sheet off and rotated on his butt. After pulling his T-shirt over his head, he stretched for his crutches and maneuvered upright. He made it to the kitchen without causing a disturbance, but when he hit the light switch and turned the faucet on, a voice came from behind.

"What's goin' on?"

Gabe finished filling the glass and drained it, then set it on the counter. He used his crutches to turn around. "Nothing. I'm fine."

"Huh." Cisco gave him a skeptical grunt.

"I had a bad dream, okay?"

"Ya wanna talk?"

"At four-thirty? Go back to bed." Gabe started toward the door, heading there himself.

"I can't sleep with you prowling."

"I'm not prowling. I got a glass of water, man."

"I see." Cisco blocked his passage from the kitchen.

Gabe sighed and sank onto one of the hard wooden chairs around the table. "I still have dreams about the explosion. Sometimes I can't get back to sleep."

Cisco stood looking down at him, both dressed in boxers and T-shirts. "Tell me about it. The parts that keep you awake."

Gabe's shoulders slumped. He gave his cousin a long stare. "Seriously? You want to do this now?"

"Why not? We're up. You want some coffee?"

"No, man. I want to go back to bed."

"Indulge me." Cisco pulled up a chair. "You've come to live here in our fair state, and I have yet to hear the whole story. I know you've been told to talk your feelings out."

He had, but now? His cousin could be a pit bull when he got a subject between his teeth. Gabe shook his head. "What do you want to know?"

"Everything. Who's Josh? You yelled his name in your sleep."

"Josh was my friend. We were close. He was marching behind me, but I got something in my eye and stopped. Josh kept going with everyone else and tripped the bomb." Gabe avoided his cousin's eyes. The explosion never should've happened. They'd cleared the village. The road was supposed to be safe.

Gabe swallowed hard. "Josh died on the spot. He never had a chance."

Cisco had the grace not to comment. Gabe didn't need advice, sympathy, or excuses. Nothing anyone said would change the outcome of that day, but he'd worked hard to overcome the guilt.

"Next thing I knew, the surgeon was shining lights in my eyes and telling me my leg was gone."

"Were you in Germany?" Cisco started the pot of coffee. Apparently, he intended to stay up.

"No. That was in the field hospital, where they put me together enough for the flight. Thirteen surgeries later, they sewed up my stump for good." Gabe rubbed his eyes. Cisco had been patient, but Gabe owed him some explanations. "The concussion turned out to be mild on the scale of TBIs. That's traumatic brain injuries. And not permanent, thankfully. I stayed at Landstuhl a week. I wasn't the best of patients."

Cisco got two cups and pulled some cookies from the cupboard where the leftovers from the party were stored. Breakfast of champions. "Not your usual heroic self?"

Gabe ignored the urge to deck his cousin. He'd hated himself and his future at the time. "I was surly and depressed." He reached for a cookie and put it down. Why was he even up?

Cisco poured his coffee and stuffed half a cookie in his mouth. "I haven't seen that side of you, myself. How'd you get past it?"

At a loss to explain, he frowned. Landstuhl had been filled with pain. Repeated debridements cleaned his wounds of bacteria, dirt, shrapnel, and dying tissue. Consciousness forced him to face the crushing weight of his failure. Afterward, eight months at Walter Reed Military Medical Center brought memories of disinfectant and the dark humor of maimed men struggling to make sense of their plight.

Cisco waited.

Gabe shrugged. "I got some not-so-tender words of wisdom from some of the other guys, and a pretty nurse dressed me down. That got my attention."

Cisco snickered.

"Once I was able to move around, they assigned me to a group. But I didn't believe in emotional trauma. To me, time was the problem. Getting back in shape was taking too long while my squad took all the hits.

Gabe leaned back and folded his arms. "I remember this one guy—Joe Phillips—who said I needed to change my expectations. "Made me furious. I mean, nothing expected, nothing accomplished, right?"

Cisco sipped his coffee. His unruly hair hung past the line of his jaw. Guys like him were targeted by sergeants when the buses unloaded for boot camp.

"Gabe the Good. You always had to do the right thing."

Gabe put his hands on the table to rise. He might manage a little more sack time. "What is it with you? Always the smart mouth."

"Sorry. I didn't mean anything by it, dude. Continue … please."

He studied his cousin. The guy could flick insults like cigarette butts. Jealousy maybe? Not likely. But Cisco had never been one to hold the rules in awe.

The old refrigerator hummed, and a new batch of ice cubes clattered into the bin.

Gabe yawned. "Long story, short—I ignored a lot of good advice until the infections set me back, and I began to see reality." His counselors said he was running from his fears. Not welcome at the time.

Cisco stood and stuck out his hand. "Well, thanks for sharing, bro'. I'm impressed with all you've come through. Not for being perfect but for trying. I know it hasn't been easy."

It hadn't. Gabe accepted Cisco's hand. Despite Cisco's irritating personality, he'd come through with this place for Gabe to live and plan. "Apology accepted. You know, I'd have stayed in DC if it weren't for you. You're a pain in the rear, but you're family, and I appreciate your help."

Gabe stood and positioned the crutches under his arms. Pinkish hints of dawn showed through the kitchen window. "Think I'll go back to bed for a while."

Cisco dumped the dregs from his cup into the sink and followed. "How'd you like the party?"

Gabe considered. "It was fantastic. Best party I've ever been to. We should do one every week." Nobody said the answer had to be true.

Green, yellow, and orange radar images crawled across the Weather Channel map on Larkyn's TV. Severe storms, with possible flash flooding, tracked north and east out of the Gulf of Mexico spawning tornadoes across Alabama, Georgia, and South Carolina, as the storm advanced. She continued to listen until the announcer gave the forecast for Raleigh. Severe storms in the early hours but nothing about tornadoes. Good.

The impatiens around her patio had started looking puny as summer waned. No need to water them tonight. Instead, Larkyn dragged the first of her heavy wrought iron chairs across the flagstone to the garage. She set it in the corner away from Matthew's bike, helmet, and riding gloves. One shoe remained from the fateful ride. Why did she keep that shoe? She sighed. The same reason she kept all the things that made him feel close.

Second chair, done. Two to go. The sky held no sign of impending rain as the setting sun tinted the blue with tangerine. The other shoe had never been found. The police report and the ER physician's statement told her Matthew had arrived in a cervical collar, his respirations maintained by an Ambu bag, his helmet askew but still on.

A powerful push didn't budge the table. Okay. Its weight should keep it from blowing away. Hands on her hips, she surveyed the sky which, again, showed no sign of a storm at all.

Her cell phone jingled from the bar in the kitchen, so she hurried inside to answer. "Hey, Sara. I was putting my outdoor chairs away."

"Oh, good for you. I'm sitting here in my apartment thinking about the party last week. Thought I'd give you a call since we haven't talked."

Larkyn had little news to share. Her work week had been routine except for trying to gather billing data for her boss Trudy Hamilton's latest project. Larkyn hated to interrupt her superiors for records they were supposed to keep, but Trudy had made the report a priority. How ironic the least helpful person was her husband, Martin Hamilton, who never had time to comply.

"So, how did you enjoy our party? I saw you and Gabe together." Sara got right to the point as usual. "Thanks for taking care of the ice for me, by the way."

Larkyn grimaced at the memory. "You need to thank Gabe for that. He's the one who did it."

"Did you like him? He's going to be sticking around it seems. Staying with Cisco until he gets a job and settled somewhere."

Ah. Larkyn had been right. Gabe's visit wouldn't be brief. "He was nice, Sara. Like I said, he saved me and the ice. Even after I almost ran him down." Now, why did she have to bring that up?

"I heard about that." Sara chuckled. "Cisco says Gabe is pretty bummed about his retirement from the Army. I think he expected to stay in his whole life. But he likes the new leg from MyoPro. It's got components Cisco and Matt tested two years ago. Your hubby would be glad to see the results in action."

Larkyn pressed her lips together. No doubt he would, but reminders of what might have been opened doors to regret. She had enough of them already.

Moving on, they chatted about the urgency of ordering wedding cakes and planning the reception in time for spring, until Sara yawned in the middle of a word.

"I should go to bed. I've been up since five."

"What for?"

"We're running something in the lab. Had to be there early the last two mornings. But tomorrow is Friday. Yay."

Larkyn didn't have that problem, thank goodness. Accounting jobs began at a civilized nine o'clock, but she still needed an alarm to get her moving. "Well, get yourself a bowl of Cheerios and go to sleep."

"Yuck. Mind if I trade that in for chamomile tea?"

"Whatever you say." Larkyn smiled into her phone. She loved carbs and dairy. But if there was a healthy alternative to anything, Sara was on it.

"Oh. I almost forgot the reason I called. You're invited to a hayride. MyoPro sponsors "Ladders for Life", a ministry for children with an incarcerated parent. The hayride is their next event."

Larkyn's smile faded. "I know nothing about kids with parents in jail."

"You don't have to. Just come along and help us feed them hot dogs and roast some marshmallows." Sara's wheedling voice continued to shred her objections. "A storyteller's coming to tell the kids a Bible story. It'll be fun, I promise."

Hmm. The marshmallows she could see, but Bible stories? Her father had raised her with the opinion that religious myths only harmed her. A person needed practical skills to tackle life, not some "mumbo-jumbo."

"I'll think about it."

"Come on. It's not for several weeks, so put it on your calendar. You'll love the kids. They're so worth the little time we get to spend with them."

While Sara made her case, Larkyn took one more look outside and lowered the back door blinds. Maybe she should put her religious doubts aside. This was about innocent children who needed guidance. Besides, as an adult, her views of God were up to her. "All right," she agreed with a sigh. "I'll come."

Whatever help Larkyn might give didn't change the fact that the Almighty's absence, in the seconds when Matthew needed him, didn't score him any points. She'd need a lot more than a children's story to convince her God cared, since he also didn't seem interested in finding the person who stole her husband's life.

After a quick goodbye to Sara, Larkyn popped a bag of popcorn and settled in for her nightly allotment of Netflix episodes. The rule had come about to save her from costly weeknight binges that distracted her from the loneliness but wrecked her mornings. When she turned the TV off, the patter of rain on the windows told her the forecast had been right.

With another night in her empty bed ahead, she changed into her cute nightgown with the skateboarding dogs and brushed her teeth.

Last in her bedtime ritual, she cradled a dark-brown bottle to her chest. Matthew's parents had taken a share of his ashes home to California. All the rest but these were scattered in Jordan Lake. Kissing the bottle made no sense, yet she continued to do so. If she'd roused herself and returned his kiss the morning he said goodbye, he might still be alive. Instead, she let him ride off into a trap—laid by fate, God, or coincidence. While she slept.

With heavy arms, she dragged the extra pillows out of her way and lay down on her side. Sara's wedding ... Ladders for Life ... storms. The cyclist she'd met a second time ... he'd lost his friend ... so easy to talk to ... an extraordinary man ...

Her breaths slowed. She turned again, burrowing into her pillow, away from the gusting wind and drum of rain on the windowpane. Hopefully, the storm would move quickly, and tomorrow would be sunny again. If only.

CHAPTER FIVE

A resounding crack startled Larkyn from her sleep. Gunshots? She blinked in the darkness and raised herself on one arm. An unearthly shriek and a foundation-jarring thunk made her cringe. Was the world coming apart? A surge of energy had her kicking at the covers and scrambling out of the bed, but her eyes were blind in the darkness. Where was the night light?

Her eyes adjusted as she listened. Blessed silence, except for the wind and raindrops. But the room smelled fresh and damp. She touched the edge of a slipper with her foot and felt with her toes for the other one.

The patter of rain sounded loud and close. Shivering, she shuffled in her slippers, arms reaching into the darkness to where her walk-in closet should be. There. She opened the door and fingered her garments until she found a hoodie. Yanking it off the hanger, she pulled it on over her gown and hugged the warmth. Much better.

Where was her phone? A current of chilly air swirled through the room as she felt her way to the bedside table, located her phone's familiar, flat shape, and unplugged it from the charging cord. A press of the button unlocked the screen bringing it to life with blinding colors. A swipe and a tap brought forth a powerful white beam.

"Thank you," she breathed to no one in particular, glad to see again. She flipped the light switch. Nothing. Right. The power was out.

Halfway up the hall, she stopped to gape. Shiny, slick leaves filled the foyer ahead. Another light source bounced beyond.

"Hello?" she warbled.

"Hello." A male voice came back, more confident than hers. "It's Ted Thompson from next door. Are you hurt?"

Oh, thank goodness. "No, not really. I'm in the hall behind the leaves. What happened?"

"Just stay there, honey. Let me see if we can get through to you."

We? Sure enough, she heard another voice.

"Let's wait for the fire department, Ted. We don't know what's damaged. Something could fall."

"Larkyn?" Ted again.

"Yes?"

"Bill from across the street is with me here. We want you to stay where you are for now. Are you okay to do that?"

"Um." The rain was soaking everything. But she had cover in the hall. "I guess. It's kinda cold in here."

"Well, grab a blanket or something. Your tree is down, and it came through the roof. If you're blocked in, I think it's safer to stay where you are."

Yes, safer was good. She wrapped the hoodie closer. The oak was the only large tree in the yard, and it was huge. Matthew had wanted this lot because of that tree. How could it be down?

A shudder passed through her as she stumbled to her walk-in closet for a fuzzy afghan. She wrapped herself and hugged its meager warmth with trembling arms. Ted and Bill would be back soon. She hoped.

What about shoes? Yes. Her slippers were soaked, and her feet felt like ice. One hand clutched the blanket while the other rummaged for socks and her walking shoes as sirens added to the disruption of the night.

Lights and shadows crossed the wall again. New voices invaded her private domain. "Close the door and stay back against the outside wall, ma'am. We'll get to you as soon as we can."

Larkyn slid down into the corner and managed to tie her shoes before the growl of a chainsaw roared to life. Head down, she huddled in a ball and covered her ears until the racket ceased. When the bedroom door finally opened, a helmeted man in a black rain suit striped with reflective tape appeared and gestured for her to come.

She tried to stand, but her legs wouldn't move.

"Let's get you out of here." The fireman grabbed her hand and pulled her up, then escorted her by the elbow through the littered foyer to the yard.

Oh, my. Larkyn blinked against the assault of dazzling red and blue strobe lights as emergency workers swarmed her yard. Someone draped her with a plastic poncho.

"Are you all right, ma'am?" A woman. Paramedic? Studied her face.

"I think so." She chattered through her teeth.

"May I take her to my house?" An older lady encircled her shoulders with a motherly embrace. The paramedic nodded.

"Come on, honey, let's go inside."

Larkyn followed without a word, glad someone had taken charge. The woman must belong to Ted. She knew them only as the retired couple who lived next door.

"Here, take that poncho off." Dena proceeded to pull at her. Why was she shaking again? The rain was chilly, but it wasn't that cold.

"I'm Dena, remember? I've got some water on for tea—unless you prefer coffee?"

"I like tea."

"Good, so do I. The kitchen's this way."

Larkyn followed and quickly regained her bearings. Dena's floor plan appeared to be the reverse of hers. Garage on the left, not right. The large room ahead opened to the kitchen. The bedrooms had to be down the hall to the right, instead of the left. Matthew called them cookie-cutter houses, but despite the similarities, something different resided here.

Navy, rust, and hunter-greens spoke of a previous decade as did the collection of Hummel figurines, commemorative plates, and fancy teacups. The atmosphere gave Larkyn the impression of a perfect grandma's house. Dena took off her jacket and hung it on the hall tree. Practical duck boots and jeans, coupled with her short, graying hairstyle suggested a woman with life experience.

"You can use the guest room, dear." Dena pointed the way. "I put some dry things out for you to wear."

Larkyn moved in the direction shown and entered another room decorated in a country theme. Her temporary wardrobe lay folded on a four-poster bed. She stripped off her nightgown and let it drop to the braided rug. Dena's faded-pink sweatpants and long-sleeved souvenir T-shirt from Gatlinburg, Tennessee, swallowed her, but they were dry, soft, and heavenly warm. By the time her shoes were retied, she'd stopped shaking, and the tension in her shoulders loosened up.

When Larkyn returned to the kitchen, Dena pointed to a line of small boxes on the laminate countertop—English Breakfast, Peppermint, Earl Grey, Cinnamon Stick. "Take your pick." She poured steaming water into mismatched mugs.

"You really are a tea fan. I am too." Dena's kindness soothed Larkyn's jangled nerves. She opened an Earl Grey packet and peeled the wrapper with steadier hands.

"Sugar's there, and I have milk." Dena set the drink on the table with a warm, friendly smile.As she clasped the warm tea mug, Larkyn breathed the familiar aroma and took her first tentative sip. A wave of fatigue and defeat brought her forehead to the table.

"Now, now." Dena's gentle voice brought her close to weeping. "Things will look brighter when the sun comes up. Help will come, and the damage will be repaired."

Oh, yes. Brighter in the daylight. The voice of an optimist. Dena's walls were decorated with happy sayings confirming her view of the world. *This is the day that the Lord has made* and *Be ye thankful always*. Under different circumstances, Larkyn might have judged them, but she couldn't fault her neighbor's goodness tonight.

"Is there someone you want to call? Family? Friends? Insurance company?"

The options left Larkyn queasy. She had insurance somewhere, and Sara could send word to Cisco who probably knew what to ask. But family? Her parents hadn't approved her choice for marriage. Then two years ago, Matthew's funeral had interrupted their trip to Europe. Another call would only cement their opinion that she was incapable of handling her life.

Dena noticed her silence. "Excuse me for being nosy, but didn't you used to be married? I remember a handsome young man who mowed the lawn and rode his bicycle early in the morning. I'm an early riser, and I often saw him leaving."

Larkyn shriveled. Was she so private a friendly person like Dena didn't know?" She cleared her throat. "Yes. I was." She swallowed. "But two years ago, he was run off the road on that bike and died."

Dena's hand went to her heart. "I'm so sorry. How did we not know that? We used to travel quite a bit, but we should've been better neighbors."

"No, it's more our fault than yours." Larkyn objected. "Matthew and I didn't mingle much." Her lips pressed together at the echo of her boss Trudy's voice, *Get out some for heaven's sake. Look beyond yourself.* She forced a weak laugh. "Since he's been gone, I've been accused of being a hermit."

"Everybody needs friends." The words conveyed understanding, not reproof. "And I'm glad we're here for you now."

Indeed. What would she have done if Ted hadn't come over with Bill? She hated to think how much scarier, or even more dangerous, this could've been.

The door burst open, and all six feet of Ted Thompson charged in. Completely drenched. "Those firefighters have got it under control." He grabbed a kitchen towel and wiped his face. "They're covering the roof with a tarp, and the power company's been alerted." He directed his eyes to the guest in his wife's clothes. "You, little lady, need to call a tree service to take down the rest of that big ole oak. What a shame."

Larkyn's heart surged. "How much damage is there?"

"Quite a lot, I'm afraid, but the good news is your car and the garage are fine. You'll need your homeowner's insurance company to send out an adjuster." He shook out his jacket and hung it over a chair.

"Uh-uh." Dena waved at him. "Look at that. Dripping everywhere."

Ted snatched it back and headed for what had to be the laundry room.

A yawn of embarrassing size seized Larkyn as the tea did its magic. The microwave clock said 6:03. It would be light in less than an hour.

When Ted returned, he washed his hands, then tipped the coffee carafe and filled his mug. "I doubt you can live in your house for a while."

Not go home? She reached for her phone and gripped it like the lifeline it was. The tension spread to her shoulders and neck.

"Let's give the crew out there some time to finish, then we'll see if you can rescue some things."

Larkyn slumped. How could she be homeless? "Can they fix my house?"

Ted smiled at her like a father. Dena patted the back of her hand.

"Of course they can fix it, honey, but it'll take some time. The first thing is to get some estimates from a professional."

Out of a hollow place that reminded her of being five, tears slid down her cheeks. Where was her mom when she needed help? Doing important things.

"I guess I better call my friend."

Poor Sara. Saddled with another Larkyn crisis.

CHAPTER SIX

Who was banging on his door at this hour? Only one possibility.

"Go away," Gabe growled.

The door swung inward. "Oh, good. You're up." Cisco barged in.

"I'm not even close to being up." Gabe rolled to his side and punched the pillow under his cheek. Was the sun even up?

"Hey, man. We've got an emergency. I need you to man up and drag your sorry behind out of this bed.

Man up? Seriously? Who was the war hero here, and who was the nerd? "Go away."

"Not a chance."

Gabe knew what was coming next. He clutched the blanket to his chin in anticipation of his cousin's predictable move. Nothing had changed since grade school. The yank came, starting a tug of war over the blanket that covered his mostly naked skin.

"Stop it." Gabe held on, even as he rolled to his back and sat up. Cisco was no match for weight training.

"Okay. But I'm serious." Cisco yielded. "We have an emergency. With Larkyn."

Larkyn? Sara's friend? The one with aquamarine eyes who ran him down with her Jeep?

His frown must've answered.

"A tree fell on her house last night. She needs help."

Gabe raised his eyebrows. "A tree."

"Yes. A bona fide oak tree of unusual size. It crashed her roof in."

"Is she okay?"

"She's fine. Not a scratch. But Sara wants us to go over there since she can't miss work this morning. She'll be available later this afternoon."

Lucky Sara. Gabe put his bare feet on the carpet, swiped a dirty T-shirt from the floor, and pulled it over his head. "Sounds like something for professionals."

"Yeah, I agree. But we gotta go provide a sitrep, if you will." Cisco had picked up some jargon from the movies. Good for him.

Gabe grabbed his crutches and bowed to the inevitable. "Do you have coffee made? Some carbs, perhaps?"

"If you mean my awesome pancakes, forget it. There's a bagel and some moldy cream cheese in the fridge. Coffee, I've got."

"Give me five minutes." Gabe found clean clothes in his drawer and headed to the shower up the hall.

The hot water coaxed his body to wakefulness. He used to be able to jump from sleep to firing his weapon in half a minute. Maybe he *was* a sorry butt.

A tree? The suds ran off his face and shoulders and disappeared down the drain. Skip the shave since this was an *emergency*. He turned the water off and toweled his body and hair. Back in his room, he tested the socket's seal and added jeans, socks, and a shoe to match the current one on his artificial foot.

"Hi." Cisco handed him a cup when he entered the kitchen. "There's your bagel. Toasted with butter and jam. No extra charge for the napkin."

Gabe sat at the table littered with crumbs. The sink contained dishes going back to Monday. Did Sara know her fiancé lived this way? He bit into the bagel and let the chewy, buttery sweetness wake him further. "Thanks." He sipped the hot brew from a thick crockery mug.

Cisco smirked. "You're welcome."

"I had planned to talk to the Hot Shot team leader in Asheville today." He swallowed and bit again.

Cisco ran water and rinsed the dishes, clattering the plates as he loaded the dishwasher. "I don't know how long this will take, cuz'. Sara didn't give details."

Gabe drank as deeply as the heat allowed and stood. Seeing Larkyn again so soon was a surprise but shouldn't have been. She was a friend of the family and part of the wedding to come. "Did she ask Sara to get us out of bed?"

"No. Sara just knew. These gals have intuition we can only hope to understand."

Gabe snorted. Good grief, no wonder he didn't understand them.

Cisco palmed his keys. "Ya ready?"

Gabe followed him outside. He wedged his six-foot height into the passenger seat of Cisco's infamous green Honda. The car had muffler issues but a stellar stereo. This morning the muffler took center stage. It thundered as Gabe fumbled for the bar to retract the custom racing-style seat. "Sara's a midget."

"Whatever." Cisco ground it into gear and backed down the driveway. He looked both ways, wheeled backward, and shoved it into first. They were off.

In a scant four blocks, albeit long ones, they pulled up to the curb.

Holy moley.

The fire department had come in force. A cherry picker from the utility company, guarded by orange cones, parked at the corner. And the roar of chain saws cut the morning's peace.

Gabe climbed awkwardly out of his low-slung seat and stood to survey the wreckage. The felled oak once stood in the backyard. Its crown now faced the street. He could only imagine the damage.

Cisco whistled low. "Let's check it out."

Heading past the garage, they met a skinny fellow wearing a tie and wire-rimmed glasses. "Hey. You can't go back there."

Cisco gave him the once-over. "We're here at the request of the homeowner. Who are you?"

"Phil Ames, Claims Adjuster, First Fidelity." His slacks and polished loafers screamed desk job.

Cisco narrowed his eyes. "Where's Mrs. Wagner?"

"Cisco!" Larkyn came running toward them from the neighbor's yard. Her hair was tangled, her eyes smudged, and the pink sweatpants she wore were loose enough for two. But in the light of dawn, she looked adorable.

She threw her arms around his cousin, who slowly responded in kind. Gabe watched her release the hug and go self-conscious at the sight of him.

Cisco stepped back. He nodded toward the wreckage. "What happened?"

"The tree." She gestured with a helpless wave in its direction. "It came out of the ground and fell on my house. Come see."

Gabe glanced at the adjuster as they passed into the no-fly zone. The fellow ignored them as he continued to snap his pics.

"Do you have your own photos?" Gabe dared to inject himself into the situation. So far, his presence hadn't been acknowledged.

"Should I?" Her eyebrows raised.

"Well, I would." He shrugged. "In case there's a dispute."

Silence.

Never mind the poor reception, his advice was solid. "There might be disagreements about the cost of repairs. Limitations to the coverage. Documentation helps."

Cisco looked at Larkyn. "Better safe than sorry?"

She glanced at him and back to Cisco. "Well, okay. I left my phone at Dena's, but I'll get it."

Cisco nodded. "Go ahead. We'll poke around till you get back."

Gabe's heart squeezed as he watched her go. *Traitor.* This was no time to get involved. He had his own problems to solve.

Circling behind the garage, they tromped on the sodden grass and gawked at the half-exposed root ball. The trunk lay at about sixty degrees against the home's rear wall. He caught sight of kitchen appliances beyond the broken glass, crushed siding, and torn insulation. Massive impact by tons of solid hardwood. Larkyn was lucky the bedrooms were on the other end of the house.

Cisco wagged his head. "What a mess." He took a few steps closer to see inside.

"Excuse me, sir. You need to move back. We're securing the premises." The fireman, dressed for action in a heavy jacket, boots, and black protective pants, was telling, not asking.

Gabe obeyed as a crew moved past carrying their ladders and spreading crime scene tape around the perimeter. Thank goodness for first responders.

Would Gabe ever be one again?

"Here's my phone." Larkyn sounded breathless as she pointed it at Cisco. "I don't know what to take pictures of."

"My cousin's good at that." Cisco passed the buck, er phone, to Gabe. "He's also done a little roofing in his distant past."

Very distant. Gabe kept his hands to his side.

"Come on, help the lady out."

Rather than argue, Gabe took the phone. How had he become the expert?

"Here." Larkyn leaned into his space. Her hair fell forward like it had the day she knelt beside him at the roadside. She unlocked the screen and tapped one icon, then another. "Just press there."

Right. The easy part.

He remembered taking photos after a grease fire in his mother's kitchen and observing the captain document weapons caches. As long as they didn't have to stand up in court, he had this.

Gabe examined different camera views and meandered away to do his job. The crown of the tree rested somewhere inside, probably in whatever room lay beyond the kitchen. The house's rear wall had buckled. He clicked, zoomed closer, and clicked again. Hanging gutters, skewed window frames. A shiver coursed down his spine. He might have become used to the shells of bombed-out buildings, and survivors combing piles of debris in pathetic attempts to rebuild, but this mess in safe suburbia took him by surprise. War was far away, but destruction could find you anywhere.

He rounded the corner to the front yard and stepped under the porch to peer inside a window. Leaves littered the floor and branches the size of his thigh poked through the ceiling with the sunlight. He snapped pictures through the glass but didn't try to enter. Last, he backed off to check out the roof line. Hard to tell for sure, but he'd bet on structural damage.

The time on this phone read a mere eight o'clock in the morning. But already steps had been taken to secure the home and start repairs. All good. Larkyn and Cisco emerged from behind the garage walking with the insurance dude. She didn't wear a happy face.

It couldn't be true. Larkyn gritted her teeth to hold another bout of tears inside. It wasn't true.

"It's not up to me," the nasty man from First Fidelity complained. "I don't make the rules. I just follow them."

"You've got it all wrong," she said for the third time. "I know flood damage isn't covered, but this wasn't a flood. It's rain damage. The tree fell in a rainstorm. I don't know why. Maybe wind and lightning, but we had no flood."

"There's flooding all around, ma'am. The weather records show a flash flood warning was issued for this area. Creeks overflowed. Your policy covers the removal of the tree and roof repair. That's all."

She exhaled. What did it take to get through to this guy?

"Show me the evidence of flooding." Cisco's cousin's voice cut in. He joined them holding her phone in the air. "I'll take pictures of it to add to our file."

The adjuster scowled.

"If you'll let me inside, I'll document the water damage for future reference. I imagine it won't be hard to prove whether or not the flooding you speak of affected this house or even this street."

Oh my. She almost smiled at the effect of his words. Almost.

"I have photos, sir," the obnoxious adjuster assured them. "Once I leave, I will submit my assessment of the claim. The owner will have an opportunity to appeal anything she wishes."

"Appeal?" Cisco joined the battle. "Why don't you just make an accurate report to start with?"

Larkyn's hopes rose. She had help. She wasn't in this alone. "I have the phone number and email for First Fidelity inside. As soon as I can, I'll call them myself."

"Why wait?" Gabe extended her phone. "Just look it up on the web. They'll have a hotline for problems, I'm sure."

Mr. Ames brushed his thinning hair back from his forehead with a growl. "Look. I was sent out here because we're flooded with calls." He seemed oblivious to his choice of words. "Go ahead and make a list of the damaged contents of your home. Include your photographs." He inclined his head toward Gabe. "I can get an estimate for the exterior by the end of the day. When you complete the Proof of Loss forms, First Fidelity will make you a full settlement offer. I urge you to read your policy first to be sure you comply with it. I believe your deductible is fifteen hundred dollars."

Larkyn's stomach sank. Matthew took care of things like this—except Matthew was gone. She fought the threat of tears. She couldn't be weak and helpless. Especially in front of these men.

Read her policy. Right. Find her policy was more like it. She had a drawer full of papers she'd been too upset to sort through after the funeral. Two years ago. What was wrong with her?

When the adjuster was out of earshot, Cisco spoke. "He sure got friendlier after you mentioned calling the home office. Good job, cuz'."

Larkyn hated conflict. "He's probably under a lot of pressure, but I couldn't let him cheat me." She wrung her hands. "I promise you, there was no flood. Ted was the first to come inside. He'll vouch for my story."

Cisco's side hug eased the weight pushing on her chest. "Let me give Sara a call. I'm sure you can stay with her tonight. I have a key, and I can let you in now if you want."

"Thanks, Cisco. But I can't leave." She surveyed the chaos and something important cut through her fog. Once her tree was gone … "Um. Do you think you could take another picture?" She made herself look at Gabe. The poor guy must wish he was anywhere else.

"What do you need?" He answered slowly.

"There's a heart carved on the trunk of the tree. Could you? Do you—"

Without a word, he left her standing with Cisco. In a few moments, he appeared again with a disconcerting wink. "Got it."

"Thank you—for everything." She took her phone from his hand. "I didn't realize pictures would be important."

"See ya for supper, then?" Cisco tapped the roof of his car. "Bring what you need for Sara's."

A bright smile covered the groan inside. "I will. Tell her thanks."

The rumble of Cisco's car faded as it turned at the end of the block. Despite people everywhere, the morning became empty again.

CHAPTER SEVEN

Larkyn's ears rang with the roar of chain saws dismembering her tree. Phil Ames had come through by sending a crew to get the behemoth off her house.

"I'm going to my friend's now." She entered Dena's kitchen where the tangy aroma of browning onions made her stomach contract. "Wow, that smells good."

Dena turned from her skillet. "Ted's grilling bratwurst for dinner. He likes them with onions and peppers."

Larkyn pushed away the longing to eat with Ted. "Thank you for everything today. Guess I'll be back in the morning."

"I'm sure you've had enough for now, but tomorrow let's see what we can salvage from your freezer and fridge. I hate to think of all the waste."

Rotting perishables? "Please. You and Ted can take whatever we find." Another yawn took over. She'd have to handle the pantry too. And her broken dishes.

Tomorrow.

The drive to Cisco's took no time. All traces of the storm had moved on leaving only windswept clouds brushed onto the sky in harmless strokes of pink and gold. A friendly breeze tousled her hair and tugged at the edges of her floppy shirt as she pulled her black carry-on to the front door and rang the bell.

"Come in. You don't have to knock." Sara held the door so she could squeeze by. "Just leave that here. We'll take it with us later." She gathered Larkyn into her arms. "How are you doing?" She peered through the open door. "Aren't you glad your car's okay?"

"Hangin' in." Larkyn inhaled and let her lungs empty slowly. Yes, thankfully, her car had been spared.

"Are you hungry?" Sara proceeded directly to the stove and stirred something in a pot. "The guys filled me in a little. Sorry, I couldn't get away from work before. We had too much to do." She tapped her spoon on the pot and rattled on. "Cisco's bringing a rotisserie chicken, and I'm making mashed potatoes. There's supposed to be salad stuff in the fridge."

Sara drained her pot of scalding, starchy water, and a cloud of steam filled the sink. "So, tell me everything that happened. What does it look like now?"

"The wind and the soggy ground seem to be all it took to knock our big oak tree onto the back of the house. The fire department came first, then a tree service was there all day, cutting it up. The hole in the roof is covered with a tarp until permanent repairs get started."

"Oh, wow." Sara stopped mashing long enough to look at her. "Where's the salad stuff?"

Larkyn blinked. "In the fridge?"

Sara set her work aside, silent for a moment. "You're barely with me." She furrowed her brow at Larkyn's face. "And no wonder. Today was traumatic, and here I am yakking away. Her arms came around her friend again. "I'm so sorry."

Sympathy. Why did it bring out the tears? Larkyn sniffed and wiped at her cheeks. "Today was terrible. Our home is a wreck. But it's not just that. All the things we shared, the only things I had left, are trashed. Literally."

The sight of firemen replayed in her mind as they hauled her damaged furnishings out like garbage. Helpful, neighborly hands had picked through the pieces for anything worth saving. Broken lamps and picture frames, shattered dishes and glassware, soggy scatter rugs and pillows—someone had to do it. But a look in the rolling trash bin had made her want to be sick.

"Everything's gone." Her voice broke as she tried to explain. "Our life is going to the landfill. It's not fair. Isn't it enough to lose Matthew? Why should I have to lose everything else? Is God that mad at me?"

"Honey, no." Sara's third hug brought more tears. "God's not mad at you."

Hurt poured from her as a bout of wracking sobs broke out. She sniffed and caught her breath. "I'm trying to be brave, but—."

"Sit down." Sara grabbed a glass and filled it. "Drink this water."

Larkyn blew her nose on a napkin and took the glass. "Why do people think drinking water helps?" She sipped.

"I have no idea." Sara smiled, and Larkyn's own lips twitched.

The squeak of hinges on the back door followed by deep voices announced the arrival of the men.

Larkyn wadded the napkin in her fist. At least the blubbering was over before she faced mixed company.

"Hey, my sweet lollipop." Cisco approached Sara with a sappy grin.

Larkyn caught Gabe rolling his eyes, and he caught her watching him. "Hi. I see you made it."

"Barely." She couldn't suppress the smile that answered his.

"How's the crime scene?" He kept his eyes on her, ignoring the lovebirds who cooed at each other over the bowl of mashed potatoes.

"They accomplished more than I ever imagined. The tree is all sawed up. The hole in the roof is covered. The water runs. Power was restored just before I left."

Cisco dragged a finger through Sara's bowl and put it in his mouth. "Mmm. Maybe add more butter?"

"It's not done." Sara swatted at him, and he went back for more—as if they'd been married for years.

"It sounds like you're in pretty good shape." Cisco smacked his lips. "Did any parts of your house escape?"

"Stop being funny." Sara elbowed him away to finish the mashing. "She's been traumatized."

Cisco flashed her a grin. "I'm sorry." Was he serious or not? Cisco and sensitivity were a rare sighting. "But hey. I brought the chicken." He reached for the grocery bag in Gabe's hand.

"Thank you, both." Sara nodded at Gabe. "Will one of you carve it up? We just need to finish the salad."

The fragrance of herb-roasted chicken reminded Larkyn's stomach again that she was hungry. She sat staring while Cisco butchered the chicken, and Sara made the salad.

When everyone took their seats, Gabe interrupted the business of serving. "Do you mind if I say grace?"

Larkyn's hands stilled. She glanced around, then bowed her head with the others.

"Lord, we thank you for this meal and for your protection of Larkyn last night. Help her to rebuild and give her your peace. Amen."

"Thank you, Gabe." Sara quietly took up the platter and handed it off as Larkyn swallowed her surprise.

The conversation included another recap of her day. The problem, she explained, was that she didn't know a good estimate from a bad one.

"I'm sure Gabe could check it out." Cisco volunteered.

Larkyn stole a glance in time to see the flash of Gabe's frown disappear.

Sara took a long swallow of tea. "We all need to do what we can. Tomorrow's Saturday. I'll help you at the house. Make calls. Whatever you need."

"Looky here." Cisco read his phone screen. "A business right here in Cary that helps with property damage claims. They have good reviews and promise to be your advocate. It says here, 'Don't take a check without a second opinion.' You might want to call them."

"Really?" Sara leaned into his space.

Larkyn's hopes flickered. "I was told to inventory the losses. You could help me with that."

"Good." Sara switched to executive mode. "What about H&H, that law firm you work for? Can they do anything?"

"There's no negligence or anything like that. I talked to Trudy earlier." Larkyn's expression twisted. "She was very sympathetic and sorry, but she told me God was looking out for me. That he knows we have a deadline for her project."

"What does that even mean?" Sara seemed genuinely puzzled.

"Trudy thinks God is the answer to everything." Larkyn shrugged. Since Gabe and Cisco seemed to be tuned to another topic, she added, "She acts like she has insider knowledge of his plans, but things don't happen that way for me."

Sara patted her hand, her eyes full of kindness. "Not to worry. You're welcome at my place for as long as you need."

Larkyn compressed her lips. In the world's tiniest apartment?

"We'll be fine." Sara squeezed her hand. "It won't be forever, right?"

CHAPTER EIGHT

Gabe hung up his phone and stared at the wall. What to make of that conversation?

According to his careful research, getting a job with a fire-fighting agency would open the door to his replacement dream. With such a sponsoring agency, he'd be eligible to compete for Incident Qualification at the arduous level—known as the Pack Test. If he passed the pack test and took some classes, he'd earn his Red Card—key to the world of wildland fire suppression.

Perfect.

The person at the US Forest Service had been one-hundred-percent supportive. Military experience was a decided plus. Already in decent shape? Terrific. Until he mentioned his amputation.

No one like him had been hired before, but the gentleman gave him the info needed to proceed. Meanwhile, he was free to begin the required classes on the web. Basic wildland fire fighting, fire behavior, intro to the command structure, and human factors on the fire line. The Army didn't want him in the infantry, but if he could find a sponsor, the Red Card would make him part of a team again. Life from the ashes and all.

Hooah! He punched his fist in the air.

All right, so the dude on the phone had cautioned him. Each case was different, but he had a chance to make this work.

Gabe changed into riding clothes. What he needed now was some North Carolina sun and balmy October air on his face. Despite what the storm did to Larkyn, the South knew how to do fall.

Cisco's rear end faced him as his cousin bent over the engine compartment of his Honda. The lively beat of Santana's "Black Magic Woman" accompanied whatever sorcery he was performing under the hood.

"Why do you drive that thing?" Gabe hoped his cousin would rise to the bait.

"Why not? She's magnificent." Cisco stood up and wiped his hands on a greasy rag.

"What does Sara think? Everyone knows it's an eyesore."

"Hey, man. She dated me for over two years, and this was my car. Guess she loves me, huh?"

Gabe shrugged. Wives could be different than girlfriends. Not that he wished the happy couple ill.

Cisco fitted a socket to his wrench. "Where you off to?"

"Nowhere special. I just talked to the guy up in Asheville. Gotta prepare for the pack test."

Cisco's head disappeared under the hood again. "That's great. What's a pack test?"

Gabe peered around Cisco. "What're you doing now?"

"Changing spark plugs and adjusting the timing."

Right. He and Cisco had tinkered like this back in the day—when their clunkers needed constant work to stay on the road. "You gonna take care of Sara's car like this?"

"Have you seen her car? Everything runs off a computer. I wouldn't get within ten feet of that thing." Cisco grunted with the effort of turning his wrench.

"It's a mighty cute Mini Cooper, pal. Don't you ride with her?"

Cisco ducked to avoid cracking his head as he ascended from the bowels of his engine. "If I must. But listen. Car arguments aren't worth it. She likes hers, and I like mine."

"Who's gonna break and trade for the minivan when the babies come?" Gabe chuckled.

Cisco glared at him. "Do not go there, man. I'm not ready for that conversation." He released the catch and lowered the hood into place with a satisfying thunk. "Now, what's a pack test?"

Gabe mounted his bike. "It's a three-mile hike wearing forty-five pounds, finished in forty-five minutes. One of the requirements for a Red Card. Can't fight fires without a Red Card."

"Well, good luck." His cousin could be a man of few words—but not often.

"Thanks." Gabe gripped his handlebars and glided down the driveway. "See ya later."

"I heard from the girls," Cisco shouted after him.

Gabe circled back. "Yeah?"

"Why don't you cruise by Larkyn's house. They might could use some help."

What? Gabe shoved hard on the pedal, propelling himself away. A guy couldn't go for his own ride without jumping into a rescue operation?

Okay, he had to admit Larkyn aroused protective instincts he'd rather leave alone. His sister called him a golden retriever type. Fine. But the need he sensed in her was deep. Not something he could deal with right now.

Peddling along the suburban streets, he noted the homes, the yards with their picket fences. Here and there, Big Wheels and bikes lay abandoned on perfect lawns. Cisco's words came back. *I'm not ready for that conversation*. Well, neither was he. And dating was only the beginning. He smiled at the thought. Cisco and Sara might end up in *that conversation* quicker than they could say 'honeymoon.'

He cruised along at a leisurely pace. No need to push until he got out on the back roads.

Larkyn was beautiful—okay, so what? A career in the Army had shown him how often family obligations tore at soldiers. The whole thing was unfair to either side. Firefighting could be the same—with long deployments that seemed to be getting longer as seasonal droughts increased around the country. Maybe he liked it that way? Commitment, sacrifice ... *did* he have a hero complex?

Gabe took a left into unfamiliar territory. Never mind, he'd circle the block and be on his way. Except the concept of 'block' didn't exist in this town. Increasingly caught in a suburban labyrinth of Courts, Ways, Circles, and Places, he looked for a way to get out.

Then the view became familiar.

Uh-oh, there they were. A long-legged blonde and a bouncy redhead. Wearing cutoffs and T-shirts.

My, my. His bike sailed into the driveway.

The ladies noticed. "Hey," Sara called with enthusiasm. "Glad you made it."

He was expected?

Larkyn followed Sara to the spot where he'd rooted his feet. A bandanna held her hair in check, and her pale skin shone with exertion. He pulled his gaze from the rest of her and focused on the house beyond. "No more yellow tape. How's it lookin' in there?"

"Come on, we'll show you." Sara waved him on.

Nothing to do but follow.

The front door stood open, and they walked into the devastation. The carpet had been ripped out, exposing the subfloor. No furniture. The kitchen bar lay in splinters. Cabinetry hung askew. The stove and fridge had been removed, and a gaping hole exposed the backyard where the sink and dishwasher once fit. The ceiling around the hole had been demolished, exposing the tarp and some attic trusses.

"How did all this happen?" He tried to take it in.

"You mean the damage or the clean-up?" Sara put her hands on her hips. "The fire department gets a lot of credit, plus, this girl has amazing neighbors. Tell him, Larkyn."

"Sara's right, my neighbors have been fantastic. Someone who deals with storm damage talked to me this morning," she added with less assurance. They're sending estimates."

A much older woman in scruffy jeans and a sleeveless blouse came up the hall. "Hey, there. Ted's making progress with the shop vac in the bedrooms."

"Gabe, this is Dena." Sara introduced them. "Gabe is my fiancé's cousin, currently staying with him. Gabe, why don't you go meet Ted?"

Why didn't he go meet Ted? Okay, Sara, why not?

Gabe followed the noise.

Ted's bent-over form vacuumed water from the carpet in a bedroom with a king-sized bed. Must be Larkyn's. He'd better announce himself.

"Hi. Sara sent me."

"Howdy." Ted shut off his machine and extended his hand. "Ted Thompson. From next door."

"Gabe DeSantis."

Ted felt the carpet with an open palm. "I'm trying to head off any mold and save this carpet. It seems to be doing some good."

Gabe panned the room. "Is the adjuster still trying to write off the claim as flood damage?"

"Oh, you heard about that? That fellow's been set straight." Ted pulled a hankie from the pocket of his cargo shorts and wiped his forehead. "We're looking after Larkyn's interests. I think Dena's adopted her."

Gabe smiled. Very good. Competent adults on the job. Not him.

"Can you give me a hand? I need to get under this bed." Ted assumed he was here to help.

Gabe moved to the far side and bent carefully at the knees to lift. She slept right here every night.

"Thanks. Now d'you mind moving this stuff off the nightstand into the bathroom? It all looks fine in there."

Gabe carried the lamp, a carved box, the digital alarm clock, and an interesting vial of powder to the bathroom. One side of Larkyn's double vanity was strewn with feminine things. The other end lay bare except for a single flask of men's aftershave. He set what he carried out of the way and turned to escape. This place was private. He didn't belong here.

"Thanks. D'you mind moving those shoes off the closet floor? I'm almost done in here." Ted gestured at a half-open door.

Gabe didn't want to probe any deeper into Larkyn's possessions, but Ted was oblivious. The guy had to be past sixty. She could be his daughter.

Not wanting to argue, he opened the door and blinked at the double rack of skirts, blouses, dresses, and pants on hangers. Purses and baskets of unknown contents occupied an upper shelf. He gathered the stray shoes in his arms.

Three months ago, he'd been a corporal. He understood his job. The men he fought beside knew theirs. "Where should I put 'em?" Gabe addressed Ted, but Ted had disappeared and Larkyn stood in the doorway.

His face warmed. No, man, this was not his life. "Ted asked me to move your shoes."

She smiled, but her face turned pinker. "It's a mess, isn't it? Just put them on the bed."

"No. It's not." Did she mean the closet or the damage? "I mean, it's very normal. Your closet ... I'm not familiar with women's closets, but ... this seems normal." *Shut up, Gabe.* He placed a pair of black high heels, two fluffy pink slippers, flip flops, and a pair of navy pumps on the mattress.

"Excuse me." Like a coward, he bailed and headed for the kitchen—then exited through the hole into her backyard where the naked rootball lay exposed to the air. Larkyn had followed him out. What happened to Sara? She couldn't leave him here.

"Thank you for coming by. It's helping me see I'm not alone. Especially without my husband here."

See, Gabe. You're not fifteen, and this is not a school dance. He stood awkwardly with his hands in the pockets of his basketball shorts. "This would be scary no matter who you are. I'm glad you have such fantastic friends."

She stopped at the edge of what once had been a patio, dropped to one knee, and smoothed the splintered flagstone as if stroking something precious.

"Matthew and Cisco built this that summer. We had plans to christen it with a cookout the day he got hit."

The cruelty of her loss touched him almost as much as his own. He watched her stand and dust the grit and wood chips from her hands.

"Yesterday, most of our possessions got tossed into a dumpster. I know it's only stuff, and I'm not hurt. The house will survive, but—what a perfect picture of my life." Her voice caught in her throat, and she swallowed. "It was already wrecked, but now it's official."

Oh, no. Not tears.

He resisted the nudge to pull her into a hug. Her troubles weren't his assignment. They barely knew each other.

His heart betrayed him, and his limbs disobeyed. He placed one arm around her shoulder, which she turned her body into, and his other arm couldn't help but come around. She buried her face in her hands against his chest while he patted her on the back.

Words came, unbidden, a silent request made to the One he'd come to know so recently.

God, please bless this woman. I don't know if she believes, but give her your peace and comfort. Help her to get through this.

Though the words weren't spoken aloud, he hoped they helped because she sure seemed lost.

Larkyn wasn't used to throwing herself at men. Comfort was okay, but other people could give her that. Why did this one feel so safe when being with him was wrong?

He'd been in her bedroom for goodness' sake, holding her shoes, clearly embarrassed. Why did she follow him outside, blubber about her loneliness, and practically ask for a hug? Most guys would run for the hills.

Easing back, she restored distance between them and wiped her tears with her dirty hands. She should wear Kleenex around her neck.

Not ready for eye contact, she sniffed and didn't move. Her sight-line hit right at his collarbone. Right at the notch revealed by his crew-neck shirt.

Hmm, quite a bit taller than Matthew. She couldn't help but notice because her cheek fit right beside Matthew's cheek, her favorite place to nestle.

Okay, this was getting weird.

"I'm sorry," she blurted. "That was awkward."

"I think it's normal." His arms hung at his sides again, where they most likely belonged. "You've lost a lot already and now the storm. It's gotta be overwhelming."

He'd called her reaction normal. Twice. Had war skewed his senses? She'd forgotten what normal felt like, but she'd take his assessment for now. Maybe even admit the hug felt good.

"You've hired contractors for the repairs?"

Had she? Sort of. Could she admit that Matthew always carried the load as if she were made of porcelain? "I talked to the guy who came by."

"Make sure he's licensed and insured."

She wrung her hands. "Sara says I could do some remodeling, but I don't know what I'd change." Without Matthew, what did it matter?

He edged away, walking toward the place where he'd left his bike. "Guess I'll go now. I was going for a ride to clear my thoughts. I have decisions to make about the future too."

He lifted the bike and stood beside it.

"Matthew said he had his best ideas while riding."

"I need a few of those." He smiled as he balanced on his artificial foot and swung the real leg over.

"I hope you find them, then ..." She didn't back away, and he didn't push off.

"Well, good luck." They spoke in unison.

"Guess we both need some of that." She smiled as he coasted into the street.

"More than luck," he called back as he pedaled off the way he'd come.

What did that mean? She followed his progress until he turned the corner, then went inside and found Dena mopping the kitchen floor.

"Dena, you're doing too much."

"Hey," Dena stopped pushing the mop. "Let us feel like we're useful for a while, okay? Our kids don't need us. They live in Charlotte, but they're always off somewhere." She pointed at the scars in the linoleum. "Guess you'll be replacing this."

Larkyn's head hurt. She looked for somewhere to sit but the table and chairs were gone. "I'm sure it needs to be torn out. Gabe asked if I'd hired anyone yet. I need to make a decision. Too many decisions."

Dena leaned on her mop handle. "His name is Gabe? He's quite the specimen. Where did you meet him?"

Specimen? She squinted at Dena.

Dena pursed her lips. "He's handsome, girl. Don't you have eyes?"

How could she not notice? But she wasn't supposed to.

"He seems to have noticed you." Dena's eyes gleamed as her lips curved into a teasing smile.

"No, he didn't." She fussed with the ring she still wore. Dirt under her fingernails. Rough, red knuckles. Multiple scratches. How lovely.

"If he offers to help, you better let him. Welcome him with open arms."

Had Dena seen her in those arms? She didn't need Dena's frustrated mothering on top of Sara's matchmaking. "I think I'll go see how Ted's doing."

"Don't you think we've made miraculous progress in two days? God's looking after you, honey." Dena returned to her mopping with a smile on her work-worn face.

Larkyn considered her neighbor and her words. "I don't deserve all this. But you're right, everyone's been great, especially you and Ted. I hope I can thank you enough someday."

Dena eyed her intently. "We just want to be the hands and feet of Jesus. Anywhere we can."

Larkyn had no answer. What did it even mean? Between Gabe's "more than luck" and Dena's talk about Jesus, she was lost. Maybe when things calmed down she'd ask. Or maybe not.

CHAPTER NINE

Larkyn opened her eyes to a close-up of red upholstery and groaned. Her back didn't approve of this lovely piece of furniture as a place to spend the night. Easing up, she trained sleepy eyes on her surroundings. Sara's room displayed some serious decorating savvy.

To complement the red divan, two simple black butterfly chairs preserved space and a fluffy cream rug brought the pieces together. A modern torchiere lamp stood in the corner, positioned well to light the small room. Larkyn retrieved two stylish white and black throw pillows from the floor. A glance at the sunburst clock told her she'd slept too long.

She stretched and toddled to the bathroom, leaving her blanket trailing from the sofa. Sara was gone and her bed was made. Her hostess left for work early. Really early. But it did help that they didn't cross paths in the morning.

With no time for breakfast, Larkyn dressed in navy slacks and a loosely woven white blouse with three-quarter sleeves. She'd brought a pair of navy pumps which worked today. Tomorrow she'd change up the blouse to create a different look. Being so far from her closet taxed her wardrobe skills, but Sara's generosity meant a lot, and she intended to minimize the impact of her presence.

The comfort of routine duties at work caused Larkyn's cloak of stress to fall off. Numbers at least obeyed the rules. With an understanding of said rules, she could master any problem. That was the theory, and it worked for her job. Today, she welcomed the numbers like a friend.

By afternoon, the friendship was over.

"Hey, get your nose off the grindstone and take a break." Georgia startled Larkyn from her fixation with the computer screen. The paralegal, and her professionally plaited hair, possessed an exotic beauty and style she owned with confidence. Today, Georgia gleamed in gold accented sandals, a canary yellow blouse, and coppery slacks that complemented her bronzed skin. Next to Georgia, Larkyn resembled a humble wren.

"I'd love to stop, but I've got a problem."

Georgia's look held a hint of pity. "Wish I could help, but math and I don't get along."

Larkyn sighed. Accounting wasn't simply math. She rubbed her forehead to ease the dull pain above her eyebrows. "Maybe I do need to clear my brain. What did Einstein say about insanity? Doing the same thing over and over and expecting a different result?"

"You got me. I'm not that close to Einstein." Georgia laughed as if she couldn't care less but waited for Larkyn to finish changing her mind.

"Okay." She sighed again, saved the data file, and closed it. The financial secrets of H&H resided with her, and this project was the Hamiltons' attempt to assess their financial health. No pressure. No pressure at all. "A break it is. But I need something decadent from downstairs."

She and Georgia descended the five floors to the lobby and ordered their drinks at the café where the coffee was a different species than the stuff they drank in their break room. Larkyn added a protein bar to appease her empty stomach, and they stepped aside to wait for their drinks.

"We missed you at lunch." Georgia, the eyes and ears of all official news-slash-gossip gave an inquisitive tilt of her head. The *we* included Kate, Martin Hamilton's relatively new secretary, who looked more like an intern than a matronly gatekeeper. But clearly, the preppy wardrobe and cheerleader smile hid something more. Else why would she work for the big boss?

"I overslept and didn't have time to pack anything. Plus, Trudy is pushing hard for this report."

"You'd think she'd lighten up after what happened." Georgia retrieved her order from the counter.

"It's a mess and gonna get worse. Today, they start the demo. I can't understand why that beautiful tree had to attack half my house."

Georgia lifted her brows. "Sounds like an opportunity to get a renovation paid for."

When the barista finished her order, Larkyn accepted her latte brimming with whipped cream topping. The two found a table near the window where they could observe the comings and goings of people they didn't know. Scratch that. *She* didn't know. Georgia was probably tracking the social pulse of downtown Raleigh this very minute.

"You don't understand, Georgia. I don't want to change our house. It's all I have of our life together—and now it's trash."

"Honey. I'm single, as you know." Georgia examined her fingernails and emphasized her drawl. "But it seems to me your life with Matthew is gone. Don't you think it's time to try something new? Redefine yourself—just a tad?"

Larkyn played with her cup, nudging it in a circle. Georgia didn't understand. Everyone knew this gorgeous friend was prowling for a husband, but Georgia's independence stood out like the boldness of her clothing. She could never understand what it was like to be a wren.

"It's hard to think about a new life, Georgia. I'm not cut out like you and Faye. You're strong people. You know what you want."

Georgia sat back. "What does Faye have to do with this? She's been gone a long time. Did you know her?"

Larkyn straightened her shoulders. "I did. She was my friend—for a while. She was hilarious and fun, and she gave me confidence. But then ... I don't know what happened. She backed off. The next thing I knew, she'd left the firm."

"Did she get another job?"

"I have no idea. I was out of it because of the accident, and I never followed up. I'm sure it wouldn't have mattered, though. Faye was going places, and having been Martin's secretary, I doubt she had any trouble getting another position."

"I'm sorry about whatever happened, but listen, girl," Georgia leaned in for emphasis. "You're just as strong as anyone here. Look at what you've come through. And look at all those numbers you deal with. I'm just saying that you have permission to have a life. You're sharp, so don't get stuck."

"Ha." Larkyn managed a smile. "Interesting you should say that. Stuck is exactly what I've been."

"So now you're unstuck." Georgia pronounced. "If that tree can't un-stick you, I don't know what can."

Well, gee. How did she miss the transformation?

Georgia tapped her phone and noted the time. "We better get back upstairs. But listen, if you want some company at Home Depot, I'm your gal. We can shop for new appliances, cabinets, paint. I'm good at all that."

"How about furniture?"

"Seriously?" Georgia's eyes gleamed.

Larkyn stood, jarring the tabletop. "Maybe," she taunted with a grin.

They tossed their cups and headed for the elevator. Georgia hurried to catch the doors before they closed on two forty-somethings right off the cover of *Men's Health*. The two talked in the code of brokers, checking their watches and adjusting their trendy ties. Out of their sight, Georgia pantomimed panting, and Larkyn sent her a stern frown. She would die before she acted like a fool over some preening executive. As soon as they exited at their floor, Georgia burst out laughing.

"Lighten up, Wagner. They were hot, and you know it."

At that moment, Trudy rounded the corner and stopped. "Just the person I've been looking for. Where did you go?"

Georgia winked from behind Trudy and made her escape with a wiggly-fingers goodbye.

"Just downstairs for a minute." Larkyn's newfound vision of freedom, wanted or not, chafed at Trudy's tone. She was responsible and got her work done. Why this pushiness? "If you mean the project, there's been a glitch, but it's coming along." Not one-hundred percent true, but close enough.

"Well, let's take a look at that." Trudy frowned.

She continued frowning at the spreadsheet Larkyn showed her. Larkyn could have told Trudy she wouldn't gain much from this exercise, but instead, she let Trudy see the work.

After several minutes, the boss's sage advice amounted to, "Keep trying."

Right. Indeed, she would. Einstein notwithstanding.

After another hour of disappointing progress, Larkyn pushed her chair back, hugged her stomach and bent forward until her forehead touched the desk. She could do this job. Why wasn't anything working? And what was so important about this ridiculous project?

Trudy cared more about these stupid numbers than she cared about Larkyn's catastrophic weekend. Like Larkyn's parents, nothing was good enough.

She stood and stalked to the women's restroom, wet a paper towel, and held it to her face. Time to calm down.

No. She wanted to stomp her foot. How could she calm down when her life was in a tailspin?

Matthew would have understood. He always cheered her up. But he was gone. She couldn't even go home to their house and hug that ugly orange pillow he loved so much.

She tossed the paper towel in the trash can and returned to her office. At least she wasn't crying again. What good did it do?

Dropping into her desk chair, Larkyn massaged her temples in a circle. Georgia was right. Sara was right. The time had come to move ahead. And while she was dumping her old life, she might as well toss her unanswerable questions. Like, why did God, if he was there at all, decide to take Matthew from her?

Releasing a pent-up breath, she straightened her shoulders. Somehow, someway, she had to start again.

She'd survived two years already, right?

With any luck, she could do a few more.

CHAPTER TEN

Gabe labored under the load he carried after only thirty minutes. The muffled impact of his boots synchronized with the cadence of his breathing, in and out. He'd chosen this trail in the woods surrounding Jordan Lake because it met pack test conditions—basically smooth, without much of a grade. The temperature was a perfect sixty-five degrees, but clouds hung low over the lake and trail as if to smother his efforts.

Following advice to start easy, Gabe was up to packing forty pounds out of the required forty-five. That was progress, but nothing compared to the ten-mile, sixty-pound weighted marches he'd survived in infantry training. 'Course both of his legs were intact at the time.

Just yesterday, he'd come across an article published back in the spring. A paratrooper with an amputation below the knee had gone back to his job with the airborne. News like that had pushed him on to fight for his return to combat. Because of those efforts, he'd done more than the doctors expected.

Until his time ran out, and the official verdict labeled him unfit for combat duty.

Dear Corporal DeSantis. You're doing great, but rehab's over. Sorry, you didn't make it.

Against the rules of his self-made regimen, Gabe stopped. Like a heel rubbed raw by a new shoe, his stump burned from friction with the socket. He uncapped his water bottle and slugged some down, giving his skin a break. He might wear a thirty-grand C-leg—the most advanced prosthetic available—thanks to Cisco and MyoPro—but it didn't matter today.

His turnaround point lay a quarter mile ahead, but painful lessons had taught him not to ignore these signs. Only rest would heal the skin and allow it to get tougher.

Gabe had never been a wimp. Massive blood loss, infections, multiple painful surgeries, muscle atrophy, and emotional trauma had made him even stronger. The fight to relearn to walk from scratch had tested him to the core.

A gaggle of cheeky crows jeered from the branches above.

"Oh, shut up," he muttered. He hated to turn back but couldn't risk the complete breakdown of the skin that covered his stump. Not with a Red Card at stake.

Limping noticeably, Gabe reached the parking lot. The placid surface of Jordan Lake lay before him. Despite the pain, he hobbled a few more steps to stand at the water's edge.

Would he ever be the man he'd been before?

Peace descended, and a higher perspective soothed his loss. The timeless God who created all this was in control. No use whining about the past. Soldiering was over. But firefighting? He had hope for that one yet.

Gabe noted the squeak as he opened the door of his truck. Yep. He had four wheels. The used F-100 had come to him through a vet named Pancho.

He cranked her up and listened. She didn't exactly purr, but aside from some minor dents and scratches that any truck worth its salt should acquire, the brakes were good, the transmission, sound, she didn't burn oil, and the tires weren't bald.

Sold. For a price he could manage. *Thank you, Lord. And thanks for Pancho too.*

The two had met at the VA's outpatient clinic, a truly depressing place. Gabe had been thinking about the untold stories represented in the room, when a swarthy fellow with a ponytail took the empty seat beside him. The guy Gabe came to know as Pancho proceeded to tell him about the AVA, also known as Raleigh's humble chapter of The Atlantic Veteran's Alliance, which in turn led to finding the truck. A considerable upgrade from his bike.

Driving back to his cousin's led him close to Larkyn's house. There'd been no complaints from the girls about bunking together, but after a week, it had to be getting old. A peek at the progress couldn't hurt.

Rounding the corner, he slowed to a crawl. No mistaking which house was hers. A truck and van convention spilled from the driveway into the street. A worker pushed a dolly loaded with boxes into the garage. Curiosity steered him to the curb, and he threw his gearshift into park.

"Gabe?"

Larkyn approached, dressed in classy business clothes. He dragged his attention from the swish of her skirt around her slender legs as she walked to meet him.

"What are you doing here?"

Good question. It seemed like a good idea a minute ago, but his sweat-stained shirt and state of un-showeredness hadn't figured into the decision. Nor did the chance she might be home.

"Hi, there. Just driving back to Cisco's." He fought the limp as he strode to meet her. "Thought I'd check on your progress. A lot going on, I see."

She turned to glance behind her. "Yeah ... I just stopped by too. Everything seems to be coming along."

Voices on the roof caught his attention. Two catlike workers flopped a layer of shingles, one at a time, over the roofing felt. The rhythmic tat of their pneumatic nail guns advanced along the row.

Gabe frowned. "You're not replacing the whole roof?"

"What do you mean? The hole is fixed, and they're almost done."

"I see. It's just that—" *Gabe shut up. Her roof is none of your business.*

"What?" She peered at him like she might inspect an unknown insect. Friend or foe?

"Well ..." Too late to let it go now. "I used to do a little construction work in the summer. Not that you have to be an expert to see that those shingles don't match."

"What do you mean, match?"

How interesting. A woman who didn't notice colors? "It's just obvious that your roof has been repaired. I mean those old shingles," he pointed upward in their direction, "are faded. Do you know how old they are?"

He might as well have asked how old her brake linings were by the look she gave him. "I have no idea. We bought this house when we married, seven years ago now. Before that? Who knows?"

The sun in her lovely turquoise eyes had gone dark. He was losing ground.

"Hey, I'm not an expert, okay. But depending on how old your roof was, it probably makes sense to reshingle the whole thing. Especially if your homeowners' insurance has a problem with a half-and-half roof."

Larkyn frowned. Worry lines creased her forehead. He might be a jerk for adding to her stress, but better now than worse problems down the line.

She tossed one side of her straight, blonde hair over her shoulder, and crossed bare arms over her silky blouse. "I think I'll let the experts decide then, if you don't mind."

"At least run it by them, okay? Before they get too far along?"

She stared at the ground, clearly not happy about a delay.

A burly guy who could match Gabe inch-for-inch appeared from nowhere in a work-worn sweatshirt and paint-spattered boots. He didn't look happy with the stranger talking to his homeowner. Once upon a time, Gabe could have taken him down in a single move. Drill sergeant style.

"Ms. Wagner? You got a complaint?"

"Hello, Buck. No. I don't have a complaint. But my friend here is asking why I'm not replacing the roof. He says the shingles don't match. Can you explain it to him?"

Buck's irritation clearly showed. "We were told that a full reroof was not covered by Ms. Wagner's insurance. Simply following orders."

Larkyn's posture said, "Satisfied?"

He ought to let it go, but words that barely sounded like his own came out of his mouth. "I wonder why not. This patch job seems to be less than ideal. If the old roof is gonna need replacing before too long, this could be a waste of money. It could jeopardize the value of her home and prevent her from reinsuring."

Buck looked at Gabe like a cigarette butt he wanted to grind into the sidewalk. "Why don't you just call the insurance company then? I'm sure they'd love your input." He made a point of turning to address the owner of the roof. "Is that all? I'd like to get back to work."

Furrows reappeared between Larkyn's eyes. "Maybe I should just check with them. I can call right now."

"Be my guest." Buck stepped back and bellowed. "Griff! Mitch! Come on down. We're done for the day."

"Wait!" she wailed. "I don't want you to leave."

Buck checked the watch on his tattooed arm. "We have other jobs, Ms. Wagner. You get my instructions straightened out, and I'll get back to the job." He hitched up his pants and tromped toward the open garage.

Larkyn looked like someone had stolen her teddy bear. And he was the thief.

Gabe rubbed his jaw. "Sorry."

"Sorry?" She straightened to her full five-foot-four inches and glared. The combination of business attire and frustration replaced his teddy bear image with another, somewhat more adult picture. Gabe averted his eyes.

Did he have the right to butt in? They were talking about a roof, not the end of the world. But didn't she want it done right?

"I know." He displayed his palms in a way that signaled backing off. "None of my business. But wouldn't you agree that now is the time to ask questions, not six months from now when you can't do anything about it?"

"Do anything about what?" She scowled. Her eyes, normally the color of sea glass, were now loaded with heat-seeking missiles aimed at center mass. "I wasn't aware I had a problem until you created one."

Leave it, Gabe. You've had your say. He ignored his own advice. "Those restorations experts Cisco told you about should have the answer. What were their recommendations?"

She blinked. "I never got any."

"What?"

"I didn't call them, okay?" She tapped one beautiful foot. "This company contacted me, and they made it sound really easy. They work with First Fidelity all the time."

Gabe ran his hand over his head, pushing his hair back, a gesture that made a lot more sense when his hair was long. Funny how old habits stuck around. But looking on the bright side, maybe the contractor was legit. Or maybe he wasn't in league with the insurance company to minimize Larkyn's payout. Shouldn't someone know for sure?

At further personal risk, he pushed. "See if you can find out how old your roof is and what your policy covers. Ask about the best practices for your situation."

Her frown began to wobble. What next? Tears? Oh, he hoped not.

He adopted a coaxing tone with room for her to call the shots. Proper negotiation technique if he remembered right. "My point is this could be an opportunity. You get it done right, and your roof will last another twenty years."

Doors slammed in the driveway and vehicles cranked. The roofing crew was leaving.

Larkyn swiped at her cheek. Where was Sara—anyone— before he hugged her again? And created complications.

"All right. I see what you're saying." The blue in her eyes had warmed—or cooled. Either way, she looked friendlier. "What should we do?"

"I think you should call the people Cisco recommended and tell them what happened." Careful not to jar their new status, he continued gently. "Ask them for a second opinion. Then you can approach your insurance company for clarification. Nothing against Buck, but his best interest might not be yours."

Her sweet blonde head bobbed. He wasn't sure which he liked more, the submissive or the fiery Larkyn. "I didn't set out to cause you trouble. Guess I couldn't stop myself." He squelched his smile.

Her subdued compliance shook him. Everything about her said *handle with care*, which he didn't need. Yet he'd slipped right into the rescuer role he couldn't seem to shake. Even in his platoon, he'd found himself defusing conflicts. A peacemaker. Maybe that was it. God said they were blessed.

"I hope to see you at my party, Gabe." She wrapped her arms around herself.

Her party. That would be the thing Sara mentioned—Larkyn's thank-you to the people in her neighborhood for helping, which he guessed now included him.

"Okay. Sure. I'll be there."

She shifted her weight and rubbed her arms against the new chill of the afternoon. "I need to get back to work."

"Right." Gabe made a move to head out himself, but her voice halted his motion.

"Thanks for stopping." The breeze caught her hair like golden strands in the sunlight and blew them across her face.

He stopped his hand from reaching out to gently smooth her hair. "No problem. Just riding by."

She collected the errant locks for herself and tucked them into place. Backing a couple of steps, she turned and left him staring.

CHAPTER ELEVEN

Larkyn headed back to work but didn't get far. Buck's high-handed ways irked her. Gabe's questions made perfect sense. She had to go back and face this thing.

Turning around at the first opportunity, she headed back to the house where the drilling and banging continued. At least the interior wounds of her house seemed to be under control.

Leaving the workers, dust, and debris, she hurried down the hall to the little bedroom office.

Matthew, posed beside his bike in full cycling gear, smiled at her from the photo on the wall. Mussed hair and hazel eyes sparkled with life, his energy and drive captured in a moment of glory.

Do not cry. She bit her lower lip with determination and took a seat at the wooden desk. Everything in the room looked shabby after seeing the renovations. Yard sale finds and consignment cast-offs, photo albums, and yearbooks, treasured once, now looked merely old and neglected. Was this her life?

No. The old might not fit anymore, and the new might feel strange, but she couldn't wallow in the in-between. With a fortifying breath, Larkyn opened the deep drawer designed for files. Somewhere in this pile of papers she'd find the age of her roof.

From the most recent on the top to the older, she dug like an archaeologist. Recent invoices, warranty statements, hospital bills, insurance statements, a bill for cremation. *Leave it.*

Down and down. Bank statements from years ago? Kept because?

There. A fat accordion folder with a crackled, yellowed label that read, *Closing 2007.* She pulled off the elastic band and thumbed through the loan documents. Nothing specific about the roof, but the house had been ten years old when they bought it and seven years had passed. Assuming this was the original roof, it was old enough to be replaced.

Satisfied, she placed a call to First Fidelity, rehearsing her words as the phone rang.

"Phil Ames."

"Mr. Ames? This is Larkyn Wagner. You handled the claim on my house after my tree fell." She took his silence for understanding. "I have a question about my roof." She recited the address, just in case. "Are you there?"

"Sure, sure. Let me pull that up." After a moment he spoke again. "What's your question?"

"The shingles being used to repair my roof don't match the old ones which appear to be seventeen years old. Shouldn't they all be replaced?"

The adjuster cleared his throat. "I see from your policy that the coverage purchased on your home does not cover replacement of the full roof unless the entire roof is damaged."

Wasn't her entire roof damaged? Just because the hole was in one spot. Larkyn exhaled. Right. This was the company that tried to pawn off her claim as flood damage. "What about the older shingles then? My roof will be partly new and partly old."

"You have a choice, of course, but what most people do is have the roof fully replaced and pay the cost difference themselves. I suggest you talk to your roofer and get a quote."

Talk to Buck? The guy who walked out? Not hardly. "Do I have to use the same person? I mean, everything else is going fine, but I don't like the way he handled my questions. He was very rude."

"You can use whomever you want, Ms. Wagner. We have a list to help homeowners out. Would you like me to recommend someone?"

Based on First Fidelity's record? "No thanks. I think I can handle it now."

"Your choice, of course. I just want to reiterate that North Carolina state law does not require insurance to match existing shingles or siding."

Siding? Nobody had mentioned the siding. Ahh, but Gabe hadn't been out back. Larkyn put her hand to her forehead. Forget it. It didn't matter. She couldn't afford replacement siding.

"I see. Thank you, Mr. Ames."

Larkyn punched the end-call icon with unnecessary force. Was it too much to expect just a little handholding? Or maybe he assumed she had a husband at home to help her navigate the terrors of wind and lightning with funds to pay for the aftermath. Such things were called acts of God. Awful.

"Mrs. Wagner?" Mr. Cooper, Jr., the cabinet maker's son hovered in the doorway. "You've got deliveries."

Outside, a Lowe's truck filled the space left by Buck and his crew.

"Where would you like these, ma'am?" A bearded fellow in a faded blue work uniform handed her a delivery invoice for a new gas stove and high-efficiency dishwasher.

"Oh, thank you. This is great."

"The cabinets have to be finished first." The younger Cooper interrupted her moment of joy.

"You want us to come back?" The man from Lowes looked bored. "We'll have to look at the schedule."

No. "How long will that be?"

"Depends."

She sighed. One day? A week? Next year? "I hate to wait, but we're not talking about a long time, are we?"

"I don't make the schedule, ma'am. But we could drop 'em in the foyer here."

Having them in the house seemed better than lost in a warehouse. "Okay. But put them by the bar here. Then get me on the list for installation. As soon as possible, please."

The man scratched the side of his jaw. "Whatever you say." He ambled out to tell his partner the verdict.

Junior leaned on his electric drill which whined as another screw spun into the wall.

Larkyn breathed a slow exhale. She had a job waiting in another part of the universe, but she needed to be here. Trudy would have to understand.

Two bulky boxes rode in on a dolly and were deposited among the clutter. Larkyn signed for delivery.

"How d'you like them?" The voice of pride called her attention back to the cabinets.

Larkyn pulled her focus away from problems. "Oh my. You're doing a beautiful job." Georgia's suggestion of a pale gray finish with stylish black pulls and knobs lifted the room to another level. Think how great the granite would look.

He nodded acceptance and stroked the face of one of the doors. "I'll finish this row and then sweep up. Tomorrow should do it."

Larkyn left him to his work and went back to the bedroom office. She restacked the papers and returned them to the drawer. Files would help. She'd get to it soon. But first, the roof. How many hundreds of dollars would it cost to do it right? Then, when this was over, she'd have to find another insurance company.

"Oh, Matthew." She closed the drawer and sat with her head in her hands. "You've really left me here with this."

Unmoved, he smiled from the wall.

Gabe had done her a favor when he questioned the shingles. For the first time, she understood why her friends pushed her to meet someone. But as tempting as it was to have help, what about love? The heart throbbing, can't-live-a-minute-apart-from-you kind.

She'd never feel that kind of love again. Couldn't imagine wanting to.

Larkyn dragged her body from the chair. While she cherished her friends, they had lives of their own.

The final answer lay with her. She had to be more responsible.

Become a woman instead of a child.

CHAPTER TWELVE

"You don't have to leave yet, you know." Sara sat in her butterfly chair hugging a sofa pillow.

"Yes, I do." Larkyn rolled the last of her undergarments and tucked them into the leftover crannies in her suitcase. Two weeks had passed. Time to get out from underfoot. Not that Sara seemed tired of stepping around her belongings or annoyed by her constant presence. But when Sara left for work, there she was, snoozing on the divan. Her stuff invaded the tiny kitchen. If Sara got home late from Cisco's, she had to tiptoe past her roommate.

"You have been more than generous, Sara. I've imposed long enough."

"You're not imposing." Sara leaned forward, smashing the pillow between her legs and elbows.

Larkyn narrowed her eyes. "I think you should check the mirror, Sara. Your nose is growing." She surveyed the floor around them. Nothing hiding, nothing missing? She sat back on her heels and pushed herself to stand.

"You got it all." Sara sighed.

A brief knock sounded on the door, and Cisco poked his head inside the room.

"You didn't have to come." Larkyn gathered two grocery bags from the kitchen counter and set them beside her suitcase and a plastic tub of toiletries.

"Hey, we can't help it if we're curious to see your new house." Cisco hugged his fiancée and kissed her on the lips.

Gabe trailed his cousin. "I'm the caboose on this train, but my cousin here insisted you might need a truck." He frowned at the sight of the luggage. All four items.

"Francisco Amato, have you no shame at all?" Larkyn cuffed him on the arm. How much did he think she had brought with her given the size of Sara's apartment?

"What?" Cisco rubbed the spot. "No need for violence. I didn't know how much you had. Women need a lot more stuff."

Sara put her hands on her hips. "Watch it, bud."

"Never mind," Larkyn waved her arms. "Everybody take something."

They formed a little parade. Everything fit in the back of her Jeep. Embarrassing but not her fault. She hadn't asked for the Army to show up.

Larkyn was right. Cisco was a conniver, but to be honest, the offense didn't sink too deep. Gabe, too, was curious to see the repairs after being coerced to photograph the damage and butting in about the roof. Buck might've been an okay guy, but his departure suited Gabe just fine.

Two cars and his truck pulled into her driveway. He and Cisco grabbed Larkyn's few possessions and headed in through the garage.

"My goodness." Sara's voice echoed as they crossed the kitchen, their shoes grinding on grit and sawdust. She sandwiched her face in her hands.

The cabinets were in, but not all of the drawers installed. The appliances stood in their places—sleek, contemporary, stainless steel. The polished surface countertops were covered with dust he could write his name in.

"Oh-my-goodness good, or oh-my-goodness bad?" Larkyn rubbed her hands together and down the front of her jeans.

"Oh, my goodness—both." Sara couldn't seem to make up her mind. "I love it. Everything's gorgeous. It's just in rougher shape than I expected to be moving back in."

Larkyn laughed. "You are such a diplomat."

"What are you going to sit on?' Sara surveyed the emptiness.

"Everything in here was ruined. I guess a trip to the outlets is next."

Gabe had never seen the before-the-storm look, but it sure seemed that God had cleared the decks for a new beginning. A jab to his belly said that might apply to himself as well.

"I'm ready when you are." Sara twirled in a circle, arms extended. "Look at all this space."

"Georgia says since we live near the heart of furniture manufacturing, we never need to pay retail."

Sara grinned. "Absolutely. We'll start with market samples and discount warehouses." She considered the open living area. "I know you and Matthew had it all together, but here's a chance to express your latent creativity."

Larkyn twisted a lock of hair on her finger, on the verge of an actual smile.

Gabe caught signs of alarm on Cisco's face. Sara was maybe just a little too into remodeling. He murmured sideways. "You takin' notes?"

Cisco pulled a face. "My poor house."

"*My* house?" Gabe teased with mock pity. "You best start thinking of *our* house, bud."

"I see you've got the flooring." Cisco ignored him and deftly changed the subject from new furniture.

Sara explored the kitchen. "Tell Cisco about your appliances." She stuck her head in the pantry, inspecting its innards. "I love gas. Can we get gas someday, honey?"

Larkyn followed Cisco who circled long narrow cartons stacked by the front door. "I guess it's okay to open one." She looked to Gabe who plunged his hand into his pocket producing the knife he always carried.

Cisco sent him a droll grin.

Mock all you want, pal. Gabe made a note to stick an elbow in Cisco's gut the first chance he got. Then he deleted the note. Were they not past fifth grade? Besides, Sara was doing a great job of hassling Cisco on her own.

"Luxury vinyl planking? Ooh, can we see?" Her voice rose to soprano range.

With Gabe's sharp yank, the tape separated and yielded a view of the contents. He lifted a plank from the top.

Cisco read the label on the box. "Light oak. Nice color. No more carpet?"

"Not in this whole area." Larkyn made a sweep with her hand. "Georgia says the hardwood will modernize, and rugs will take the color scheme and style whichever way I want to go."

Cisco interrupted whatever ideas Sara might have for new floors. "I like carpet. Glad you could save the hall and bedrooms."

"I know." Larkyn sighed. "At least one thing will be the same."

"How are you going to have your party in the midst of all this mess?" Sara had moved on.

"It'll be in Dena's yard. I'm ordering barbecue. Meanwhile, I'm going to be eating a lot of take-out myself."

"Sounds good." Gabe cast his vote. He'd come to appreciate the southern version of smoking meats.

"Thanks. I hope so." Larkyn met his smile with less than convincing confidence. "I didn't thank you for the roofing advice. You were right to question Buck. I have to pay for the added shingling, but it's the smart thing to do."

Gabe nodded, something pleasant rising in his chest. Her praise shouldn't matter that much, but it did.

"We'll see you on Saturday then." Sara hugged her friend. "Come back to my place if it gets to be too much."

Larkyn smiled. "Hey, I've got my bed and running water. The floors are going in tomorrow. A little clean-up, and like Gabe said, it's almost done."

Gabe ran a hand over his hair. It took emotional effort to break out of the victim role. He'd been there himself, and this woman was coming along.

CHAPTER THIRTEEN

Dena popped through the screen door onto her deck, oven mitts on her hands. "Thought I heard you out here.

Larkyn looked up from unloading containers of pulled pork and slaw from Smokey's Pit. If Matthew had been here, they would've had to include Texas beef brisket or go home. But he wasn't.

Ted joined them. "Beautiful day. The Lord has blessed us for sure."

Did God control the weather? Considering what happened to her house, it seemed less thorny to believe in chance. But it sounded nice coming from the couple who'd graciously agreed to host her neighborhood thank-you party on top of everything else.

"Howdy, friend. How can I help?" Sara sauntered into the yard in a denim skirt and cowboy boots, her red hair flaming. Adorable. Cisco obviously agreed as he tracked her every move.

Dena waved. "Welcome, welcome. Can someone fill the cooler with ice for me?"

Larkyn sighted Gabe on Cisco's heels.

"Hey," he called to Larkyn. "I'm your ice man, remember?" He had the audacity to wink.

Argh, Larkyn had done her best to ignore that part of the engagement party. But his dark-brown eyes twinkled with warmth like a dash of cinnamon in her coffee.

"Bless you," Dena gushed and pointed him to her kitchen.

Gabe headed off in his jeans and snug Henley T-shirt—a distracting combination. Larkyn turned from the view of his disappearing back, dismissing the way his hair suited the angles of his face now that he'd let it grow some.

She greeted the neighbors as they trickled in. The chatter increased, and bursts of laughter told her the guests were fine.

"Don't you think we need to eat?" Larkyn sidled up to Dena who signaled Ted in a way only decades of marriage could accomplish.

"Right." Ted nodded, then boomed. "Attention here. Larkyn has something to say."

She did, but the last place she wanted to be was center stage. With a big smile to hide her nerves, Larkyn faced the crowd. Nobody frowned, and nobody jeered.

"I just want to thank all of you for coming to help me. Some of us have hardly met, but you stopped whatever you were doing and tackled what you could." She called out names and specific things without once needing the list she'd tucked away in her pocket. "I'm so grateful to have such wonderful neighbors." The catch in her voice surprised her. "Um, please enjoy the food because we've got plenty."

"Hold on." Ted stepped back in. "Let's thank the Lord before we start."

People bowed their heads and stilled their hands. Larkyn followed suit.

"Father in Heaven," Ted intoned. "We thank you for this beautiful afternoon and for fellowship with our neighbors. Thank you for protecting Larkyn and for the work that's restoring her house. Bless this food we have before us and those who prepared it. Amen."

When Larkyn opened her eyes, Gabe was looking her way. How was she supposed to react? She didn't know the rules and wasn't sure she wanted to. Life was hard enough.

In the years she'd known her boss, Trudy, she'd never asked personal questions about her faith. Maybe because Trudy advertised for God as if he could be drawn upon like a checking account. But how would Larkyn know? She'd never opened an account.

"Hey, Gabe." Sara swallowed, dabbing at her mouth. "I met this guy at MyoPro. He's getting a leg like yours, and he also lost an eye. I told him about that veteran's group you hang out with. I think he's interested in adaptive sports."

"Oh, cool. Where did he serve?"

"I didn't ask, but I got his email. You can contact him if you want. We deal with the Warrior Transition Unit at Fort Bragg all the time. Y'all could be a super resource for the wounded soldiers down there."

A shadow crossed Gabe's face. "The WTU is for guys who are staying in. But give me what you've got. I'm not sure how long I'll be involved if I pass the Pack Test, but I'll be glad to introduce him to the guys on the cycling team."

Larkyn stopped chewing at the reference to biking. "Cycle team?"

"The Atlantic Veteran's Alliance has an informal group. Some guys use hand bikes, and some have standard bikes like me. Riding's a positive motivator to keep the guys—or gals—pushing forward."

"Isn't it funny how God steers our lives in new directions?" Ted shook his head. "We can be going along according to plan and all of a sudden, wham. Everything changes."

Not funny at all, Larkyn wanted to say.

Gabe swallowed a bite. "I can't say I welcomed being *steered* at the time, Mr. Thompson, but I did come face-to-face with God, which was a good thing. Maybe the best thing that could've happened to me."

Ted nodded his understanding. There it was, like a secret club. So pleased with themselves. Larkyn studied the ice in her cup. It might be nice to know how Ted was steered. Dena too, for that matter. How would they feel if one of them were taken away like her husband was? If the person at fault were unknown and running free?

"What brought you to faith, son?"

"The end of my career." Gabe tugged the leg of his jeans up to reveal his shoe and metal ankle. "I got caught in the blast radius of a bomb that destroyed my friend. That's when God became personal."

Larkyn held her breath.

Dena stood by Ted and put her hand on his shoulder. "My husband can be pushy. Don't feel you have to explain."

"I don't mind." Gabe seemed remarkably comfortable with disclosing the details in public. "I was raised an Italian Catholic in Brooklyn, New York. My mom insisted we go to mass, catechism class, and all that stuff, but it didn't mean a lot to me."

"But now it does?" Dena smiled.

"Well, no, ma'am. Not really. But God came out of the stained glass. He's helped me every day, which is good because my life's been pretty much wiped out, and I'm not sure where I'm going from here."

Dena's eyes shimmered as she smiled at Gabe. "Believe it or not, that's not a bad place to be. I will pray for you, Gabe. God has a plan. He's always ahead of us on the road."

Really? Larkyn stifled her irritation. She stood. "I think I'll get the dessert."

Sara joined her in the kitchen.

"How's it going over at the house?" Sara asked as she scooped ice cream onto bowls of golden, pastry-topped peaches.

"It's going great. Since you saw it, the kitchen's finished and the floors are in. I've looked at some furniture Georgia likes, but if we can shop together, I'd love your help with decisions." Larkyn paused and swallowed hard. "The home I shared with Matthew is gone—" She couldn't finish.

Sara patted her shoulder. She didn't have to say a word. The truth was obvious. Change had come whether Larkyn was ready or not.

"Hey, where's the cobbler?" An impatient guest, who sounded suspiciously like Cisco, shouted.

"Keep your shirt on. We're coming." Sara tossed the empty carton, and they each picked up a tray.

When Larkyn took her seat again, the men's conversations had turned to sports. A group of moms chatted while the kids ran loose. This was her party, and everyone belonged somewhere but her.

Cisco nudged her. "Ya wanna play a game of corn hole? I need to teach someone a lesson." He nodded toward his cousin who'd attracted the attention of a few of the female neighbors.

"Why?"

Cisco looked bewildered. "I need a reason?"

Larkyn shook her head. Did this attitude come from being Italian, being cousins, or just being Cisco?

"Come on." He tugged at her arm. "You can't poop out on your party."

"Nobody's pooping out." She let him pull her to her feet.

"Who's pooping?" One of the cavorting boys screeched to a halt.

"The birds." Cisco ducked. "You better watch your head." The child whooped and took off to spread the news.

"Oh my gosh, Cisco." Sara caught the end of the exchange. "Is that how you're going to raise our children?"

"Come on, soldier-boy." He called to Gabe, ignoring the question. "Leave your fans."

"Excuse me." Gabe stepped back from his conversation. He put his face in Cisco's. "What's your problem?"

"We're playing this cornhole game. You and Larkyn against me and Sara."

"You'll be sorry," Larkyn declared.

Cisco smirked at Gabe's uncertain frown.

Gabe apparently decided to take the challenge, because he followed as they crossed the grass and took their places.

Sara went first, releasing her bag of dried corn in a slow arc toward the board with the hole in it. Complete miss.

Gabe's turn. No score.

Cisco put his bag of corn on the board for one point and strutted.

Larkyn aimed as if she were going to bowl a strike, took a step, and let it fly. Bam. In the hole.

"Beginner's luck," Cisco muttered.

Gabe smacked her hand with a high five.

After several rounds, Larkyn continued to drive up the score. At twenty to twelve, Gabe's toss scored the last point.

"Yes! "He punched at the air. "Teach who a lesson?"

Larkyn gasped as he swept her into a one-armed swirl.

"You had a ringer." Cisco waved a hand in dismissal.

Gabe laughed. "You pushed us into this, bud."

Larkyn caught her breath as her feet landed on the grass, and the world stopped spinning. They were only playing a silly game, but something inside her surged, making it hard not to whoop out loud.

Sara's enigmatic smile didn't help. "I think we're all going to enjoy that hayride."

"Hayride?" Larkyn cocked her head to the side.

"Ladders to Life, remember?" Sara grinned. "Next weekend?"

CHAPTER FOURTEEN

Larkyn hustled across some farmland that had to be at least fifty miles from home. Not according to her directions, but the drive had sure been long. Whoa, where did all these kids come from?

Her ankle turned, and she stumbled on the uneven ground. Despite running late, she slowed her pace and took in the scene. Rowdy boys and girls swerved and dodged each other on the rutted field in a fierce game of tag. Hoisting her paper grocery bag higher in her arms, Larkyn aimed for the adults and the smoky aroma of roasting hot dogs.

"Hey, Larkyn. Good to see you." Greetings from some of Matthew's former colleagues at MyoPro made her smile. She'd seen a few at Sara's engagement party, and they remembered her. How sweet.

"Thanks, it's good to be here." She called back, realizing she meant the words.

"Sorry I'm late." She caught her breath as she pulled up beside Sara who quickly moved browned, juicy wieners from the grill to an aluminum pan with tongs. "Tell me what to do."

Sara wiped her forehead with the sleeve of her plaid flannel shirt and pointed to a pair of plastic gloves. "Put those on and get these hotdogs into buns."

Larkyn stowed her belongings under the portable table and got busy. As she worked, a whistle pierced the bedlam and most of the craziness halted.

"Hey! Listen up." Gabe, dressed in jeans and a US Army T-shirt, issued the order with the authority of a drill sergeant.

"The mess line forms here." He pointed to the ground at his feet. "Tell the cooks what you want on your dog, take a bag of chips, then sit wherever you want. We'll bring the drinks."

He nodded to Cisco and some of the other men, then watched his troops obey. "And don't forget your napkin."

Gabe strode by as Larkyn replenished the open box of Doritos, Lays, and SunChips. "You can have seconds, but only after you finish what you have." With a wink and a softer voice, he added, "Be sure to save room for the cookies."

Trying not to stare openly, Larkyn marveled at his display of authority—and the humor and kindness beneath it.

Before the kids could disperse, he barked again. "Attention everyone. Time to police the area." A few of the kids exchanged funny looks. Police? Perhaps not be the best word to use for clean-up around this crowd, but Gabe rolled on.

"This is Team Alpha." He raised the hand of a boy on his right, then turned to the left and found another leader. "You are Team Bravo. Whoever has the heaviest bag of trash at the end of the game wins."

Wins what? He didn't say, but armed with their black-plastic trash bags, the teams raced to clear the ground of litter.

"Hey, what do we have for prizes?" Gabe approached the server's table where the women were cleaning up.

"You mean you don't have anything?" Sara glowered. "What were you thinking? We can't lie to these kids."

Larkyn raised her hand like a child in school. "I brought some Tootsie Roll Pops." Why, she didn't know, except that she'd never been allowed to have them when her parents were around. "They're under the table."

"You did?" Sara's astonishment said little for her faith in Larkyn.

"Atta girl." Gabe grinned his approval and smacked her palms in a double high-five.

Cisco retrieved the paper sack from under the table. Tossing her vest and scarf aside, he revealed a Costco-sized bag of candy and crowed, "We got prizes."

"Don't give me a heart attack like that again." Sara formed a circle with her hands as if to strangle Gabe.

"O, ye of little faith." He pulled a cute, one-sided smile.

The teams presented their bags to Gabe, everyone crowding around him. Making a show, he struggled to lift each one, comparing them twice. With a baffled look, he tried once more, then shrugged dramatically. "I have to declare a tie."

Cheers erupted, and the kids pumped their arms in the air. "Pri-zes," they chanted.

Larkyn could hardly dispense the suckers fast enough, so Sara ripped a bigger hole in the plastic and grabbed handfuls to give away while Gabe staggered, wiping nonexistent sweat from his brow. What a ham—the Cisco side of him.

The remnants of the day faded to a pink glow as the sun dropped below the horizon, taking its warmth along. Larkyn hugged herself and retrieved her vest and scarf from the ground. They'd done their part. Others would supervise the hayride.

She tilted her head at Gabe. "I had no idea you were a cross between the Pied Piper and Kindergarten Cop."

"Aww, shucks." He mimed a modest cowboy, then extended a courtly elbow. "You ready to take a ride, little lady?"

"Why yes, sir. I believe I am." She ducked her chin and curtsied.

Gabe found a comfortable spot on the bed of hay and closed his eyes. As soon as it got quiet, the Pack Test occupied his thoughts. He should be well on his way to acing the thing by now, but setbacks were killing him. God knew the questions haunting his thoughts. Something had to give.

Fragments of young voices singing camp songs drifted through the encroaching darkness as the wagons creaked along. Truthfully, getting out with these kids was the highlight of his week. The horses snorted. He caught a whiff of fresh manure.

"Look at that!" Excited shouts broke into his reverie. The wagon rolled to a stop.

Who-ee. Someone had built an awesome blaze.

"Who's in charge here?" Cisco looked at Gabe who looked right back at him.

"This is your deal, man. Corporal DeSantis is retired. I hear marshmallows calling my name."

"Gotcha." Cisco shrugged and took off to catch up with Sara.

Gabe surveyed the scene. Okay, a brief perimeter check wouldn't hurt.

The microprocessors in his leg handled the bumpy ground with ease. He couldn't fault that training in the least. Now, if the skin on his stump would just cooperate.

He saw no sword fights with burning sticks or dangerous pushing. The lure of more sugar seemed good enough to keep the troops entertained. Excellent.

He spotted Larkyn on her knees helping a timid-looking tyke hold her stick in the fire. The child wore a miniature jean jacket embroidered with flowers, and her head was covered in rows of plaits fastened with pink barrettes. What a cutie.

By the time the two finished, he'd strung a couple of marshmallows on a branch and carried them to Larkyn who watched her little friend run off.

"Did you see Sherice? Isn't she adorable?"

"Yep." Gabe loaded his own stick. Someone else was mighty cute too, but he had no right to say so.

They stood together as close as they could to the heat. Larkyn rotated her stick with absurd patience while Gabe set his ablaze. Within seconds, he blew out the fire with an enormous puff and swallowed the blackened goodies.

"Another lesson of childhood," he mumbled through a full mouth. "He who hesitates is last."

"It's *lost*," she said with an indulgent smile, content to gently brown her marshmallow.

"No. Last. As in, misses out on everything."

Her delicate fingers extracted the marshmallow with care befitting a surgeon. "Oh, you mean competition—survival of the fittest … or fastest?"

If she grinned like that all the time, he might be lost himself. "Yep. Hang around and you'll get the idea."

"Not sure I want to." She looked for a place to wipe her fingers.

He offered her his shirttail. "It's washable."

She chose, instead, to wipe them down her jeans. "So are these."

Ahh, so they were. And nicely fitting as well.

Cisco interrupted Gabe's questionable appreciation. "Hogging the marshmallows?" He snatched the bag.

Gabe made a face at his departure. "Did Matthew act like that with his siblings?"

Her grin disappeared. "I don't know. I wish we'd talked more about things like that."

Never talked about his childhood? How bizarre. This woman was a puzzle, but she'd managed to fly in under the radar and capture his attention. The more she forgot to be sad, the more she disrupted his agenda with foreign ideas.

"Hey, you guys, come sit with us." Sara trotted by with the blanket she'd brought aboard the wagon. The leaders had wrapped up the marshmallow roast and now herded their charges into a semi-circle in front of quiet flames that gently consumed what was left of the logs.

After a brief spell of jostling for position, the crowd settled. Larkyn sat sandwiched between Gabe and Cisco, while Sara sat in front, resting on Cisco's chest. Gabe leaned back with his hands behind him and crossed his ankles, sharply aware of the woman at his side.

She seemed ready for arctic conditions with that scarf wrapped up to her ears. While everything about her said fragile, he'd seen changes since the tree had bashed her house. Too bad any guy who pursued her would have to compete with a ghost.

His cousin pulled his future bride closer, nuzzling his nose in the crook of her neck. Cisco had scored big with Sara. Watching them raised questions Gabe couldn't answer. If Plan B succeeded, Gabe would wind up under another starry sky washing soot off his face and trading survival stories with his buds on a firefighting crew. But what if it didn't?

What was so wrong with the scene right here? More to the point, why were those eyes and lips that seldom smiled so hard to get out of his mind?

CHAPTER FIFTEEN

Wedged between solid male bodies on either side, Larkyn felt sheltered by two Rocks of Gibraltar. Cisco provided half the warmth, but she couldn't escape Gabe's presence. Here he sat, dressed in a flimsy cotton shirt, no jacket, looking perfectly relaxed and comfortable—as if he couldn't be rattled by anything.

"Once upon a time on a night like this one, a shepherd sat by his fire guarding his flock of sheep." The woman storyteller wore a long skirt and dangly earrings. With the scarf around her hair, she looked like a gypsy. "He made sure his sheep had good grass to eat and water to drink as they grazed until the sun went down." She paused to let them imagine the scene.

"Can you hear the sheep calling, *baa-baa* to each other as the flock gathered for the night? It was time for the shepherd to count the lambs to be sure everyone was safe. Why did he count? Because predators lived in the darkness. Who knows what a predator is?" She looked for raised hands.

"A bad guy?" a voice called out.

"You could say that." She nodded. "Sheep's predators in Bible times were wild animals—bears, wolves, or lions. Wouldn't one of them love a tasty lamb for dinner?" She shivered causing her earrings to sway. "But the shepherd stayed alert. Every night, he counted his one-hundred sheep to be sure that all were with him.

"But this night, the shepherd frowned and started again, touching each one as he counted." She tapped the heads of several children. "Ninety-nine sheep. Oh no." She pressed her hands to her cheeks in dismay. "How many was he supposed to have?"

"Uh-hundred," the children shouted back.

"That's right, one-hundred—somebody was missing." She let that sink in before raising helpless hands. "What do you think he did?"

Larkyn studied the wide-eyed listeners as several spoke up with their answers.

"He couldn't do nothing till the morning."

"He yelled for the lamb to come back."

"He was mad."

"No, he was sad."

Had their perspectives come from real life? Probably.

The story lady continued. "This shepherd was very brave. He lit a torch from his fire and carried the flame into the dark. He searched everywhere until he found his lost lamb. Then he picked it up and carried it back in his arms."

"Do you believe this?" Larkyn whispered to Gabe.

"The story?"

"Well, yes, but I mean the Bible."

"Yeah, I do."

"All of it? The flood and the Garden of Eden?"

"As far as I know, I do. I accept it. I don't think it's a lie."

"Well, not a lie. But an allegory—or symbolic? Not literally real."

"Ssshh." Cisco shushed her. "I'm tryin' to hear."

Gabe put his lips near her ear and whispered. "Maybe now's not the time for a theological discussion. But I can tell you I don't question what I read in the Bible."

She nodded, the issue of Bible validity got lost in the warmth of his breath and the scent of his personal nearness. Long dormant desires to be held and even kissed surfaced like tiny bubbles trapped underwater. This could not be good.

Larkyn peeked at Gabe's profile as the storyteller finished her lesson. His Italian background showed in his olive skin tone and dark hair. He was handsome but not in the airbrushed way of magazine models. Gabe's face bore the lines of someone who'd gone through horrors and emerged with beautiful scars. He had a gentle side to go with the strong, and she saw someone she trusted. Matthew was carved into her heart as clearly as the heart in the bark of her tree. The tree and its promise were gone, but little by little, Gabe had become more than just part of the package with Sara and Cisco. Gabe was his own man—and he was very much alive.

"You are God's little lamb," the storyteller told each child as she handed them a flannel cutout shaped like a sheep. Even the older kids seemed happy with the gift.

Larkyn pondered her own world-class collection of Build-a-Bears and her Beanie Baby menagerie. Material things didn't translate into love when she was growing up, but these strangers had shown the children they had value in a simple lesson. Sara was right, Larkyn needed to be here.

As the wagons rolled out, Sara and Cisco hogged the blanket. And why not? She had the foresight to bring it. Larkyn shook her head at Gabe's coatless condition. "Aren't you cold at all?"

"Hey, you haven't experienced cold until you sit in a hole all night in Afghanistan. In the mountains. In January." He chose a place to recline, dismissing her concerns. "I'm pretty sure my temperature gauge got broken."

Cisco snorted. "And I suppose you marched ten miles in five feet of snow, uphill both ways?"

"No, I didn't." Gabe shot back. "More like twenty miles."

Larkyn watched him get comfortable on the hay, ignoring his cousin, lacing his fingers behind his head.

"Ah. There's the big dipper." Gabe pointed.

Larkyn craned her neck. "Where?"

Gabe patted the hay beside him. "Try the view from here. It's nothing like the stars you see in—" He shielded his mouth from Cisco's sight, "an unnamed country far away. But it's pretty nice."

What could she say? No thank you. I don't care about seeing pretty stars?

In fact, she loved the night sky. She and Matthew used to lounge on the sand at Jordan Lake after a long day on the water and locate the constellations. She'd always wondered about what might be out there beyond their sight, even beyond human knowledge. She might've been small, but to Matthew, she mattered. He'd been her hiding place under the vault of the heavens.

Gabe gave up and enjoyed the stars by himself. A sharp finger poked at her conscience. How nice did a person have to be for her to treat them like a friend?

She scooted closer on the seat of her jeans and leaned back to lie on the hay. *Oh.* A brilliant crescent moon ascended from the horizon accompanied by a dramatic pair of companions, Jupiter and Saturn. Someone had spilled a bucket of stars across the blackness. The dipper stood out as always.

She wondered aloud. "Is that why they call it the Milky Way?"

Gabe continued to look at the sky. "Is what why?"

"You know. The stars. They look like spilled milk." Their quiet conversation dribbled along.

"They do?"

"Somebody thought so." Where was his imagination? Didn't they call it the Milky Way for a reason? Even in foxholes?

A giggle pushed for escape from the lockdown she had on her heart. Cisco's jabs at Gabe about everything. Gabe's own parries like an agile fencer, inflicting strikes of his own.

The giggle found a crack.

He rolled to one elbow with an inquiring look. The wagon, the world, were lost in the darkness, but his face was close. If Sara noticed, nosy questions were ahead. For the moment she didn't care.

"I was thinking about how grand it must have looked in Afghanistan, but how you can hardly mention the word without Cisco jumping on your case. It seemed funny."

"I like it when you laugh. You don't do it often enough." He narrowed his eyes. "Of course, that was not a laugh. Sounded more like a strangled pigeon."

"Oh really?" Her chances of scoring against him were next to zero, but so what? "Strangling a pigeon is no laughing matter, mister. That should be reported."

"My point exactly." He kept his features neutral. "Laughing is serious business."

"What?" Okay, she was lost. Had lost. But when verbal sparring didn't work, one could resort to hay.

Larkyn grabbed a handful of straw from beside her and tossed it in his general direction hitting nothing. Unimpressed by her pathetic effort, he resumed his position on his back. *Okay*. She scooped a double handful and targeted his peaceful face. With total success.

What in creation had she been thinking? Victory lasted mere seconds as he coughed dust and spit dried grass. One hand shot out like lightning fastening around her wrist. She sucked in air.

"No. I'm sorry. Please forgive me. I'll never do it again." In her head, this was a game, but a hammer in her chest attacked with solid blows. Fight? Run? Play dead?

His other arm encircled her like steel. She drew into a defensive ball.

He smelled like aftershave. Sandalwood and citrus? His breath carried the barest hint of burned marshmallow along with something minty. The voice of Captain Hook growled.

"Do you know what we do with troublemakers?"

Bravado was all she had. "What? I don't see any planks. Guess you'll have to let me go."

His arm loosened but didn't release her. "I have to say, that attack on me was very un-pigeon-like of you."

Out of comebacks, she sighed. "Pigeons have their moments too, I guess."

His laugh warmed the air around her, and his eyes lit up like twin flares of delight. In her?

"Just so you know," he advised with mock seriousness, "I had a lot of experience standing up to my older sister."

Ohh, he compared her to his sister. That was safe. Hadn't she wanted safe?

His retreat to his own space, supported on one elbow, left her in the cold. "What about you? Any brothers to defend your honor or teach you how to defend yourself?"

She picked at the straw on her vest and brushed stray hairs from her face, tucking them behind her ear. "Neither. I'm an only child."

"Cousins?"

"Nope. Just me. A lonely waif locked in the turret of my father's castle."

"Come on."

"It's true." She pressed. For an unknown reason, it felt important he understand. "I hate it for you that your father left, but you were lucky. I wished for a brother or sister for a long time until I gave up. I doubt my parents planned on having me, and they certainly didn't want another kid."

He studied her. She shrugged. It didn't matter anymore. Or it hadn't while she had Matthew.

"Larkyn, God meant for you to be." The seriousness in his dark eyes wouldn't let her look away. "If I learned anything from my brush with death, it's that even if you don't feel deserving, life is a gift to be thankful for. You don't want to throw your life away, and you don't want to have any regrets."

She didn't answer—she couldn't.

"My advice," he said. "Live your life. The one you have. The one you want. And don't let anything stop you."

CHAPTER SIXTEEN

Larkyn shut the door and took her customary seat in Trudy's office. The leather armrest of the chair she sat in was the color of mellow eggnog and felt soft as a well-worn glove. If she could afford something this nice, new furniture might appeal. Trudy paired them with bold accents of black and turquoise, but Larkyn favored a more soothing combination. Maybe grey-blue and sage green like the colors at Jordan Lake.

Trudy broke into her fanciful illusion with an apology for not acknowledging the report she'd rushed Larkyn to finish. The dynamic duo had just returned from Scottsdale, Arizona, where Martin presented the keynote address at a conference on business ethics. Kate had complained about how cranky Martin had been and how many times she had to retype his speech.

"Let's see what you have." Trudy extended her hand for the printouts.

Larkyn passed the folder across the desk. While Trudy read and skimmed the tables, Larkyn steadied her foot which jiggled with a mind of its own. Despite her father's disappointment, avoiding this kind of pressure was why she'd avoided the CPA world. Let her be a simple bookkeeper with ducks that stayed in their rows.

"You've done a lot of work, my dear. Thank you." Trudy smiled.

After the struggle to put this report together while doing her normal work and living in chaos at home, was that all Trudy could say? "Did I accomplish what you wanted?"

Trudy glanced down at the file and put her hand on top. "I'll look at this more closely, but don't worry. I can tell you did an excellent job."

She could *tell*? "Do the figures show what you wanted to see?"

Trudy reached for other papers and shuffled them into a stack. "Don't worry about it, honey. I'm sure they are very helpful."

Larkyn balked. *I am not your honey. I'm a professional.*

In the past, she would have been relieved and grateful for the praise, but today it felt like a brushoff. Except what about all those weeks she'd wished for work she could do in her sleep? Now, she wanted significance?

Such contradictions came from listening to Gabe. *Be who you are, huh?*

Larkyn wiped her hands on her wrinkled linen slacks. If Trudy was finished, she might as well get back to her desk and her little job.

But Trudy leaned forward in the way she often did before prying into Larkyn's life. With a probing look, she began. "I haven't been the friend you deserve lately. Here you've had a terrible thing happen to your house and who knows what all. I can't take time for a long lunch, but I can ask Kate to call downstairs for a couple of salads. Stay and catch me up?"

"Um. Okay, sure." What else could she say?

While they waited for their lunches to come, Larkyn recounted recent happenings. Trudy touched the stylish cross hanging from her necklace. "My goodness. Sounds like God has been looking out for you through your friends. Nothing's too small to escape his notice, you know. He's numbered every hair on your head."

Larkyn fiddled with her wedding rings. Everyone probably thought she should take them off. She unlinked her fingers and lay her hands on the arms of her chair. What about the hairs on Matthew's head?

"I can see he might be looking out for me as you say, but why did the lightning strike my tree in the first place? Did he forget, or did he want for this to happen?"

"Sweetheart."

Trudy had an explanation that Larkyn didn't want to hear. Heat rose to her cheeks. Who cared about the tree? She wanted her husband back. To live his whole life. With her. Like they planned.

"Everything that happens in this world is not God's will." Trudy tilted her head as if the truth were obvious. "If our ancestors in the Garden, and every person since had trusted God and never disobeyed, the world would be perfect as God intended. But we know that didn't happen."

"And now we have to live with it." A point of pressure built in Larkyn's chest, as if Trudy's tidy explanation had lit a fuse. If they continued down this road, she'd lose control of the bombs inside and maybe destroy their relationship. No one wanted to see her temper tantrum. Not her mother or her father or anyone else.

"We live with the consequences, yes, but not alone." Trudy regarded her for a moment, not a speck of doubt in her eyes. "Jesus paid for our forgiveness, and he's here to comfort us when things get bad. His life sets us free from the effects of sin if we allow him to. He loves you, child. Try to believe that."

Did believing make it true? Perhaps her father's scorn for religion was set too deep in her mind. "I don't know why I can't, Trudy. It doesn't seem real."

"Do you read the Bible?"

"Sometimes." As in almost never. The small New Testament and Book of Psalms the chaplain in the hospital had given her could be anywhere. She'd gone along with the chaplain when he prayed with Matthew's parents who'd come out from California, but nothing took away her fear that he would die. Everyone could see how that turned out.

"Try reading a little every day." The woman across the desk looked earnest. "God's Word is alive. It reaches into our hearts. Jesus said the truth will set us free."

Set her free? She was on her own. She had too much freedom already. Larkyn crossed her arms. She'd always obeyed her parents, except when she married Matthew. After that, she *wanted* to follow her husband. The two of them were free and happy together—period, exclamation point.

What about God's rules? He was famous for them.

Before she could pelt Trudy with such relevant questions, something she'd never have the nerve to do anyway, Kate announced her presence. "I've got your salads, Mrs. Hamilton."

"Thank you, Kate. Just set them here."

Kate complied with a peek at Larkyn. Yes, lunch with the boss today.

Two clear plastic boxes revealed crispy green romaine, chicken grilled just right and a packet of creamy dressing. A caddy held two plastic cups of tea on ice with lemon. Yum. Could they just enjoy the food?

Trudy blessed the salads and added a prayer for Larkyn's peace of mind. She asked God to give her grace to understand and know the truth about his love for her. Surprisingly, the angry knot in Larkyn's chest gave way to the urge to cry. A tear trickled from the corner of her eye, but she dabbed it with her napkin and gulped the untimely meltdown away with a healthy swallow of tea.

Trudy smiled. "It's okay to cry, you know."

And it's good to get through emotional minefields without blowing oneself to pieces. Larkyn's lips formed a compliant smile before she speared the lettuce.

CHAPTER SEVENTEEN

Gabe's blaring alarm clock penetrated the depths of his sleep. How long had it been beeping? His fingers closed around the obnoxious source and silenced the alarm. The explosion dream had struck again, but he'd been able to dismiss it quickly and fallen right back to sleep. Making progress.

He flipped the covers off and reached for his crutch. His laptop, on the floor, sat open from his search the night before. What a joke. The Forest Service recruitment specialist understood his situation. Gabe had combat experience. His Army record proved he could operate in a demanding work environment, deal with long hours and high stress. But after all these weeks, he hadn't been able to find a sponsoring agency willing to take him. There might even be a policy against it.

Gabe made his way to the shower where the hot spray pounded his shoulders and back. Would he ever get past the stigma of having a missing leg? Someday, some lucky guy would come along and prove it could be done. Why couldn't it be him?

Dressed in baggy shorts and a T-shirt, Gabe grabbed a bottle of water. Despite the discouraging report, time to get to work.

His times were improving, even fully loaded, but what did it matter if he never got to take the test? Gabe shook off the negativity and cranked his truck intending to drive to Jordan Lake. On second thought, the body adapted to predictable demands. He'd seen a shady suburban park on his way to the AVA. A change of scene might help.

The drone of landscape mowers greeted him. Sunlit orange, red, and gold leaves fluttered from the trees and decorated pathways occupied by joggers and faithful early risers, walking their dogs.

He stretched, then hefted the weighted backpack with a grunt. In minutes, his gait hit a comfortable rhythm as his muscles warmed to a steady, aggressive pace, eating up the pavement. At this rate, he would make his target time.

"Excuse me." A jogger in spandex veered to pass him as he finished a loop around the park. Her ponytail swung with every stride, as her two perfect legs drove like efficient machines. The distance between them increased, and soon, she'd rounded a curve and disappeared.

The pack's straps dug into his shoulders, but Gabe pressed on. Pain was normal. The job would be tough. Firefighters carried heavy equipment, cut paths, dug trenches, and hiked up mountains. The test was called arduous for a reason.

Approaching mile two, his breathing was fine, but his left leg throbbed and felt heavier with every step. *Aw, come on.* Was this normal pain or the beginning of something more?

"Slow is fast, Gabe." His PT spoke from the past. "If you keep overdoing it, you're going to get another infection, and you know what that means. Be patient. You can only push so hard. You'll get stronger, but let your body guide you."

The answer pierced his hope like a toddler's balloon. His body cried to stop.

Blast. How could this happen again?

The litany of warnings he knew by heart crashed in. Keep on and damage the skin on his stump. Again. Break from training and lose the conditioning he'd gained. Either way spelled failure for now.

Gabe pulled up at the parking lot and stopped. He shed his pack to the grass and stood with hands on his hips. He'd be stupid to go another step much less another lap.

The sun slipped behind a cloud, leaving the morning breeze to chill his sweaty skin. Gabe sank to the ground and gulped from the water bottle. Beautiful colors of fall disguised the fact the leaves were dying. Like his dreams. He'd vowed to never give up, but what was the alternative? Try again next season? When he'd be that much older?

If these doors didn't open, what would he do? Who would he be?

The automatic sprinklers came on and peppered him with cold spray. Perfect. He picked up his pack by one strap and lugged it to the truck, refusing to limp.

Gabe entered the kitchen and found his cousin pouring batter onto a skillet. His empty stomach seized upon the aroma of bacon, coffee, and the sizzle of pancakes on the way.

Cisco turned from the stove and slapped him on the back. "Hey, cuz. Where ya been?"

"Out." Gabe picked up a carton, poured a tumbler of orange juice, and downed it. Then ditching the surly approach, he added, "Smells good."

The front door opened and closed with a bang. "Hi, guys." Sara strolled in, her hair full of bounce and her green eyes bright.

Cisco gave her a quick kiss. "Want some breakfast?"

"I've eaten, thanks." She sat next to Gabe. "I'll take coffee, though." She stole a piece of bacon from the platter.

Cisco handed her a steaming cup of coffee, then passed a stack of plump hotcakes from his spatula to Gabe's plate. "Syrup's there."

"Thanks." Gabe doused them and took three slices of bacon while Cisco poured another batch of pancakes. "Since when did you become a cook?"

"Oh, I've got a lot of secret talents. Ain't that right, darlin'?" Cisco winked at Sara.

Sara harrumphed. She scrutinized Gabe over the rim of her mug. "Are you a bit more haggard than usual this morning, my almost brother-in-law?"

Gabe liked directness to a point. He swallowed a huge bite of sweetness. "I'm trying to figure out what's happening to my life."

Cisco sat down and took the rest of the bacon.

"What's wrong with your life, Gabe?" Sara pushed this time. Usually Cisco's job, but hey, now they were a tag team. "Does this have to do with that test you're training for? How's that going, by the way?"

"It's about getting my leg blown off and being forced to deal with helplessness and the end of my career." Wow. Sarcasm, too? He sounded like a whiny brat. Not to mention that he'd just laid himself open to all manner of snarky comebacks. Instead, they ganged up with silence.

Cisco shared two extra pancakes and pushed the maple syrup at him.

"Thanks, but I can feed myself," Gabe snapped.

"Whoa." Sara set her coffee down.

Gabe crossed his arms like a five-year-old. "Sorry."

Cisco leaned toward his future bride, "Soldier-boy's afraid he won't pass the test even though he hasn't tried yet."

Gabe scowled. His cousin's put-downs were getting old. Why couldn't they have a normal conversation?

Sara put her hand on Gabe's arm. "Don't listen to Cisco. He's being a jerk." She continued to search him. "The hayride was great, and I know you had fun. Did something happen?"

This had nothing to do with the hayride. Gabe disengaged his prosthesis and exposed his stump. He peeled back the stocking liner to assess the damage. Raw, red skin but no blood. Rest and antibiotic cream should fix 'er up—along with the patience he seemed to lack.

"I am so sorry." If tenderness could be bottled, Sara would be rich. His cousin did not deserve her.

He blinked to dispel the tears that threatened to spill. What was wrong with him?

"I had another flashback last night. I'm working my tail off to get ready for this test, but I need a sponsoring agency, and no one's interested in a guy without all his limbs. Now this." He motioned at his offending thigh with contempt. "I went out to train, and you can see what happened. What am I supposed to do?"

"I know you could get this for yourself." Cisco set a cup of fresh coffee before him, and Gabe acknowledged the gesture with a nod. He could use it, strong and hot.

Sara watched him brave the first tentative sip. "Maybe you should give it a day or two before you decide what this means."

A day or two? He'd been at this for a couple of months and the pattern kept repeating. Maybe it was time to seriously pray—again. God had brought him all this way. But for what?

Cisco took their plates to the sink. Gabe lounged and sipped his coffee.

"Okay." Sara pushed her hair back, a completely futile gesture. "It's not an answer to the rest of your life, but try this on. The new *Interstellar* movie comes out on Thursday. Why don't the four of us go?"

The four of us. Hmm. They were an entity now? "Has Larkyn signed off on this plan?"

"I'm sure she'll be fine with it."

"You didn't ask her? Isn't that presuming a lot?"

Sara hitched her purse over her shoulder as she stood. Her green eyes seemed to peer right into his head. Maybe she should've been a shrink.

"All right, Mr. Manners, let's do this correctly. You call Larkyn and ask if she wants to go to the movies with us—and let me know. Right now, Cisco and I have a date to taste wedding cakes."

Their departure left the kitchen quiet. Cisco's Honda growled to life and thundered away, leaving him alone.

Gabe leaned on his elbows with his head in his hands. *Father, forgive my rotten attitude.* He sighed and spoke softly, "Show me the way up, around, or through this mountain, because I've hit another roadblock."

No voices answered, no writing appeared on the wall, but his mind cleared and his mood improved. Okay, then. What about this movie thing? He'd done right by not agreeing immediately. Sara meant well, but neither he nor Larkyn needed to get swept up in someone else's agenda.

What did he want for his life? Aside from a new career?

Gabe had never dated much. Cisco was the ladies' man. Relationships were available in the Army, but falling in love while fighting a war didn't make sense to him. Nor did temporary liaisons grounded in lust. His mother's struggle after his father deserted their family stayed with him like a watchful eye. With one heart to give, he'd given it to the Army until the Army broke up with him.

Flinching a little at the pain, Gabe reattached his prosthesis and dragged himself down the hall to care for his wounded stump. An interesting thought percolated to the surface. Wildland firefighters deployed like soldiers for long periods of time. They worked as a team with life and death in the balance. Did that explain the attraction? As much as he hated to admit it, his cousin's insults might have a point. Did being a hero ease the rejection from his dad?

Gabe treated his skin with meticulous care and then sat on the edge of his bed. Larkyn Wagner had never expressed an interest in anything but Matthew. Gabe had no right to cause waves in her little world. Yet, it was only a movie, and she could say no. Judging by the hayride, the odds were probably even.

With his stump clean and dressed properly, Gabe picked up his phone. Surprisingly, her answer mattered.

Come on, Larkyn, say yes.

CHAPTER EIGHTEEN

Larkyn brushed her freshly shampooed hair. Straight as a stick her mother would say—as if straight were a flaw. Kate had straight hair too. It hung halfway down her back like a gorgeous platinum waterfall.

In a quick motion, she installed a black plastic clip at the back of her neck and ditched the brush. Good enough. Tonight was no big deal. A simple movie with friends.

Who was she kidding? Gabe, not Sara, had asked her to go. And she'd said yes. The plans included Sara and Cisco, sure, but the arrangement sounded suspiciously like a double date.

How many times had she checked herself in the mirror? The cranberry cashmere sweater and silver pendant looked striking together, but the pendant, a Valentine's gift from Matthew, was a little fancy.

Should she take it off? Gabe wouldn't know where it came from.

Would it matter to him if he did?

Argh. She did this—analyzed—when she was nervous. The evening would run its natural course. Besides, skinny jeans and ankle boots dressed the sweater down.

Her doorbell chimed. No time left to dither. He was here.

Gabe's smile dissolved her tizzy in warmth. He raised his brows. "Hi. You look great."

"Thank you. So do you."

Not what she meant to say. But who could help it with those black denims and that seasoned leather jacket? Add the creamy pullover with his rich brown eyes, and you had a potent combination. A flush seeped up her neck.

Slipping on her coat as he held it for her, she busied her hands with her scarf, not daring to meet his eyes again so soon. "Are the others in the car?"

Gabe shifted his weight. "There's been a little change." He cleared his throat. "Sara's mom called as we were about to leave her place. Her sister's husband, Phil, had an encounter with a chainsaw. He's in the emergency room, going to be fine, but Sara needed to be there for Jean. The movie fell off her list."

A chainsaw? Larkyn stilled in the act of shouldering her purse.

"Look, I understand if you want to cancel, but they insisted we carry on."

Larkyn could imagine.

"Hey, we're halfway there." Gabe read her hesitation clearly. "It'll be fun."

His persuasive tone did wonders with her doubt. It would be a shame to waste all her worry about this night. She gave him a hesitant smile. "I guess we could."

Her weak assurance seemed to be enough. Gabe stepped back, held the door, and let her take the lead as they left the house.

"You're driving Cisco's car?" Larkyn gaped at the infamous green Honda.

"I loaned my truck to some guys from the AVA who had to move. I wasn't supposed to need it."

"The Veteran's Alliance? They have the cycling team, right?"

"That's right. I think we talked about them at your barbecue. I've gotten more involved since it's looking like I'll be around here for longer than I thought."

Gabe held the passenger door. Inside, the car looked perfectly normal except for the custom seats. "I've wondered what it would be like to ride in this thing."

"Tonight's your lucky night then." He flashed her a grin before he closed her door.

Larkyn fastened her seatbelt while Gabe got in and adjusted his legs. He turned the key and the engine growled, then rumbled.

"Was it hard to learn to drive?"

He touched the gas with his good foot, eased off the clutch, and backed into the street. "I had to get the feel of it again" He moved the stick from reverse to first. "But never fear, I'm tested and approved for vehicular operation. Some guys learn to drive with two prosthetics."

"I'm impressed." She observed the process of driving with new appreciation. His hands held the steering wheel at ten and two. A fine white line snaked across the back of his hand from between his thumb and first finger. The scar had faded against his skin which even in November was tanned. How much did he work out to keep those muscles fit? Training for firefighting, no doubt.

Larkyn folded her hands in her lap and stared at them, instead of him. Here they were, on their own. If he found the sight of her wedding rings awkward, he hid it well.

The ride to the theater took less than fifteen minutes. A long line had already formed. Larkyn read the lighted display. *Interstellar*—Sold Out.

"Looks like we missed it." Gabe's eager expression fell. "Do you have a second choice?"

If he wasn't giving up ... She scanned the list. Romantic comedy—no way. The spy movie started thirty minutes ago. She hated horror.

"What about the war movie?" She referred to the only acceptable choice.

"If you don't mind, it works for me." He lifted one shoulder in a tentative shrug.

"Um, Brad Pitt works for me." She smiled.

"All righty, then." His crinkly grin landed smack in her heart, lifting it like a weightless balloon. She wasn't a total dud, even if her heart felt tethered to Matthew most of the time.

She and Gabe joined the line of couples and families doing this very normal thing as if they were normal too. Gabe stepped to the cashier's window. Larkyn reached for her purse.

"Got it." He pushed his credit card through the opening in the glass.

Of course, he did. They were on a date.

Two tickets later, Gabe stopped at the concessions bar. "I can never get past the smell of theater popcorn. Would you like some candy? Anything to drink?"

The aroma of buttered popcorn was her weakness too. "I'd like some Cheerwine, thanks. As long as you share some of *that*." She laughed at the giant refillable bucket. "They charge an arm and a leg for refreshments, you know."

"I'm gonna need a discount then," he said with a straight face. "What's this Cheerwine stuff?"

She explained the soda was a local thing. "I can't really describe the flavor, but you can try mine if you want."

Finding seats in the semi-darkness was no trouble since everyone else had gone to see *Interstellar*. She passed him her cup, and he took a sip with his straw.

Lines creased his forehead. "Cherry? Dr. Pepper? Sort of?"

"Mere knock-offs." She smiled. "Cheerwine goes back to the end of World War One. A guy from Salisbury, North Carolina, invented the drink just a few miles from here."

"Hmm. It's okay, but I'll stick to my regular Pepsi." He dug into the popcorn.

Larkyn slipped out of her coat as the lights went down. He arranged it for her over the back of her seat. Their hands collided over the popcorn bucket in a way that felt both alien and familiar. Her arm relaxed when his shoulder brushed hers, and she had no desire to move away.

The lights dimmed, and before she had time to analyze these contradictions, the screen exploded with the sights and sounds of combat. In seconds, they plunged into a heavy assault between tanks firing shells at troops on foot.

Larkyn gripped the arms of her seat. She was about to experience his world.

Neither spoke as the credits rolled. Larkyn wasn't squeamish, but the violence of war sobered her. Quietly, they joined the crowd spilling out of the theater. The story had been vintage World War Two. Even though times and weapons changed, soldiers faced the same things. The fearful, the courageous, the hardened, and the broken, all bled the same. And as Gabe knew firsthand, some of them lived, and some of them died.

He stood on the verge of stepping off the curb hands in the pockets of his leather jacket looking like he belonged on the screen himself. "Would you like to get some coffee or dessert?"

Larkyn's reflexive negative answer got lost in the word *dessert*. "If you don't already know, I'm a sucker for chocolate cake. I know a place that has the best in the world."

"You do?" His teasing grin was almost as inviting as the cake.

"I do." She tilted her head with a splash of attitude.

"I think you better prove it." He cupped her elbow as they stepped off the curb together.

A quick drive brought them to Madeline's, her favorite restaurant since childhood. Mullioned windows invited them in to taste what the cooks had concocted tonight. Whiffs of hearty clam chowder, the yeasty aroma of fresh bread, and the chatter of people enjoying themselves wrapped her in a welcoming hug.

A friendly hostess led them past a lavish, tiered display of baked goods. Diners hovered over soups, salad bowls, and tempting plates as she and Gabe slid into a cozy booth. An oil-lit candle flickered beside a pottery vase spouting a single, purple mum.

When their server returned with coffees and dessert, Gabe's face confirmed her choice. He gaped at the plate and at her. "It looks like half of a meatloaf."

"Triple-layer, double-chocolate," Larkyn grinned. She added cream to her cup of decaf until it resembled the perfect shade, then she sampled the meatloaf. "Mmmm." Her moan brought a laugh from Gabe. "What?" She swallowed creamy frosting.

"My sister does that. She gets into tastes. But her weakness is pistachio cream cannoli with chocolate chips."

"I didn't realize I was so obvious." She took another bite. "What do you moan about?"

A second passed while Larkyn's brain caught up with her mouth. If she bolted now, maybe she could call Sara. But Cisco would be there, and they'd want to know why she fled her date.

She glanced away. "Can you forget I said that?"

"Now, why would I want to forget?" Gabe leered.

She turned her flaming cheeks to face him. "Because I'm mortified?"

He straightened his features. "What for? I know what you meant."

A tear streaked her burning face.

"Come on, Larkyn. I know you're not flirting with me. I know that Matthew is on your mind, and you're embarrassed to be here."

Oh no. She shrank against the back of the booth. Was it true? She'd never meant to make him feel that way. "I'm sorry. You've been a perfect gentleman, Gabe. You've paid for everything, and now we're here at my favorite place. I'm not ready for this, am I?"

"Not ready to have a friend?" His soft voice soothed her rampaging shame.

With impeccable timing, their waitress reappeared and rested her hip against the table facing Gabe. "How're y'all doing?"

Gabe drew back a few inches. "We're doing fine. The cake's outstanding."

"Glad you like it," she cooed and held eye contact. "We're a little bit famous for our desserts."

"You good, Larkyn?" His question reminded the waitress there were two at the table.

"I'm fine, thanks." She pondered the exchange as his admirer took her coffee pot elsewhere and returned her attention to Gabe. "Can we start over?"

"Whatever you want." He took a bite of cake and slowly withdrew the fork from his mouth with a conspicuous groan. "Mmm-mm. This is amazing."

Larkyn threw her napkin at him.

"What?" He raised his brows and snatched another big bite.

"Maybe we need two pieces." She cut into her side to catch up. "He who hesitates is last, right?"

"You weren't supposed to remember that." He pulled the plate to himself, and Larkyn huffed. He grinned and slid it back.

Larkyn positioned the plate squarely in the middle. "Truce?"

He raised his hands in mock surrender.

"Very funny." She took another bite—careful to stifle any sounds of pleasure. "Seriously though, the movie seemed intense. Did you find it true to life?"

"It was pretty good. Can't fault the special effects. But it's hard to experience reality when you're sitting in a comfortable chair." A far-off look crossed his face. "War can be boring too. But those are the times to take advantage of, 'cause no one knows when we'll be called to march or the next attack will come."

"Why did you want to go back so bad?"

He stared at the cake.

"We shared it all, the good and bad, y'know?" He looked up. "We were brothers, willing to die for one another." Sorrow glinted from his eyes. "But everything changed with that IED. Josh was gone. My leg, my whole body, wrecked. I left the platoon. I left the country. I lost my mission, my friends, and ultimately, my career." He looked at her directly. "All I ever wanted was to get back to the infantry. Until it became painfully clear it wasn't going to happen."

Their stories weren't so different. Gabe had every right to be bitter, but Larkyn didn't see it.

He lounged in the corner of the booth. "I lost it for a while, and that's where Cisco came in—with his connections at MyoPro. I appreciate everything MyoPro did to get me this miracle leg, but I hate being sidelined when my buddies are over there fighting. I'm healthy. I should be doing my part."

Larkyn could argue he'd already done his part, but she didn't try. For that matter, what right did anyone have to the comforts and pleasures of home while others paid the price for our way of life? "You've done more than most of us."

Gabe laid his fork aside for the moment. He seemed incredibly comfortable with the conversation as if they were the only ones in the restaurant. "My mom was against me joining. She talked me into taking classes in junior college, but I think she could see that my poor grades came more from a lack of interest than lack of ability. I mean, look at my cousin." He scoffed good-naturedly. "Anyway, I enlisted at twenty-two which made me the old man, but I was finally where I was meant to be. I know the military's not for everyone, but it was a perfect fit for me."

"Forgive the comparison," she tilted her head, "but we're a little bit alike that way. Both of us lost our dreams come true. Now we're looking for what comes next."

Well, not exactly. She hadn't been *looking*. Not forward, anyway. She'd been going through the motions while Gabe had been fighting for his new start.

The pretty waitress stopped at their booth again. With so many tables, her attention was remarkable.

"You ready for something more?" She managed to convey two meanings.

Gabe looked at their half-eaten cake and then at Larkyn, ignoring the intruder's preference for his side of the booth. Larkyn barely shook her head.

"Just the check, please."

"You sure there's nothing I can do for you?"

Gabe looked at Larkyn again. "I think we're good."

"Yes, we're fine." Larkyn got perverse pleasure from using the plural we.

With one last move, the waitress slipped the bill toward him allowing her fingers to linger.

"Thanks, ma'am." Gabe waited to pick it up.

With no reason to stay any longer, she sashayed off, swallowed in the mix of diners and busy staff.

Larkyn observed her exit. "Do you get that a lot?" She turned back to her date whose only answer was a reddish flush at the neck of his sweater.

"Let's get out of here." He placed a couple of bills, plenty to cover their order, on the table, then stopped. "Excuse me." He called to a passing busboy. "Can you get us a box for this?"

"Sure. Just one sec." The young man kept moving and came back promptly, leaving a plastic container as he hurried by.

Larkyn grinned. "You read my mind."

"How could I not?" He grinned back as she filled the box with leftover chocolate cake. "Come on." He scooted out of the booth and took her hand. "Let's escape. I've got an idea."

He kept her hand as they wove their way to the front.

Once outside, she took in a breath of cold air. The brilliant moon had risen high. Despite the wool thickness of her coat, the touch of Gabe's fingers grazing her back caused her heart to hitch. Like he'd found a long inactive, secret button.

"Can I show you a beautiful place I found? It's not far." He waited for her to slide into her seat.

"Um, sure." It had to be getting late, but going home now felt like closing a book in the middle of a sentence.

Larkyn buckled up while Gabe got the engine rumbling and the heater blowing. He asked her to close her eyes.

"What for?"

"Trust me. It's a good surprise."

He found the stereo and turned the music low. Larkyn absorbed the mellow sax that filled their intimate space. Her back and shoulders surrendered to the contours of Cisco's custom seat as Gabe backed out of their parking spot and waited to enter the highway. She was almost thirty. He'd been twenty-two when he went in. How old did that make him now? With one last look at the firm lines of his profile, she imagined him dressed like the soldiers she'd seen. Desert camouflage. Heavy vest. Weapons everywhere. She knew he'd been alert, smart, disciplined, brave. Now he chose to be here with her, and he wasn't ready to end their time together.

"I hope your mystery place is worth it," she said before closing her eyes.

"It is," was all he would say.

After a couple of miles, he asked, "How ya doin'?"

"Very well." She breathed a sigh. "You sure know how to make a girl sleepy."

"Oh, cool," he snickered.

Too content to raise an apology for how that sounded, she rode on.

Eventually the car slowed. It made a turn, crunching onto gravel, and stopped.

"Don't peek yet. I'm coming to get you."

He eased her from her cozy shelter and kept her hand tucked into the crook of his elbow as she baby-stepped on the rocks. The breeze carried a musty smell as it ruffled her hair. She hunched her shoulders into her coat to block the cold.

Gabe brought them to a halt. "You can open your eyes now."

Sight confirmed the presence of water, a lot of it, reflecting split fragments of silver off its quiet surface. A few bright stars pricked the sky. The shoreline came into focus, along with familiar landmarks. A sandy beach. A dock.

She reclaimed her hand with a jerk and hugged herself against the throb in her chest.

CHAPTER NINETEEN

Gabe's arms hung limp as Larkyn started for the car. His date for the evening seemed to be on the brink of a breakdown.

"Wait. Please." He wasn't ordering, and he wasn't begging. What was he doing?

"This is Jordan Lake." Her hands flew toward the watery expanse before they covered her face. "I ... we ... came here all the time. It's like *ours* ... I come here when I miss him, because ... some of his ashes are in this lake."

Gabe's heart compressed. How was he supposed to know that Jordan Lake was holy ground?

Concern for Larkyn's feelings battled with frustration. It would be nice if he had experience in relationships like this. Or if Larkyn was a normal person.

"If I'd known this would upset you, do you think we would have come?" Being rational. That's what he was.

She didn't run off, but her body language screamed defensive or maybe scared. He dared to put his hands on her shoulders and look into her eyes. Black obscured most of the striking aquamarine. Not fifteen minutes ago he'd seen the person under the shroud. The woman was funny and cute ... and precious.

Potential responses whirled through his brain. Don't minimize. Don't enable. Don't destroy her precarious trust.

Like he was God?

Her gaze dropped, so he removed his hands from her shoulders. "What can I do?"

She pursed her lips and shut her eyes. Her chest rose and fell. After a moment, she looked at him again. "I'm sorry. This is not your fault. Maybe you should just take me home."

Slicing disappointment took him by surprise. He'd analyze that later. Right now, he had to save this night and maybe a piece of himself. Words came from nowhere and clung like a burr. "Is that what you want?"

The lake lapped gently at the shore, pushed by a breeze, and wispy cirrus clouds lit by the moon rode the currents aloft.

"I don't know." He heard defeat in her voice, but it didn't sound final.

"Let's walk out on the dock."

She looked in that direction, seeming to ponder the prospect of walking sacred ground with someone who didn't belong here. Except he did. He'd found Jordan Lake on his own and found its peace for himself. Whatever came along to stir its surface, the stillness below in its tranquil depths gave comfort.

"Why did you bring me here?"

He shoved his hands in the pockets of his jeans and examined his shoes for a moment. "Just an impulse. I love this place. Thought maybe you would too." He didn't add that sharing personal things with her felt natural. That he'd never experienced that before, even with women he seemed to have more in common with. He hadn't come here to start a fight. "We were having fun."

The wind played with her hair as she turned to keep it from escaping the black clip thingy she'd put in the back. If things were different, he could imagine helping her loosen it altogether, allowing the wind to have its way. But things were not different, and he tried not to make them worse.

"How do you do it?" Her attention landed out on the horizon somewhere.

"What do I do?"

She looked right at him as if to extract an answer from everything she saw. "Move on. Release the anger, or guilt, whatever it is. Be free. Have fun again."

"You look cold. D'you want to get back in the car?"

She nodded, distracted as if coping with being at Jordan Lake was enough to handle. The desire to take her in his arms felt disconnected from what was obviously real to her. Instead, he held the door open for her and closed it. His therapist would say she needed to talk. Unless she insisted on going home, he was ready to sit here a while.

She fidgeted with her hands and swiped an escaping tear. "I'm not mad at you, Gabe. I'm in shock that you brought me here."

"I can see."

"I know you've been through a lot that I could never understand, but so have I. What I want to know is how you can put the past behind you." She paused and touched two fingers to her lips. "That's not right. My problem's not forgetting the man I was married to, it's how to remember him without shutting down the life ahead of me. It's only been a little while that I've even cared about having a future."

"I've been there, Larkyn. Not where you are exactly. I didn't lose a wife." Seriously, what could he know? He'd never opened his heart to that degree in the first place. "But I know about the process that grief takes. I also know it's different for everyone."

"But you're over your grief."

"I'm getting there day by day. With God's help."

"Oh? And how does that work?"

Gabe rubbed the back of his neck. Did he sense sarcasm or genuine interest?

This wasn't the first time Larkyn had alluded to issues with God. She seemed to be searching even if she couldn't admit she was.

"If you want to know how faith works for me, I can try to explain."

She turned in her seat to face him. "Please, I want to hear."

"I've never told anyone this story before. He glanced away and sent up a silent plea to have the right words. "It's hard to explain. You'll understand why in a minute."

She waited hands clasped in her lap.

Here goes. "When we were hit, I was unconscious for a little while, but something happened. What came next wasn't a dream, but—maybe a vision?" Her face gave nothing away. She might be wondering if he was crazy, but he'd started, and he would finish.

"Anyway, a man who looked like Jesus—I know he *was* Jesus—appeared beside Josh. It's like he showed up to be with him in his death. Then, suddenly, he was squatting down beside me. He didn't speak, but I knew I would be okay." As the memory unfolded, Gabe forgot he had an audience. He felt the dry, baking heat, and tasted the dust in his mouth. Heard the voices yelling like in his dream.

"I came to, and Jesus had disappeared. Pain took over, but I heard the Apache landing. After they carried me aboard, I'm blank until I woke up from surgery. A few weeks later in Germany, before they sent me back to the States, I struggled with depression, and honestly, I didn't want to live.

He hesitated before plunging on. "One night, I had another dream about the explosion where Jesus appeared just like before. All he did was sit there as my leg bled, but I could see his face, and I felt peace."

Her aqua eyes widened.

"There's not a doubt in my mind Jesus was real. More real than anything. It changed my life, Larkyn—permanently." What else could he say? This was his story. Sharing took all worry from him. No one could steal what God had done.

"Wow," she whispered.

"You don't have to say anything. It's okay, whatever you think. I'm not trying to convince you of anything."

"Well, that's good." She stared out at the night through the windshield.

The moon's light glinted off ripples on the lake. His training route began not far from here, sequestered in the pines.

Larkyn tilted her head. "It's a lovely story, and I'm glad it happened to you. I just don't see how it applies to me."

"Why not? I think if you ask him, God will find a way to reach you too."

"I've prayed before, Gabe. For Matthew in intensive care. And when I was a child, I prayed for a sister."

Her sigh sounded resigned but not cynical. There could be hope.

She continued. "My father hates God. Not that I believe my dad's got anything figured out. He and my mother ... let's say we've never been close." She snorted gently as if she found the concept absurd.

Gabe remembered the hayride. Her parents hadn't wanted her. Growing up like that had to warp your trust.

"My dad said people who believed in God were fools. He called them weak and accused them of making up myths as a crutch to get through life."

Gabe was not of a mind to argue, but her dad's claim was nothing new and easy to shoot down. "I've heard that before. Maybe even wondered about it myself when I was young. But look, we all use crutches. Some depend on money to feel secure. Some go for positions of power, popularity, or education. All can be crutches. But think about it, Larkyn. The things we depend on will fail at some point. The rich and successful die the same as the poor do. Alone."

She bit her lower lip, and her face took on a ghostly pallor in the moonlit car. "That's what I'm afraid of, Gabe."

He strained to catch the whispered words. "What do you mean?"

Head down, she spoke to her lap. "Being alone. Always, all my life. Then Matthew came. I think Matthew became my crutch."

Larkyn cringed at the truth coming out of her mouth. It didn't mean she loved Matthew less. Never. Yet, the fragments of her life before and after Matthew died made more sense.

Her father's harsh judgment of people who found comfort and strength in religion had taught her she could only make him proud if she was strong and successful. But she hadn't been strong. She'd been lonely, and she'd been scared. An ugly duckling in a family of eagles.

Even grown up, her decision not to pursue work in a big accounting firm had disappointed her parents. Her marriage as well. Not that they disliked Matthew, because they didn't even know him, but they hated her decision to skip the society event her mother expected to stage.

Childish, maybe, in retrospect, but insisting on her own way seemed adult at the time—an attempt to be herself. Matthew had given her love and value. Which meant she never had to pretend. He liked her as she was. He'd fallen in love with her as she was.

Heaviness settled in as Gabe trained his soft, dark chocolate eyes on her. "Are you saying I won't feel alone if I believe in God? *He's* supposed to be my crutch?" she pondered.

His expression lit with surprise. "Yes. That's exactly what I'm saying. We all need God, and he wants a relationship with you. He wants to be your Father."

Did she want another father? Only if he differed from Peter Baxter. Her father wasn't a bad man. If he were, the rejection might have been easier to take. He loved his work and always had time for his students. His daughter was the problem.

"How can I live up to what God expects?"

"Can you look at me, Larkyn?" He waited until she surrendered. "God doesn't expect anything from you. He wants to *give* you things. He wants to love you and protect you."

"He didn't protect Matthew." An obvious contradiction. "That's another problem I have with God. How can you trust someone who lets you down like that?"

Gabe had nothing to say for a moment, and her heart squeezed. For a moment, a way out had seemed possible. A way to join the happy people again.

He reached across the console to take her hand, and his warmth engulfed her fingers. "God doesn't promise to make us immune from the bad things that happen in this world. I do find the more I listen to his wisdom, the better things work out, though. He does promise to be with us all the time. His Presence makes every situation better."

Gabe made faith sound so logical. Yet she had troubling, unanswered questions. If she got entangled in them all, what would happen to the beautiful hope that her life could change?

Larkyn spoke more to herself than to him. "I can't ignore my questions. I can't pretend."

He squeezed her fingers lightly. "God's not afraid of questions, you know."

She studied the face that invited her into his peace. Look at him, for goodness' sake, a woman's dream come true, offering her his secret.

Indecision brought her to the edge of a cliff. Christians called it being saved, but this felt like the opposite. Letting go would destroy her. She tightened her grip on his hand. "I want to believe you, Gabe. My boss, Trudy, Dena, and now you—all of you seem so sure it works."

"It's a decision, Larkyn. From my experience, if you say *yes* in faith, God will take care of the rest. I come up against questions all the time, but I don't lose faith in his love. My problems might not disappear, but I'm not on my own to solve them."

A smile edged her lips. "Like the girl in *Miracle on Thirty-fourth Street*? 'I believe. I believe. I know it's silly, but I believe?'"

"Then do it." He stretched to reach her other hand. "Tell God you choose to believe he sent his Son Jesus to save you. That Matthew couldn't, but Jesus can."

She waffled for a moment more, straining to be sure. "I'm sorry, Gabe. It's getting late. I promise I'll think about this."

He nodded, a deeper softness in his eyes—as if he wanted to kiss her. No, he was merely worried about her and God.

Why did that make her sad?

CHAPTER TWENTY

Larkyn came to her senses entangled in her flannel gown. She pushed the uncomfortable pillow from under her head and massaged her neck. Rising on one elbow she dislodged another pillow from its nest against her chest.

Ugh. The clock on her bedside table had said two o'clock when she'd given up and moved to her new sofa. Now, dim light filled the living room, brightness framing the edges of her curtains. At least today was Saturday.

She kicked away the blanket freeing her legs and shocked her feet on the cold, bare, plank floor. *Get rug soon* went onto her mental list. After a quick trip to the bathroom, she donned her slippers and robe and scuffed along to the Keurig.

The gurgle and aroma of brewing coffee promised revival. Nine o'clock.

The date on the opened carton of cream looked iffy. A sniff settled the matter. *Yuck.* Black coffee it would have to be—if she wanted to function.

A few moments later, her head rested against the cushions of her comfy new chair with a warm mug cradled in her lap.

Last night ... oh, yes. Gabe, God, and chocolate cake. Oh, and don't forget Jordan Lake. What a lethal combination.

Despite its rocky middle, the date had ended well. A warm feeling rose in her chest having nothing to do with hot coffee. Gabe hadn't kissed her, but she was pretty sure he wanted to. That thought and others had kept her awake. Until she left the bed she'd shared with Matthew.

Larkyn sipped her bitter drink as she surveyed the room she had begun to love. It now had cloud gray walls instead of tan, oak floors instead of beige carpet, and smoky grey upholstered pieces scattered with a collection of pillows.

Yep, her stuck and boring life had come unstuck. Someone or something had fired a gun and the old mule she was used to riding had become a galloping horse. Time to stop the jouncing and find the reins.

She lifted her mug and swallowed with a grimace.

The accountant in her thrived on logic. If she was A, lonely, and wanted C, a happy and fulfilling life, she needed B. According to Gabe, B equaled God. God didn't guarantee perfect circumstances, but he would be her Father and the crutch that never failed.

Padding to the sink, she poured the nasty liquid down the drain of her new enamel farm sink and gazed through the window into the space once filled by her tree. Wet grass. It must've rained. If Matthew were here, they would turn on the gas logs and snuggle.

Did God snuggle? Could he sit across a candlelit table and hold her hand?

Larkyn didn't mean to be flippant. If Gabe's encounter with Jesus was true, he sounded nice. Not distant like her father or disappointed in her like her mother. Trudy's answers seemed to come from a box. She didn't understand Larkyn's battles. If anyone could help it would be Dena. She turned away from the overcast sky and headed for her bedroom. The time had come to ask.

Larkyn zipped a UNC hoodie over her turtleneck sweater and crossed the yard to her neighbor's house without an invitation. The drizzle had ended, and though the ground was damp, Ted hailed her from newly cleared green swathes of grass that resembled a vacuumed carpet. The scratch of his rake had created tidy piles of leaves destined for disposal in plastic bags. If only all of life's debris could be so neatly dispensed with.

Before she could knock, Dena met her at the door in a pair of her signature polyester pants and a sweatshirt emblazoned with the logo of her church, Faith Community Fellowship.

"Welcome. What a surprise." She pushed her door wide, releasing the fragrance of cinnamon and vanilla that didn't come from a candle. "I was just about to cut into a loaf of zucchini bread. Come and join me."

Dena's kitchen personified Southern Country. From the ironed café curtains to the souvenir salt and peppers, to the trailing ivy that graced the windowsill. How different from Larkyn's stainless steel and polished granite.

"Tell me how you are, my dear. Enjoying being back in your home?"

Larkyn shrugged out of her jacket and hung it over the chair back. "You and Ted should come over and see how it looks. I can't believe I haven't invited you before."

Dena placed a generous slice of nut-filled bread on a plate and set it next to a tub of spreadable butter. Larkyn's mouth watered, and her tummy rumbled at the sight of a much-delayed breakfast. Steam wafted from her teacup as Dena filled it from a squatty teapot. "Thank you. This is just what I needed."

"You're very welcome." Dena sank onto one of her highly padded seat cushions and cut a second slice.

Buttery sugar and spices practically melted on Larkyn's tongue. "Mm. Yummy."

Dena's pink powdered cheeks rose in approval. "Thank you. It's one of Ted's favorite recipes."

More evidence of Dena's well spent decades. Larkyn took a second bite.

"Other than a burning desire for the company of old folks, what brings you out this morning?"

Larkyn's throat tightened. "I couldn't sleep last night." She squeezed a fist in her lap against the unexpected urge to cry.

Dena clucked with sympathy. "Is it the house?"

"No." Larkyn pushed past the tears. "Do you remember a person who came to the picnic? His name was Gabriel?"

"Oh, yes." Dena gave her a knowing smile. "The handsome soldier. I remember him."

Ah, Gabe had made an impression, as usual. "We had a conversation about faith in God." Her heart did a little flip-flop. This was harder than she thought. "That's why I couldn't sleep."

Dena's attention zeroed in on Larkyn. "What about your talk upset you, dear?"

"I didn't know I was upset." she backtracked. "But later …" She'd been so close to buying in, to jumping off the cliff and trusting. But she couldn't do it. "I'm not religious, Dena. I never considered it seriously, ever. My father said it was foolishness."

She toyed with the spoon she'd used to stir her tea. "But when Matthew was dying, I found out his parents go to church, and he'd been baptized as a little boy." Tears pricked her eyes again. "I didn't know."

A quick swallow, and she forged on. "After his death, my boss, Trudy, took me under her wing and started giving me advice from the Bible." Her gaze strayed to the walls where Dena's sayings put forth their wisdom. "It's clear you and Ted believe in God. Now Gabe tells me this miraculous story about how Jesus became real to him. I don't know what I believe."

Was that true? Was she just unwilling?

All the while she'd been speaking, Dena peered intently, as if trying to get inside her mind. Downright unnerving. Yet Dena was kind. She never pushed.

"You've heard from a lot of people." Dena's focus never wavered. "The death of a loved one often stirs up questions, as it should. But I can't tell you what to do, honey. No one can."

Tears slid down her cheeks.

"Let's try this." Dena handed her a tissue from a box on the counter. "Try to put into words what you *do* believe about yourself and your life."

Larkyn blew into the tissue. The story wasn't complicated. "I tried to be who my parents expected, but I couldn't. With Matthew, it was easy. He wasn't disappointed in me. He loved me, and I loved him." Simple. She twisted the tissue. "When he died, my happy ending ended. I believed my life would be one way, then everything changed. I didn't know how to live without him. I was sad. I was angry. I was scared. But I was beginning to adjust, you know?" She took a long breath, searching for the next chapter. Dena sipped her tea.

"When I say adjust, I mean I learned to cope. I learned to live with less. No expectations, no disappointed dreams. Just make it through the day." Her shoulders lifted and sagged again. Pretty pointless.

"Meeting Gabe, and then the storm ... shook things up. The damage feels terrible, but I can see some good too." She wrinkled her nose. "Then last night we got in this conversation."

Dena chewed slowly, as if pondering every word. Larkyn loved that about her friend. She took a hurried bite and continued her tale.

"Gabe says that God is for me. I don't have Matthew, but God is here. Instead of being alone, I'm supposed to lean on God. It sounds simple, but it's not. I don't feel God's love. I don't *know* him, and I have no idea how to change."

Dena didn't seem worried by her story. She didn't jump to God's defense like Trudy would, explaining every argument away. In a calm voice, she asked, "Is there something you wish *could* be true? Something you'd like to believe about God?"

Great question. Larkyn broke off the corner of her zucchini bread and put it in her mouth. The glaze on the crust was her favorite part.

"To know he's real, I guess. Know he likes me and won't let me down if I trust him. Gabe doesn't feel alone with God around."

Imagine if she could too.

"The story feels like a fairy tale. I'm not the same as Gabe. Or you." She made a helpless gesture.

Dena got to her feet. "Sit tight." She left and returned holding a beautiful book with a leather-like, purple binding. Embossed vines curled down the spine and around the edges. Silver script read *Holy Bible*.

Dena laid it on the table and asked, "Why do you think you're here today? Not in my kitchen, but on planet Earth? Matthew's not here anymore, but you are. Why?"

Because I didn't meet a maniac on the road? Larkyn sought a less combative answer. She wasn't mad at Dena but at herself, because she couldn't understand. She couldn't be sure of anything anymore.

"I never belonged anywhere until I met Matthew. I can't even say I'm here because my parents wanted a daughter.

If I have to answer, I'd say I'm here by an unfortunate accident."

Dena opened her book. She paged to the middle and found the spot she was looking for. "This is Psalm 139. I'd like to read two parts if you don't mind."

Larkyn shrugged, then found her manners. "Sure. Go ahead."

Dena's index finger pointed to the lines as she read. "For you created my inmost being; you knitted me together in my mother's womb. I praise you because I am fearfully and wonderfully made." Her finger slid down a space. "My frame was not hidden from you when I was being made in secret." She looked as if to be sure Larkyn was listening then moved down another line or two. "Your eyes saw my unformed body; all the days ordained for me before one of them came to be." She raised her head. "There's your answer. The beginning of your life, and why you are alive today through God's eyes."

"Can you read that again?"

Dena did. Then she closed the book and leaned on her elbows, giving Larkyn the full attention of her faded, kind, blue eyes. She explained.

"From science, we know you began as a cell. Half of your DNA is from your father and half of it from your mother. That completed cell divided, then those two divided, then those four, and so on, until your entire body was formed. And every cell contains that original DNA. It's your physical identity. But, honey, you are much more. Your human soul has a unique personality, and your spirit is made in the image of God. Isn't that amazing? How can you be an accident?"

She was unique, for sure. But the rest? "Dena, I don't mean to be dense, but God could have set the world up and let it go to carry on. That would explain why the earth is so beautiful and at the same time so full of sorrow and pain. Why didn't he stick around and keep his creation beautiful?"

The back door banged open, and Ted blew in with a gust of the earthy scent of fall. "Whew. That wind. I rake the leaves one way and the wind scatters them another. I'm quitting for now. What're you gals up to?"

Dena pointed to the plate that held her zucchini bread. "Cut yourself a slice of this, Ted. Warm the kettle for tea if you want."

Ted blew his red nose on a napkin and swiped at his tousled thin hair. "'Scuse me, ladies." He took the knife and sliced a hunk off the end of the loaf. "Think I'll heat my coffee and go to the other room."

Larkyn marveled. Had Dena politely signaled Ted to get lost? "I guess that means I don't have to rake my leaves, either." She smiled, hoping to ease his rejection.

"Not till this wind calms down." He chomped on the sweet bread while his cup warmed in the microwave. "Carry on. I've got some important golf to watch."

"Does Ted like golf?" Larkyn squinted after him.

Dena laughed. "He's joking. He's probably going to nap in the chair."

Larkyn smiled. "You've been married a long time, haven't you?" So had her parents, but she remembered distance. Formality, not banter.

"Almost fifty years. But where were we? I can warm up your tea, or we can finish our talk another time."

"Please, let's finish now." Talking to Dena was digging up more questions, but excavation first seemed the way to go. Like demolition in her kitchen, or drilling her tooth before putting a filling in.

Bad example. Too painful. Or maybe the cost of real change?

"I believe you asked me why God didn't stick around." Dena opened the fridge and pulled out a bowl of cherries. "These were on sale. I don't know who has cherries in November, but I love them. Help yourself."

Larkyn popped a cherry in her mouth and chewed. She worked the seed discreetly out as Dena found another spot in her Bible.

"This is the Book of John who was a disciple of Jesus. He wrote this down so others could know what happened."

Larkyn took another plump cherry. Sweet and tart. She could eat a dozen.

Dena marked the place with her finger on the page. "I am the good shepherd. I know my own and my own know me, just as the Father knows me and I know the Father; and I lay down my life for the sheep."

Once again, she skipped a few lines. "I lay down my life that I may take it up again. No one takes it from me, but I lay it down of my own accord. I have authority to lay it down, and I have authority to take it up again. This charge I have received from my Father."

She remembered the children's story. "The shepherd is Jesus?"

Dena nodded. "Yes. He calls himself a shepherd because people back then understood sheep and shepherds. These verses show us that God didn't abandon the world. People abandoned him. They listened to a serpent who told them they could be like God and broke the one rule God had given them."

Larkyn puckered her brow. "Aren't there ten rules?"

Dena chuckled. "That came later. Let's stick to how the shepherd laid down his life. You can take this Bible home and read the Book of John. It's a solid start to knowing Jesus, which is what will help you most."

"I can't take this, Dena. It's yours, and it looks brand new."

"It is. But I have many Bibles. Please take it."

Dena meant for her to keep this Bible. Another look at the purple binding and Larkyn couldn't wait to take it home—to turn the paper-thin pages and discover what it said.

"Before you go, let me explain one last part." Dena folded her arms on the table.

"Jesus came to the earth, born as God's Son because the sheep had left God to go off on their own. They no longer lived in the Father's love but became God's enemies, and the world got worse and worse. Attitudes and actions that go against God are called sin, and the penalty for sin is death."

A chill ran up Larkyn's arm. "How scary." Duh. Why did she have to say that?

Dena paused at the interruption, her expression soft and her voice gentle. "Without God's solution, it's very scary." She laid her wrinkly hand on Larkyn's. Dena's wedding rings twinkled modestly, not like the gaudy three-carat rock that Larkyn's mother wore. "Honey, while it's true that sin leads us inevitably to death, God had a plan from the very beginning. Jesus was that plan."

"He lays down his life for the sheep." The words cycled in her brain, trying to gain traction.

"Exactly. As a man, he took all the blame for our sin into himself, received the death penalty for us, and took our sins to his grave. But, as it says here, he didn't deserve to die. He had the authority to lay down his life which he did, and then he was raised to life again, leaving our sins behind in the grave."

Larkyn's brows pulled together. "How do we know this actually happened?"

"It's historical fact, with more evidence emerging all the time. People who set out to prove it's false have not succeeded. Many have come to faith instead."

Dena sat back in her chair. "I've been teaching children and adults the Bible for many years. The truth is available to everyone, but the reader has to have an open heart."

"Do you think I have an open heart?" Larkyn cringed inside. Was Dena embarrassed for her?

"I think you do. If you came here today, asking to understand, your heart is open. A hard heart refuses to be touched. But God understands that too. He softens hearts."

The familiar ache in her throat dissolved. Maybe God had been softening her heart all along.

"I want to read this, Dena. I feel like I'll get it if I try."

Dena closed the book and pushed it toward Larkyn. "You enjoy this, dear. I'll be praying for you."

Larkyn stroked the beautiful cover, tracing the embossed design. It was remarkably similar to the vines carved into the chest holding the bottle of Matthew's ashes. The design associated with her grief now had a different meaning. Warmth as subtle as chiffon settled around her shoulders. Well-being surrounded her heart.

She and Dena finished their snack. Ted snored in the living room. Her remarkable peace didn't leave the whole way home.

CHAPTER TWENTY-ONE

Gabe examined his stump again. He'd pampered it for several days, but he didn't trust it yet. Once compromised, his scars took time to recover, a process he'd interrupted with his zealous training. Skin-protecting salve and clean, dry sock liners were the best he could do for now.

Ready in old jeans and a faded sweatshirt, Gabe combed hair that was long enough to need the attention of a barber and made his bed the way he'd been taught. After leaving a note for his cousin about the AVA meeting he was late for, he scuttled through a heavy mist that couldn't decide between fog and outright rain.

His buddy had returned the truck with a full tank. Nice. Nothing like a practical thank you.

Forced to poke along with the Saturday traffic, Gabe reviewed the near disaster of last night's date. Fortunately, he'd redeemed himself with an offhand comment about riding back from Jordan Lake the day they'd met. For reasons he had no clue about, Larkyn had pulled out of her mope.

"Wait." She'd raised her head. "You don't mean at the party, do you?

He dared a teasing grin. "Nope. I mean the first time."

"Aargh. It's taken me so long to forget that. But you forgave me, right?"

Forgave her? Good grief. "There's nothing to forgive. I was fine, except for the hideous bruises."

She cringed. "You don't know what I suffered over that."

She suffered? He held onto the comeback on his lips lest his teasing set off more trauma. Instead, he'd reminded her of the leftover cake, which she immediately fetched from the floor of the car and sliced into minuscule bites with her plastic fork. By the time he hit her driveway, she'd nibbled the cake to death. Seriously—nothing left. Not a single crumb.

Gabe peered through the misty rain and steered to park between the only two vehicles in the lot, a truck and a classic Mustang. No wait, sheltered under the eaves of the clapboard house sat Pancho's Harley. Where was everybody else? Gabe's wipers swished a time or two while he transitioned from wondering if he should've kissed Larkyn after all and focused on the meeting ahead.

His boots clumped across the wooden porch, and he turned the tarnished brass knob. The old home was well past its prime, but its foundation seemed strong. Inside, someone had cut the original rooms into offices and gathering spaces for groups.

Gabe took a seat in one of the metal folding chairs around what served as their conference table. Pancho sat at the head flanked by Raoul-something on one side and Gus Allenby, who went by Allen, on the other.

Pancho tossed a pen which Gabe snatched out of the air. The job of secretary seemed to have lended up in his lap along with the small notepad that followed.

"Let's get started, amigos." Pancho studied the calendar he'd removed from the wall and flipped pages. "We've got four or five months to put together this charity ride for the AVA. It sounds like plenty of time, but believe me, it's not." He focused on each man at the table—all three of them. "It looks like we're the team behind this." He rocked back on two legs of his chair.

Gabe twirled the pen in his fingers. For the new kid in town this was bad news. Where were all the dudes he'd met riding?

As if he could read minds Pancho answered, "Here's the deal, Gabe. Raoul and Allen have been around a while. They understand most of the guys come and go. Our riders make up the strongest group, but most aren't into raising funds." His chair came down onto all four legs. "We'd like to reach more guys, provide better sports facilities, and develop relationships with other organizations who offer the big-ticket services. Things like construction of handicap-accessible housing, legal aid, and counseling."

Whoa. Pretty ambitious, considering their *sports facilities* consisted of an outdoor basketball court on cracked concrete and an understocked weight room. The kitchen floor sagged in the middle, and the toilets barely flushed.

"What fundraisers have you done before?" Gabe ignored the negative for the moment.

"Not much." Pancho shrugged. "That's why this place is a dump and why we don't have better adaptive sports programs for the vets in our community."

It had never been Gabe's intention to take on the problems of his fellow vets, but this situation should not exist.

"Doesn't A stand for Alliance? Where are the other chapters?"

"It's a loose affiliation. We do get support from the greater organization, but it's up to us if we want to get ahead. Some groups have grown, and some, like us, are hangin' on."

"All that's cool, Panch, but I say we stick to our first mission which is sports." Allen pushed his thick, black-rimmed glasses up on his nose. "Make this a place men and women want to come to. Right now, the bar down the block gets more interest."

"I agree," Raoul added his two cents as Gabe drew a row of diagonal lines then crossed them in the opposite direction. "We help 'em build confidence through physical challenge, and maybe they see there's more to the future than they thought."

Gabe contemplated the crosshatch pattern he'd made on his notepad. "What if we expand this event? Put everything we have into building it up, invite vets from Virginia and South Carolina, and call it a regional competition. Ask the riders to get sponsorship to cover a hundred-dollar entry fee—"

"Hey, I like what you're sayin'." Pancho halted his roll. "But that entry fee will cancel too many folks. I say we keep it minimal but ask sponsors to pay dollars-per-mile. If we lengthen the race to a marathon, that could be substantial."

Allen tapped the table with a knuckle. "I have a friend with a print shop who might donate some fliers and banners. The riders could talk it up in their churches and stuff."

Gabe jotted.

Raul nodded. "We should ask for donations of everything we can. Water bottles, protein bars, bike tune-ups. We could even sell advertising in a program if your printer would do that too."

"I can ask." Allen shrugged.

Gabe looked up from his notes. "This is good. Expansion of the race, donations, sponsors. We also need publicity. War casualties are in the news. What if we got a reporter interested in what we're trying to do for disabled vets? If we had some video, they might carry the story."

Allen turned to Pancho "We're talking about spring, right? Armed Forces Day is in May. Or better yet, Memorial Day. The City might promote us."

The energy in the room had gone from a flicker to a hum. Gabe sensed major possibilities *if* they could get it together. A big if. He'd once believed all it took was desire and hard work to make a dream come true, but recent failures had taught him otherwise.

"Who's gonna produce a video for nothing?" Pancho voiced Gabe's doubts. "We're a committee of four, remember?"

Silence followed and Gabe squirmed. He'd instigated the push for expansion. A look at this house spoke clearly. The self-image of every wounded vet begged to be repaired.

Gabe took the leap. "We're only four now, but if we get this rollin', others will catch on. I vote we set the date for Memorial Day and go for broke. If Raoul will line up publicity, I'll figure out how to make our video."

Pancho threw up his hands. "I'm not against this fellas, but it's ambitious. I want a vote. All in favor?"

Three ayes plus Pancho's nod.

Pancho leaned forward, fingers splayed on the table. "Okay, DeSantis, your plan's approved. Come up with something good."

Monday came along with work. Larkyn hadn't heard a word from Gabe since he left her Friday night.

Had their evening been disappointing? Was he sorry they even went? Or did their date hardly register with him? What did she wish would happen now?

If nothing else, Gabe's story had provoked her into seeing Dena. Their conversation, at least, brought good.

Larkyn rose from her chair to rinse the tomato bisque soup from her thermos in the break room sink. Georgia worked on her Lean Cuisine, and Kate didn't eat at all.

"What's wrong with you, girl?" Georgia chided Kate over a bite of Chicken Cacciatore that smelled the same as every other frozen meal in plastic. "Starvation is not a healthy weight loss strategy."

"I'm only skipping once in a while, okay?" Kate's diamond flashed under the fluorescent lighting.

Another engagement. Yow.

"I want to fit in the wedding gown I've got my eye on."

"That's what alterations are for." Georgia cracked. "I plan to find me a man who likes a little meat on the bones. What about you, Larkyn? I don't see you counting calories."

Larkyn hedged. She hated taking sides, because if she did, it usually led to scorn that her genes made her thin by nature. "I try to eat healthy, but I slip all the time. I love cream too much to measure every teaspoon."

"We noticed," the two chorused.

Larkyn had heard comments about her milky coffee all her life. But she chose to see drinking something tasty as a sign of common sense.

"Speaking of food," Georgia continued. "What're y'all doing for Thanksgiving?"

Dreaded question.

Kate eagerly shared. She and Kierke, the exchange student she'd fallen for, were headed with her large family to their cabin in the mountains near Blowing Rock.

Larkyn knew Sara and Cisco were flying to Brooklyn, so Sara could meet his parents. Now Gabe was going too. According to Sara, he hadn't seen his mom since he'd arrived at the big hospital in Maryland via military transport. He hadn't seen his sister and her family since his second deployment. And to top it off, Dena and Ted's children in Charlotte had invited them to visit.

"Larkyn?" Georgia prodded. "You going to baptize that beautiful kitchen with a Thanksgiving feast?"

"Um, not exactly."

"What? Why ever not?" Georgia pushed in her typical way.

Larkyn hated the looks of pity that were bound to cover their faces. Thanksgiving might be the biggest family event on the Southern calendar. She stalled by packing her insulated lunch tote and zipping it shut. "It'll just be me this time. Everyone else has plans."

Kate looked stricken. "Come to the mountains with us. We don't have an extra bedroom, but you could have one of the couches."

Super. She could be shoehorned into Kate's family tradition, like sewing a third leg onto the turkey. "That's a very kind offer, Kate, but I'll be fine. What about you, Georgia? I know you have plans."

"Yes, ma'am." Georgia swallowed her chicken and pointed her fork at them. "I'm drivin' to my grandma's house in Laurinburg and sleepin' till noon. Then we're going to the K & W Cafeteria."

Ever gracious, Kate commented first. "That sounds nice, Georgia. Very restful."

Georgia laughed. "That's the way I see it. My granny's ninety, and she can't do all that cookin' anymore. I live the closest, and I'm not married," she waved her bare left hand. "It makes sense, and we'll have fun. I always feel better after spending time with her."

Larkyn agreed. Everyone needed a grandma, and Dena was almost hers.

Later that afternoon, Trudy flagged Larkyn down on her way to the ladies' room.

"Hi, Trudy." She'd bet money her boss would leave for Wilmington soon.

"Martin and I are going to Marge's early. Just wanted to say Happy Thanksgiving and hope you have a good weekend."

Yep. Larkyn murmured her thanks and good wishes, but Trudy had more on her mind.

"Next week, when this holiday is over, I want to talk to you about maybe doing something special for Christmas. Here in the office. Think about what the staff might enjoy, okay?"

"I—okay." Martin had agreed? She covered her shock with a smile.

At five o'clock, Larkyn cleared the surface of her desk and locked her files. Three days and her cell phone still lay mute. Not a word from Gabe. Had he already left for New York?

The elevator doors parted, and Larkyn joined the exodus. A fellow on crutches stood backed up in the corner. She sidled away to make room and clutched her purse. Was the sight of crutches a warning? Don't reach for Gabe that way? Was she reaching? Did God truly have answers for her?

CHAPTER TWENTY-TWO

Gabe's obnoxious cell phone ring dragged him out of a dead sleep. Where? He groped over the side of the bed toward the source of the sound. His pants. He dug his phone from the pocket and answered the beast.

"DeSantis." His standard identification clicked.

"Uncle Gabe?" A childish voice reeled reality in.

"Hey, bud." He fell back onto his pillow and stifled a yawn. Robbie. At eight o'clock.

"Are you up?"

"Sure," he lied. "What's going on?"

"Well … uh," the little guy's words meandered out, "Mom said I shouldn't call till you were up, so I'm glad you are."

Gabe chuckled. "That's good, Robbie. What did you need to talk about?"

His sister's youngest had taken a while to warm up to him, but fascination with the intricacies of a bionic leg drew him in. With a million questions asked and answered, Robbie forgot to be shy. By the end of Thanksgiving Day, they'd become pals.

"When can we go to the carousel? Mom said we could go when you came."

This time Gabe's yawn escaped big time, and he got himself upright. "Tell ya what. You give me time to take a shower and make a phone call. Then we'll talk about plans." He kept it vague. Who knew what Sylvie and Paul had actually promised.

He didn't mind getting out with the kids. They'd done their best being cooped up at Cisco's parents' house for yesterday's food fest, and from the feel of it, his body could use a few dozen sit-ups, some pull-ups, and a jog around the track. Which it probably wouldn't get.

"Okay." The connection dropped.

Atta boy, Robbie. Short and to the point.

Some seriously strong water pressure woke Gabe up. Sweatpants and a T-shirt would do until the day's plans were clear. Barefoot, he hobbled to the kitchen on one crutch, poured coffee from the pot, and hitched to the settee by the window. Without their leaves, the trees lining his mom's residential Brooklyn street left their second-story view unobstructed. He faced a solid row of decades old brownstones, cars parked parallel to the curb, and a sunny crystal-blue sky. Nice.

Gabe got comfortable on the settee and punched in Larkyn's number. It took a few rings for her to pick up.

"Hello?" Her voice was shy and tentative. The way he remembered her.

"Hey." His mind went blank.

"Gabe?"

"Yeah … Uh, hi. I meant to call you sooner. Did you have a happy Thanksgiving?"

A pause. "It was quiet but fine." He sensed the reserve in her voice. "How was yours?

"Anything but quiet."

Nothing.

Okay. He could carry this a bit longer. "There were nine of us at Cisco's parents' house. My sister's kids, Liza and Robbie, kept things lively. They had me doing tricks with my leg to show them how it operates. I ate enough to hibernate till spring."

"That sounds fun. What did you eat?"

"Oh, man. Let's see. Sylvie made the antipasti tray with olives, salami, prosciutto, a couple of cheeses, and marinated mushrooms. Mom brought her homemade pasta sauce for cheese-stuffed manicotti and some stuffed artichokes. Aunt Elena cooked the turkey and dressing, Italian green beans, and mashed potatoes. Then we had apple pie, pumpkin cannoli, and panna cotta with berry sauce and chocolate chips."

A giggle broke her silence. "I had to ask."

His heart warmed at the change in her tone. "I know. But the women are great cooks, and I think they like to show off. You're not allowed to pass on anything. Good thing I'm not staying long."

She didn't answer. Huh. Good or bad?

"Larkyn?"

"Yes?"

Gabe grimaced to himself and rubbed his hand across his forehead. What had he done to warrant such a lack of cooperation?

Duh, his head dropped back. Such an idiot. How long since the movie and everything else that happened that night? A week? He should have called sooner. A lot sooner.

Why hadn't he? Interesting question.

"Listen, I should have called before this ..." She appeared to be waiting for him to go on. "I enjoyed the time we spent together. The movie was good, and I appreciate what you shared at Jordan Lake. I'm sorry I didn't follow up."

Follow up? C'mon Gabe—it wasn't a meeting. "I mean I hope you had as much fun as I did."

"It was fun, Gabe. Some of it was hard, but I enjoyed it. You've been a wonderful friend."

Talk about lukewarm. A wonderful friend? *You didn't kiss her dude. How is she supposed to know you wish you had*?

"I'd um, like to redeem myself. Would you like to go out again when I get back? Maybe dinner? Something special."

"There you are!" A big voice from a little mouth burst into his mother's apartment from the floor below. "Are you ready yet?" His nephew's grin stretched all over his face, revealing a space where one tooth was gone.

"I said I had to make a phone call, Robbie." He held the phone to his chest. "I'll be through in a minute."

Robbie jiggled in place like a puppy wagging its tail. "Who is it?"

"Excuse me, Larkyn," Gabe spoke into the phone. "I have a juvenile delinquent to deal with here."

Larkyn replied, "I don't want to keep you," and Robbie asked, "What's a juv-el duhlinket?" at the same time.

He ignored Robbie.

"My nephew wants to go to some carousel today. I need to tell him I hate carousels. I think we'll go to the library, then maybe shop for new underwear."

"Noo." Robbie shook his head and waved his arms like he was signaling a plane to stop. "We need to go to Swing Valley and Slide Mountain. It's really fun."

Gabe reached out and pulled him in with one arm, so his face was squashed in Gabe's shirt. "Larkyn? Can I call you later—maybe tomorrow? Think about dinner, okay? I want to hear all about your quiet Thanksgiving."

Robbie wiggled but Gabe held on, making sure the kid could breathe while he finished with Larkyn. "You there?"

"I'm here." Did he hear a smile in her voice? "Go have fun, Uncle Gabe. And I'll look forward to your call."

"Thanks, Larkyn. Talk to you later." He'd almost called her sweetheart instead of Larkyn. But like the kiss, that might be moving too fast. Then again, what if he didn't move fast enough?

CHAPTER TWENTY-THREE

Larkyn's Friday could be summed up in two words. Gabe called.

After days of preoccupation with *the date*, her suspense had ended. The second-guessing, the decision to forget the date and get on with just being friends—all erased.

She'd spent Thanksgiving at Jordan Lake, sitting on the dock wrapped in one of Matthew's sweaters, gazing at the horizon, and questioning the past twenty-eight months of her life in light of Dena's wisdom. Had she gone there to grieve the past with Matthew or the loss of a future with Gabe?

Her mind in knots and her limbs weighted with too many regrets, she'd driven home in a funk. With no interest in holiday cooking, she forgot to eat but opened her purple Bible instead. God knew her frame, huh? He'd ordained her days? That would take some convincing.

Turning pages at random, her gaze landed on the book called Isaiah. She'd read, "For the Lord is a God of justice; blessed are all those who wait for him."

Right there. What she wanted for Matthew and herself was simple justice. Did she dare believe justice could happen, after all this time?

After Gabe's call on Friday, she'd gone on a cleaning spree to make up for the malaise of the day before. Hunger struck as well. A hearty beef stroganoff called her name. Time to go to the grocery store. But first, she'd make a quick list.

Half an hour later, she walked through Henderson's automatic doors and snagged an empty cart.

"Larkyn Wagner?"

She twisted around. Who?

"Hey. It's Faye. Remember me?"

Oh my gosh, it was. And wasn't. The woman speaking had the same luxurious auburn hair, the striking features that reminded Larkyn of Faye Dunaway, and the beautiful figure to go with all that. But … the hair was falling out of its ponytail, she wore a flannel shirt with faded jeans and tired, grimy sports shoes.

"I know." Faye interrupted before Larkyn could get her first words out. "I'm a mess."

Well maybe, compared to what Larkyn remembered. Faye's wardrobe had rivaled Georgia's. Or maybe Trudy's.

"I came down to do some work on my condo and needed carpet cleaner." She held her bag aloft.

"Faye. My goodness. What do you mean? Where do you live now?"

"In Westminster, Maryland."

"Oh." Larkyn backed out of the way of incoming shoppers, and Faye stepped aside with her. "When did you move?"

Faye hesitated, then exhaled. "It's a long story, honey."

"How long will you be in town?"

"Only a couple of days if I can manage everything. My mom and dad are keeping Mallory so I can take care of things here. I rented out the condo for a year and a half, but I need to sell it. Before winter, if I can."

Larkyn drew her brows together. "Who's Mallory?"

"Oh, dear. Of course, you wouldn't know." Faye pushed a lock of hair away from her face. "I'm sorry. I've been working so hard, and seeing you is such a surprise. You look the same, I might add."

"Thanks. I think." She paused, at a loss over the odd reunion.

Faye exhaled, seeming to make a decision. "If you have time, would you like to meet up later? I'm gonna need a break by dinner time. We could get something to eat and catch up."

With nothing but blank spaces mocking her from her calendar, Larkyn didn't hesitate. "Sure." She smiled. "Why don't you come to my house? Do you like beef stroganoff?"

Faye flashed an eager smile and pulled a cell phone from her pocket. "Give me your address, and tell me when to be there."

Faye Arthur, who'd gone from distant to disappearing without a word, sat in her kitchen sipping Perrier with lime.

Larkyn put the broccoli on to steam and tested her boiling pasta. "How did your afternoon go?"

"Not bad," Faye spoke from her perch on one of the new barstools. She now wore a pullover sweater and corduroy slacks. Her pert ponytail hung from a scrunchy with no loose ends and peach gloss coated her lips. "I've scrubbed everything washable. The carpet will have to do because I can't afford to replace it. Painters are coming next week. After that, my realtor will handle the sale."

The challenges of selling from out-of-state and other neutral topics occupied the conversation while Larkyn selected bowls and transferred the meal to the table.

The bread. With a mitted hand, she removed the cookie sheet from the oven and slid soft yeast rolls into a basket.

"You didn't have to do all this for me." Faye took a seat at the table.

"Oh, I enjoyed it." A lot more fun than cooking for one.

Faye opened her napkin and placed it on her lap. "Your house is beautiful."

"Thank you." A recently added rug in shades of blue and coral pulled the living room together. "We had a storm and the tree out back fell on this part of the house. I had to move out. It's only been a few weeks since they finished the renovation."

Faye surveyed their surroundings. "Wow. I love it. Where's Matthew tonight?" She reached for the salad bowl.

Larkyn froze. She should've prepared for this. "Matthew died." There was no other way to say it. "Over two years ago now."

Faye set the bowl down. "Are you kidding? No, of course you're not. Why do people say that?" Her hand bridged the gap between them and squeezed Larkyn's wrist. "I'm so sorry."

Larkyn let her shoulders droop. "I've been lost without him."

"Two years ago? After I moved, I guess."

Sad memories vied with the fragrance of beef mellowed by mushrooms and sour cream. Larkyn plucked a roll from the basket. "I spent a week at the hospital, and when I came back to work after the funeral, you were gone. Kate was Martin's new secretary."

Faye filled her salad bowl. "Oh, her name is Kate? How's she doing?"

"Fine." Larkyn puzzled over the question. "She's getting married soon."

"Well, good for her."

"Please, have some stroganoff." Larkyn nudged the dish. She took a turn with the salad as Faye spooned sauce filled with noodles and sirloin onto her plate.

"What happened, if you don't mind me asking." Faye placed her hands in her lap as if such a delicate question shouldn't be asked through a mouthful of food.

Larkyn agreed. "Let's talk after we eat."

"Oh, sweetheart." Faye frowned, as serious as she'd ever seen her spunky, self-confident friend. "I didn't mean to pry."

"You're not." Larkyn rushed to reassure. "I'm glad to tell you, but let's enjoy the meal while it's hot."

Faye dug into her food. "I'm starving, and this is delicious."

"Me too. I didn't cook at all yesterday. I think I was pouting."

Faye wagged her head as she chewed. "I can hardly believe he died. How tragic."

Changing the subject hadn't worked, but Larkyn's appetite had sprung to life. She spoke between bites. "I'm doing better. Getting the house repaired has forced me to take charge of things I've never had to do before."

"You're telling me." Faye raised her glass in salute. "Wait till you have a baby out of wedlock and see how fast you grow up."

Larkyn's jaw went slack. Okay, now they were even.

"Oops. There I go." She tore her roll and buttered it. "Whatever comes into my head comes out my mouth."

This was the Faye she remembered. The one who flitted through life at the office as if she owned it. Faye had modeled confidence, while Larkyn gained strength by association.

Faye bit into her roll. "These are delicious, they taste like you made them from scratch. Did you?"

Huh? "Faye. What are you doing? You can't just blurt a confession like that and not explain."

Faye finished chewing and swallowed. "You're right. I'm not ashamed of my daughter. Her name is Mallory Jane. She'll be two in February." She let those facts settle before going on. "You're the math person. You've probably got it worked out already."

Larkyn did. Faye had been pregnant when she moved. "You left H & H and moved because you were having a baby. I can understand that."

"Let me show you her picture." Faye reached for her phone and tapped on the screen. She scrolled and handed the phone to Larkyn. The face that beamed out was as ravishing as her mother. Startling wide blue eyes fringed with glorious lashes, peered into the lens from a face of innocent joy. Mallory sparkled. Larkyn wanted to hug her.

"She's adorable. Like an angel."

"She's *my* angel." A mother's pride filled Faye's voice. "I miss her, and I've only been gone a day. I wish you could see her. This trip is purely business, though. I've got to provide for her future."

Larkyn swiped the screen to view more pictures until they stopped showing Mallory. "Is this your mom and dad?" She turned the phone to face Faye.

"Yes. They've been fantastic. That was taken a while ago as you can probably tell."

Larkyn nodded. A much younger baby lay in her grandma's arms.

"My mom was diagnosed with breast cancer about six months ago. She looks different now."

Larkyn admired the trio. "I'm sorry. How is she doing?"

"She's doing well. But she can't be my daycare for Mallory like before. That's another reason I need to sell the condo fast. Childcare is terribly expensive."

Larkyn could only imagine the weight of such responsibility. She handed the phone back. "What about her father? Is he involved?"

Faye placed the phone face down beside her plate. "No. And I never want him to be."

Another shocking statement. "I'm sorry, Faye. I want to hear everything about you and Mallory, and I want to share about Matthew too, but I can hardly eat with all these bombshells going off. Can we continue after dinner?"

Faye tucked her phone away. "Hey, no problem. There's even more." She filled her fork with stroganoff and mused aloud, "I have a suspicion our meeting was meant to be."

CHAPTER TWENTY-FOUR

Larkyn's dinner guest called home to talk to her daughter and report on her day while Larkyn loaded the dishwasher. Faye's delight in Mallory came through their giggles as did the tension over the condo when the adults conversed.

"Thanks for dinner and for cleaning up." Faye pocketed her phone. "So much better than a fast-food drive-through."

Larkyn smiled. "I'm glad we ran into each other." Despite Faye's troubled situation, her freedom was contagious, like before. "I couldn't help overhearing you and Mallory. You're a great mother, but I know being alone is hard."

"Thanks. I try." Faye gathered her hair and refastened the ponytail. "Do you have coffee?"

"Of course." Larkyn gestured to the Keurig and opened one of her spacious new drawers to reveal a collection of pods and teas. "Fix what you want. I'll make tea for me." She filled the electric kettle with water, set it back on its base, and turned it on. "I'm curious. Why don't you want Mallory's father to help you?"

Faye grimaced. "I'm going to tell you, but please don't share this with anyone, okay? I mean you still work there, and you have to keep this confidential."

Larkyn got the feeling she had when her dental appointments came 'round. Probably nothing, but a dip in her stomach just the same. "I will." She breathed her promise. "But you're making me nervous. What are you talking about?"

"Sorry." Faye bounced over the word. "It's just that her father is someone you know." She paused again.

Larkyn braced. Shake the answer out of her or run in the other direction? "O-kay."

Faye squeezed her eyes closed and pushed her confession out. "It's Martin. Hamilton."

Wait—what?" Larkyn hadn't heard right. No way.

"He's the father." Faye pursed her lips. "And he doesn't deserve to know she exists."

Larkyn laid her palms on the countertop, ignoring the bubbling kettle. "He didn't know you were pregnant?"

"Oh, he knew. His plan was for an abortion." Sarcasm laced her tone. "We fought. I don't know what I thought—that he'd be happy or something?" she scoffed. "I couldn't handle being pregnant on my own, so I ran home to Mom and Dad, humiliated and full of disgust for myself and my behavior, but most of all for Martin."

Martin. Their boss. Old enough to be Faye's father.

"He's a snake, Larkyn. A complete phony."

All right. Obviously, Larkyn hadn't known Faye very well—and she sure didn't know her boss. If Trudy knew about the affair, she hid the truth well. Perhaps she had reasons to keep it a secret. Would Trudy overlook an affair if she wanted to save the firm?

Impossible. She'd never condone abortion.

"Is that why you asked about Kate?"

Faye shrugged. "Yeah, sort of. My vindictive side coming out. I bet she's young and pretty."

Indeed, she was—is. "I think I'll plead the fifth on that." Larkyn hated to bring Kate into this mess in any way. Her work demeanor was entirely different from Faye's. But nothing excused Martin's behavior as a boss. Or a husband.

"So you moved home, and your parents helped out, but then your mom got sick. Faye, Martin has lots of money. He could help you. He's supposed to help you."

"I don't want his help."

"What about when Mallory asks about her father?"

"I'll make something up," Faye flicked her wrist as if she'd discarded that question long ago.

They stood at the kitchen counter. The kettle had turned itself off. Neither spoke as they finished fixing their drinks and then wandered to the sofa.

Faye kicked off her shoes and crossed her long legs yoga-style while Larkyn tucked her ankles beside her in her favorite position.

Faye blew over the rim of her cup. "It's your turn, sweetie."

Oh, gosh. "I guess it is ..." Larkyn dragged her mind away from her boss and Faye—together. She took a deep breath and remembered the day.

"Matthew loved to go out in the early morning to ride his bike. Sometimes he went with other guys and would be gone a couple of hours. But on that Saturday morning, he went alone. I was half-asleep when he kissed me goodbye and said he'd see me for breakfast." Larkyn twisted her hands in her lap. The sharp protruding diamond on her left hand cut into her palm. "I'd barely finished my shower when a sheriff's deputy rang the bell and told me there'd been an accident."

Reliving that moment didn't kick her with the same force anymore, but at the time she'd been shocked and barely able to stand. "The deputy drove me to Duke Hospital's trauma center. By the time we got there, Matthew was ready for surgery."

Faye's forehead creased as she listened, her lips pressed together in a line.

"We never did find out exactly *how* it happened, but luckily a woman drove by and called 911. She was concerned about a dog that wouldn't leave the side of the road. He kept barking, and she was worried he'd get hit by a car. A sheriff stopped and noticed a bike in the weeds at the bottom of the ravine. Then he found Matthew, unconscious."

Larkyn paused to swallow some tea and regroup. "He stopped breathing on the way to the hospital. They placed him on life support and attached a halo to stabilize his neck which I found out later was broken. His chances weren't good, but I kept hoping he'd wake up." Her voice caught. Faye sat pale and motionless. "He lived for six days in the ICU."

Faye croaked and cleared her throat. "What road was he on when this happened?"

Larkyn's mouth went dry. Something wasn't right. "Buckley Road, over near Umstead State Park."

"You said Saturday. Not Labor Day weekend."

Larkyn set her cup down with shaky hands and hugged her stomach. "Yes—no. I mean yes—Saturday, two days before Labor Day."

Faye covered her face and moaned. "Please no."

Larkyn's stomach pitched. "You're scaring me again."

"Oh, Larkyn." Faye rocked and continued to moan. "I was there. I'm sure we saw the same person."

Larkyn snapped. "Stop, Faye. What are you talking about?" Her heart raced.

"Martin drove me to the airport," Faye whispered. Her hands still covered her face. "I never should have let him."

Larkyn bent in half, her jaws clenched tight. Could they erase the past few minutes?

When Larkyn looked up, tears streamed down Faye's cheeks. "The sun came up right in our eyes. There were a few trees, but we came around the curve. The light was blinding." She choked out the words in pieces. "We never saw him ... until ... oh, my gosh ... he was right beside my window."

Matthew! Larkyn covered her ears, but Faye kept talking.

"I screamed. Martin slammed the brakes."

Larkyn dropped her hands from her ears. She could hardly breathe. How she'd longed for this moment when the truth came out. And the punishment to follow. She expected a stranger she could freely hate. Not a friend. The truth was worse than not knowing.

Faye grabbed for Larkyn's wrist, but Larkyn jerked her arm back.

"We didn't *hit* anyone. I know we didn't. Martin stopped. He checked the rearview mirror—but then—he pulled away. I told him we had to go back and see what happened to the bike, but he wouldn't. He kept on *driving*."

Unbelievable. A cold calm blanketed Larkyn. She spoke in an even voice. "If you didn't hit him, what did you do? How did he end up dead?"

Faye hung her head. She wrung her hands. "I guess we forced him off the road."

CHAPTER TWENTY-FIVE

Gabe winced as the old floor creaked under the weight of his steps. He'd sneaked out early to take a run while everyone slept. Now, he looked for a pan to fry an egg and a toaster for some nice Italian bread. He swigged a glass of OJ and extracted a skillet from the cabinet with a minimum of clatter. The eggs hid behind all the Thanksgiving leftovers they'd ignored in favor of pizza at Brooklyn Bridge Park on Friday.

What a day. His sweet niece, Liza, at seven and a half, behaved like a proper little lady. Her intelligent brown eyes and chestnut hair resembled her mother's, but the spunk that drove Sylvia to wrestle with him hadn't shown itself in her daughter. Liza liked braids, though, and Gabe liked to pull them, an affront she handled with dignity beyond her years.

Robbie, the rascal, proudly sported a fresh butch cut. Gabe had asked where his hair had gone, and the boy's disdain cracked him up.

"It's a soldier-cut, Uncle Gabe." *Don't you know?*

The pan heated while he scrambled two eggs, found the toaster oven, and read the dials. Where was the setting for golden brown?

The eggs came out rubbery and blueberry preserves saved the toast, but he wasn't complaining. A glance at the oven clock convinced him he'd let Larkyn sleep long enough. If he waited too long, little people would appear and end his quiet time.

A groggy voice mumbled across the miles. "Hello."

Oops. She sounded pretty wrecked.

"Hey, sleepyhead. Sorry to call this early, but I didn't want to get side-tracked again."

"Gabe? Oh, I'm glad you called. I was going to try to reach Sara as soon as I woke up."

"What's up? Anything wrong?"

"Everything." Fully awake, she sobbed into the phone.

"Tell me." He ducked out into the vestibule. His terse reply reflected more his military experience than a lack of sympathy toward the woman in distress.

She didn't seem to notice. "Oh, Gabe. I found out last night what happened to Matthew." She caught her breath. "My friend, Faye, and Martin, my boss—. The accident happened the way we feared on that narrow road. Now she doesn't want to expose her daughter. But we have to go to the police."

"Can you slow down?" He knitted his brows and softened his tone. "I'm not getting all of this."

A quick huff, and she started over. Bumps and muffled sounds accompanied her words as if she were moving about. "I ran into my boss's old secretary yesterday. I hadn't seen her since she left her job, about the time that Matthew died."

"Okay." Gabe strained to hear.

"She had no idea about what happened to him because she'd moved, but as I told her about that day, she fell apart. She and Martin were driving together the very same morning."

Gabe pressed the phone to his ear, letting her rush on. "They forced a cyclist off the road and into a ravine.

Martin didn't want to be seen with her, so he didn't stop. They didn't report the accident. It was Matthew, Gabe."

He rubbed his stubbly chin and held back a curse. "That's disgusting."

"Yeah, I know." She exhaled noisily. "They'd had an affair, and Faye got pregnant. He was taking her to the airport, so she could go home. Her parents live someplace near Baltimore." The details didn't matter, but he let her ramble on.

"Martin thought the rider was probably okay, but there's no excuse for leaving the scene. Faye needs to report what she knows, but she can't let Martin know about their daughter. Or so she says. She's afraid he'll expect to be part of her life."

Gabe pinched the bridge of his nose and followed the drama as best he could.

"Faye agreed to go to the sheriff and report the accident, but she insists on calling a lawyer first. She's determined to keep this secret, which means she can't say she was pregnant or Mallory will be exposed."

Gabe understood that part well enough. "Keeping the secret plays into his hands, Larkyn. If Faye wants to keep the baby covered up, her story falls apart. That child is the motive, the reason her story's believable."

Larkyn had nothing to say.

He tried another tack. "How're you holding up?"

"Oh, Gabe." She sniffled. "I hardly slept all night. I'm stunned. But the worst thing is that my boss, a person I see every day, has been hiding the truth the whole time. He's been lying and faking, and I don't know what Trudy will say." Her voice wavered. "We're supposed to be friends. I can't believe she knows about any of this. What if Martin goes to jail? I can't imagine the scandal."

Gabe searched for something helpful to say but didn't find much. "Could he go to jail?"

"Oh, yes. We looked it up. Leaving the scene is a felony if the victim dies. It'll be worse for him as an officer of the court. Ethical standards of the Bar Association and all. Plus, Martin's well-known. Faye thinks he'll get off, no matter what."

Gabe snorted. "Except, *she's* getting a lawyer?"

"Right." Larkyn panted like she'd been in a race. "Here's the other thing. If a passenger in the car fails to report an accident they're involved in, that person's just as liable as the driver. Faye's scared. She can't risk being sentenced to jail, but we're hoping for leniency if she comes forward now."

Gabe paced the landing above the stairs. "Maybe you need a lawyer too."

"I don't know ..." Larkyn's fire gave way to uncertainty. Gabe longed to give her a hug. "We're going to wait to see what Faye finds out today."

Sure, but what a mess.

"Um, Gabe? If you want to pray, please ask for a good lawyer who knows how to handle the situation. He needs to be cheap. And pray that justice is done."

"Gladly." He regarded the phone in his hand. "You're asking me to pray?"

"Yes, I am. I've been thinking since our date. I talked to Dena. I went back to the lake on Thanksgiving. I even have a Bible now."

Lord? Gabe opened his mouth and a prayer fell out. "Thank you, God, for drawing Larkyn's heart to yours. Please give her all the wisdom and strength she needs for this situation. Comfort her and lead her by the hand. Give her peace."

Silence.

"Thank you," her quiet gratitude touched his heart.

"You're welcome." He breathed. "Is Faye there now?"

"She's here in town to put her condo on the market. She'll be dealing with her realtor and getting the condo ready until Monday when the law offices open. She wanted to go home to Mallory, but I think she's committed to seeing this through."

"I hope so, kiddo." He leaned against the wall in the stairwell and rubbed his eyes. "We're all flying back tomorrow. Can I come see you?"

"Yes! Please. I was going to accept your offer of dinner, even before."

She was? Awesome. "I miss you, Larkyn."

"You do? What about your family and all the fun you're having?"

"The trip's been perfect, but I'm rethinking the goals I had before the blast. Civilian life looks different now. I guess I'm ready to accept what it offers." That's what he wanted to say? To this woman? Now?

"How nice."

Ouch. "Wait." He stood away from the wall. "What I meant to say is that I like you. I want to come to your house when we get back."

"You do? Tomorrow?"

"Yep. Our flight's at three. Should be at RDU by five. I'll call as soon as we land."

"I'll be waiting."

Yes! "I'll see ya then. Oh, uh, remember that God is with you."

Running feet drummed below. He ducked back into the apartment and closed the vestibule door. The day no longer belonged to him.

"I know." He heard the excitement in her voice. "God did this, Gabe—uncovered the sin. He's going to give me justice and punish Martin for what he's done."

Larkyn's statement troubled him, but he'd think about that later.

CHAPTER TWENTY-SIX

Gabe palmed his keys and skirted Sara's suitcase, parked for now in the foyer. The flight from LaGuardia had been brief, but a certain someone had checked her suitcase, and it was seven-ish by the time they got to Cisco's. He'd dropped his duffel in his room. Unpacking could wait.

Sara cocked an eye, one hand propped on her hip.

"Don't give me that look." He eyed the door.

"Whatever you say." She looked entirely too smug for his liking. "Tell Larkyn we're rooting for her."

"I will." He turned the knob and got out before the cold rushed in. North Carolina had gotten the memo—time to import some winter.

He unlocked his truck and blew on his hands as the engine warmed. Defending his country from the other side of the globe had been a privilege, but seeing old friends, family, and the haunts of his youth had awakened neglected parts of his heart.

A time for every season. He quoted Solomon to himself as he drove toward Larkyn's house.

Her porch light glowed, and warm light shined from behind the drapes. The door flew open as soon as he knocked.

"Come in." She stepped aside to give him room and zinged him with a breathless smile that shot sparkles from her aqua eyes. Who was this woman? Where was the hand wringing?

He took in the fuzzy sweater and stretchy, tight pants before his arms encircled her and pulled her against his chest. She nestled like a kitten.

"Hi," he breathed into her hair.

"Hi, yourself." She drew back just enough for him to see her face. "I hope you're hungry."

Oh, man. If you only knew. He released her slowly as a spicy aroma reached him. "You're cooking?"

"Only some soup."

"Not any soup I've ever smelled before." His empty stomach gurgled.

"The recipe's called white chicken chili. Come and see."

When she lifted the lid to the cast iron pot and stirred the contents with a wooden spoon, a tangy combination of cumin, onion, garlic, and something different wafted out. Mmm.

"I know chili, and this ain't it." He leaned over to sip from the spoon she offered. "Wow, this stuff's got a kick."

"I use green chili instead of red, and chicken instead of beef." She covered the pot and turned to open the oven door. Gabe savored the sight of her willowy form as she bent to her task. More rich smells assaulted him.

"Cornbread." She announced over the golden muffins emerging from the heat. With skill, she emptied them into a basket and closed the towel lining. "You can put them on the table."

While she ladled the chili, Gabe obeyed. Then he carried both bowls to her new table. They were seated and

Gabe blessed the food. The scene felt as natural as the sweep of her hand, brushing back her hair.

Gabe's tongue tingled from the fire in his bowl. *Green chilis, huh?* They didn't put these in lasagna. "Where did you learn to make this?"

"From a recipe I found online. I've always loved ethnic foods."

He sensed that might be half of the story, but tonight she'd made the dish for him. "Maybe I can taste the flavor better when my mouth calms down." He picked up a muffin and watched as butter melted into the cornbread's texture."

"Try your muffin with this." She presented a jar of honey and watched him slather it on. "Honey helps dispel the heat."

Gabe ate slowly, savoring the flavor of the soup while enduring the burn. Lots of cornbread and honey later, his tongue no longer noticed.

"Do you think they'll have enough to arrest Martin?" Larkyn seemed to have stored this question until she couldn't hold back anymore.

"Honestly, I have no idea." And being honest, he had to ask, "What will you do if they don't?"

"I can't imagine." She frowned. "After all this time, if nothing happens? How could that be?" The sparkles faded from her eyes. "I'm afraid that when the news breaks, people will have to take sides."

A likely scenario. Loyalties would be tested. "That's something to consider."

Larkyn twisted a lock of hair around her finger.

"I refuse to back away. The old me would hide at home, but I'm not the one who should be ashamed." She glowered, her eyes deepening to a stormy hue. "I need to show up and face them."

"What you're doing will take courage. I'm proud of you."

"Proud?" Her brows pulled together, wrinkling her pretty nose. "I'm terrified, and I hate feeling that way. Being scared of Martin makes me furious." The storm intensified.

Gabe regrouped. "I understand. You're angry because he should be scared, not you. You want to turn the tables on him, right? That's what we should pray for."

Her head popped up as if surfacing from the deeps. "Hold on." She left the table and came back with a purple book. Seated again, she opened the volume to a bookmarked page.

"Listen to this in Psalm 37." She glanced at him, then down at her page. "'Commit your way to the Lord; trust in him and he will do this: He will make your righteousness shine like the dawn, the justice of your cause like the noonday sun.' Isn't that beautiful?"

Indeed. Gabe had clung to verses like that himself. "How did you find the verse?"

"Dena gave me this Bible. It's helping me, Gabe. I'm starting to understand who I am for the first time in my life."

"And who is that?"

She looked at him blankly. "Well ... I'm the person God made. I'm his child."

His lips pressed into a smile. She'd come a long way from the orphan child who doubted her parents wanted her. "I agree, but do fathers always do what their children want? Do they give them what they ask for every time?"

She frowned. "Of course not. But listen to this part. 'Be still before the Lord and wait patiently for him; do not fret when men succeed in their ways, when they carry out their wicked schemes. For evil men will be cut off ....'" And it gets better. Her finger moved from place to place, and he saw the underlining. '… the power of the wicked will be broken, but the Lord upholds the righteous.'"

Her gaze pierced him. "Don't you believe this?"

He drew a breath and let it out. "I believe, but I've made some assumptions in the past. I've learned that I don't always understand God's ways of working things out." He smiled at the lovely woman across the table, full of hope she'd never had before. Her jaw tightened.

"We're supposed to trust God, Gabe. We're supposed to have faith and count on this book to be true."

Where had she learned all this? The words were true, but there was so much more to faith than getting exactly what you want when you want it. "I'm glad you're trusting God, sweetheart." The endearment escaped his lips as if he'd used it all his life. "I'm glad you're reading the Bible and applying it to your life."

He held back on the *but,* sensing he'd only confuse her. Gabe knew, once again from experience, that elation and disappointment had to be weathered and absorbed. The key for him had been clinging to the character of his Father. Believing in that endured if God didn't perform the way he'd hoped. Still wasn't answering as he'd hoped.

Her tension dissolved before him. "You called me sweetheart."

His muscles went slack at the implication of his confession. How ready was he? Was she? He tendered a question. "Do you see yourself ever falling in love again?"

"I didn't think so … I didn't want to …"

She seemed reluctant to let him down. He waited.

"But that's changed." Her breath released with a whoosh.

Gabe's heart kicked in his chest, but caution won out. "What do you mean by changed?"

Emotion glinted in her eyes. "Ever since we met, I've been uncomfortable. Off-balance." She wavered slightly to demonstrate. "I thought being Matthew's wife was all I was, and grief was my link to him. Then I lost the house we shared. I learned about being created by God." She offered her palm in his direction. "You said so yourself, Gabe, when you told me to 'Be who you are.' Well, I'm trying. I'm more than a grieving widow. I want to live my life."

She wasn't declaring her love, but he hadn't expected her to. "I'm glad." He reached for her hand across the table. No, not good enough. He stood up and approached her with his hands extended. She took them and rose to meet him. Gabe gathered her in his arms again. "I'm very, very glad."

He closed his eyes as clarity overwhelmed him. How they'd changed. He from a frustrated soldier, a disillusioned vet, to the man who held the former Mrs. Matthew Wagner as if they belonged together.

He loosened his hug, and her face came up as he'd hoped it would. Without shifting his gaze from her unblinking eyes, he bent to touch her lips with his. What could have been chaste and simple, turned stirring and deep. His eyes drifted shut as she leaned into him, her scent and feel soaking into his soul.

Kate and Georgia compared notes on their long holiday weekends as Larkyn opened her leftover chicken chili and placed it in the microwave. She entered ninety seconds and ignored the laughter behind her as she listened to the hum and watched the seconds count down.

"Earth to Larkyn," Georgia broke through her musings. Larkyn turned and faked a smile. "Sorry. Distracted."

Kate tilted her head with a sympathetic look. "Are you all right? I hope you had a good weekend."

"I did. All my friends were out of town, but I had a nice time anyway." She referred only to Thanksgiving, which seemed like weeks ago instead of days. "Gabe came back on Sunday and stopped to see me."

"Who is Gabe?" They spouted together, nailing her in their sights.

Ahh. This was what happened when your brain went on break.

"Haven't I mentioned Gabe before?" Innocence personified, she blinked.

"No, you haven't mentioned Gabe before." Georgia mimicked Larkyn's voice. "That's something we would've noticed."

Kate swept the lengths of her fashionably straight hair over one shoulder, just like a Pantene model. "No, Larkyn. You most certainly haven't mentioned Gabe."

Ding. Her ninety seconds were up. Good. She turned to open the microwave. They waited as she carried her lunch to the table.

"So, are you going to tell us or not?" Kate prodded, a no-nonsense tone in her voice.

Did Larkyn have a choice? "Gabe's my friend, Sara's fiancé's cousin." Sufficiently vague and uninteresting.

"And ... ?" Georgia rotated her wrist.

Larkyn sighed. Couldn't she eat in peace? "And ... he's my friend too." That wasn't going to be good enough, she could already tell. "He *is*, okay?"

They waited her out.

"All right, fine. We met in September at Sara's engagement party." No need to mention the part about almost hitting him. "He helped me get my roof fixed right. We saw a movie together." *And he kissed me.* No—they didn't get to know that.

"You're dating." Kate grinned. "How wonderful is that?"

"Absolutely." Georgia raised her palm, and Kate high-fived it.

They were delighted for her. And that felt good. Larkyn tried to suppress a smile, but her lips rebelled. Okay, she could admit to being happy.

"Was that so hard?" Georgia beamed. "What's he look like?"

The memory of his embrace warmed her cheeks. This was getting out of hand.

Once again, they waited.

"He was a soldier until a few months ago when he got hurt by a landmine. He's Italian, and he's got brown eyes and dark hair." She couldn't bring herself to describe how fit and strong he was, the epitome of a hero. Or how his eyes twinkled when he was joking, and how gentle he could be when he talked about God.

"Ooh, la-la. He sounds exotic." Georgia's romantic imagination took flight. "Is he anything like David Giuntoli?"

Who? "I don't know." Larkyn shrugged.

"Yay for you! Congratulations." Kate bundled her trash and stood. "Wish I could stay to hear more, but I've got stacks waiting on my desk. Martin's expecting some people."

Larkyn's tummy took a tumble. Right. Soon those people would be detectives. When they showed up, would she want to flee or have a front row seat?

Georgia's attention shifted as well. "Sorry to desert you as well, sweetie. I've gotta go. Got a stack of papers to prepare for court. It's Mia's case."

Larkyn relaxed. The inquisition was over.

Oh, wait. Mia handled family law. *Don't be silly*. There couldn't be a connection.

Larkyn barely tasted her chili in the silence of the break room. Would those two nosy newshounds be her friends when the rest of the story broke? That part wasn't silly. Now if she could avoid Trudy and her Christmas plans, she'd make it through the day.

Her stomach churned on its spicy contents. She had to stop worrying. Last night with Gabe she'd argued for faith. Today, the Bible seemed far away. In four more hours, she'd be talking to Faye. Hopefully, Gabe would help.

His kiss still warmed her lips. *Oh, Matthew. Do you mind that Gabe is more than a friend?* How much more, she didn't dare dwell on. Only that she found herself beyond the shallows—where her feet couldn't touch the bottom.

Larkyn took her dirty dish to the sink and rinsed it under hot water. The Bible had told her not to fret, to wait patiently for the Lord. Okay.

A prayer formed in her heart. *God, you didn't come through when I was a child, but you have to come through now.*

CHAPTER TWENTY-SEVEN

Larkyn changed into exercise pants and a well-washed, droopy sweatshirt. Then she paced. She'd been home for thirty minutes. Did Faye know that?

The forecast called for snow. One of her favorite things. But today it added to her list of worries. Where was Faye? Maybe she should call.

Finally, the doorbell rang. Larkyn bolted to the foyer and flung open the door. Faye at last. Looking as pretty as ever.

"I'm so glad you got here. Come in." She panted for no reason.

Faye stepped in, and Larkyn checked the weather before she shut the door. Her streetlight reflected off a low ceiling of dense, dark clouds that did not bode well.

Faye unzipped her fleece-lined jacket and tossed it over the sofa back. Her wool pants and stylish sweater complemented a figure not changed at all by having a baby. She shed her white knit hat and smoothed her wavy tresses. "Brr. I'm so glad I brought something decent and warm to wear."

Larkyn blurted, "What happened?"

"Let's sit down. Do you have coffee?"

Was the news so bad that Faye had to stall? "Sure, the Keurig's ready, but all I have is dark roast." Larkyn scurried to the kitchen and grabbed a mug.

Faye selected a pod. "This is great."

Larkyn rummaged and found a box of biscotti. "Did you eat? I have a few leftovers."

"This is fine, thanks." Faye took a piece of biscotti and watched her coffee cup fill.

Larkyn fidgeted but held her tongue. *Please let the news be good.*

They sat at the dining table. Larkyn folded her hands and looked hard at Faye, her patience at an end. "What did your lawyer say?"

Faye took a breath and set her coffee down with unsteady hands.

"His name is Tony Aguilar. He was very understanding. I was hoping there would be some room for negotiation since this was an accident, but even if Martin didn't mean to make Matthew crash, we left the scene. We didn't call for help. Tony thought that reporting what I've learned would result in leniency. So, we went to see the police."

Larkyn sat straighter. "You went to the police already? What did they do?"

Faye shifted as if her chair was uncomfortable. "Hold on. Let me finish."

Larkyn closed her lips and tried to hold still as Faye explained in her slow, precise way.

"Tony also said that I should put Martin's name on Mallory's birth certificate, to establish my claim that we had an affair, and for other good reasons like child support. If Martin tries to contest it, he'd have to take a paternity test. And that would prove my point."

"Which is good, right? Why are you acting so strange?"

Faye sipped coffee and avoided Larkyn's eyes. "It's complicated, but to answer your question, yes, we talked and then we went to the police. They plan to visit Martin tomorrow and get his statement. He doesn't know they're coming."

Larkyn reached for Faye's elbow, resting on the table. "I don't understand. You don't seem happy."

Faye cocked her head and finally looked at Larkyn. "I told you before, I don't want to give him a father's rights. I told Tony that we have to do this without involving Mallory."

Larkyn rocked back in her chair. If the pregnancy was off the table, then Faye had no leverage. If Martin denied her story, what could they do? His word against hers.

No way. What an absurd conclusion.

"Will they arrest him?" Larkyn searched for a shred of hope. Nothing like handcuffs to show him he's in trouble.

Faye looked pale and drawn but faced her straight on. "They can't. They have to get a warrant first, and a judge will only issue one for probable cause. They can question Martin, but if he denies my story, there's not a lot they can do."

What? *No.* "How can you say that? Murderers don't get to say 'Sorry. Nope, I didn't do it.'" Did Faye think she was stupid?

Her friend's expression said as much. "Look. It's all about evidence. People say, 'I didn't do it' all the time. Don't you watch TV?"

Larkyn glowered as Faye explained.

"The police checked every lead they had after the accident, which wasn't much. As I told them, there were no other cars on the road at the time. Any security video they might have gotten from the airport doesn't exist anymore—or if it does, Martin never got out of the car. They can ask my neighbors if anyone saw me leave that morning, but who's gonna remember that? Even if someone does remember that day, they can't prove it was Martin's Tahoe without the license number or some other identification. I'm sorry, Larkyn, there's just no evidence and no leads."

It all made sense, but she couldn't let it go. How could she ever? "Your eyewitness testimony doesn't count?"

"Honey, think about it." Faye looked like she'd been run over herself. "It's my word against his. He's a big lawyer. I'm the fallen woman. Even if it went to trial, his lawyer would make me out to be the liar. He could paint me as vindictive."

Even if there was a pregnancy to hide? And a child to prove it? Unbelievable. "So, if there's no hope at all, why are they going to question him?"

Faye's shoulders dropped as if she were weary of the whole thing and tired of explaining to Larkyn. "From what I understand," she sighed, "they'll interrogate him and use their techniques to intimidate or catch him in contradictions, but again, Martin is a lawyer. He's used to such things. He won't be easy to trick."

Well, Larkyn couldn't sit here and do nothing. She stood and paced to the sink and back. The one thing that could swing this had been declared off-limits. She towered over Faye who slumped in her seat.

"You do understand our only hope is if you testify about being pregnant?" She paced back and forth again. "Tell them he refused to stop because the police would come. The accident report would show the two of you were together. The story would make the news, which he couldn't allow to happen." Larkyn turned on her heel and made another round to the sink. "Then you use the DNA to prove that the baby is his, another thing he had to cover up. It speaks to motive, Faye. Makes your story credible."

Faye covered her face and shook her head. "I'm so sorry."

"You're sorry?" Larkyn squeaked. "Sorry that Matthew died? Or sorry you refuse to tell the whole truth?"

The story couldn't end here with Martin still in charge and nothing accomplished. Her anger fizzed like soda trapped in a bottle. Heat rose from Larkyn's neck and engulfed her cheeks. She could see the awful outcome. Faye would look like a liar and Larkyn like a fool for believing her. Not just a fool, but a traitor to her employer. There would be absolutely nothing she could do.

Faye's silence fueled her fury. She could sit there looking pitiful, but Larkyn's husband was dead.

"Tell me again," she bit off her words with sarcasm, "why is it so bad to admit that Martin is Mallory's father?"

Tears rolled down Faye's cheeks. Larkyn grabbed a box of tissues, ready to throw them at her, but with restraint, she pushed them across the table. Beating up Faye didn't help.

Faye wiped at her eyes. "I don't care about my reputation, but I don't want to risk him becoming part of Mallory's life—and mine." She lifted one hand and let it drop. "He wanted to kill our baby, Larkyn." She wiped her nose. "How can I let him be her daddy—even on paper?"

Larkyn lowered herself back into her chair. Martin was Mallory's daddy, regardless, but she understood Faye's feelings—to a point. Knowing what Larkyn now knew, she never wanted to see the man again, either. But what about Matthew and justice? What about consequences for breaking the law and lying?

What about God?

Where was he in this mess?

The women sat in silence until Faye stirred. "I better get back home. Bad weather's coming."

Home? "Home to Baltimore or home to your condo?"

"Both." She stood with another sigh and headed to the sofa where her coat and hat lay. "I've done what I can."

Larkyn gaped as her so-called friend put on her coat and retrieved her purse. Faye snugged the hat down over her glorious, sexy hair.

Larkyn tailed her to the foyer with a grip on her tongue. If she said anything more, she'd regret it.

But the pressure in her chest exploded anyway. She spit her words like something nasty. "You're really leaving? Just walking away? Do you know what I'm sorry about? I'm sorry you're too selfish to do the right thing. Go back to Maryland, Faye. I was better off before you came."

CHAPTER TWENTY-EIGHT

Cisco hollered through the closed bathroom door. "Sara's comin', and she's bringin' a pizza. You wanna see if Larkyn can join us?"

Gabe opened the door and let the steam escape. "Sure. In a minute." He couldn't deny the zing the mention of Larkyn's name produced, but he kept it cool. There would be no end to the grief if Cisco suspected his nosedive into romance. Gabe rubbed his scratchy chin. If Larkyn was coming, he could use a shave.

Gabe had news of his own to share tonight. He'd been offered a job at the AVA before the trip to Brooklyn and had officially accepted. Pancho had big plans. The guy had almost finished a social work degree. He understood that Gabe had little to offer but his heart. Apparently, that was enough.

"You still primping in there?"

"Bug off, Cisco." Gabe rinsed his razor and tucked it away in the drawer. He patted his cheeks with a small splash of a cologne saved from some long-ago Christmas. Hopefully, he wouldn't smell like a flower shop. The label called it woodsy. Hopefully, woodsy was good.

Larkyn arrived at the same time as Sara, who carried the heavenly aroma of fresh-baked dough and cheese in an extra-large box. Cisco kissed her awkwardly as possession of their dinner changed hands. Gabe and Larkyn exchanged a look and by silent agreement kept their greeting low-key.

When they all took seats at the table, Larkyn seemed distracted, but Gabe went ahead with the blessing. "Thank you, Father, for watching over each of us and giving us means to enjoy this meal together … except for the mushrooms. Amen." Larkyn cut him a look.

"Hey, God has a sense of humor." He lifted a slice dripping with stretchy mozzarella.

Sara dragged a slice of her own over the edge of the box and onto her plate. "He has to, I think. Look at giraffes. Or flamingos."

"What have you got against flamingos?" Cisco folded his crust in half before taking a monster bite.

"Nothing. They walk backward, though."

"Backward? They do not." Cisco chewed and gave her a superior look.

"They do. Their knees bend the wrong way."

"Who's to say they're wrong? Maybe ours are backward," Mr. Argumentative countered.

Gabe inspected his pizza for hidden mushrooms. Yep, he'd gotten them all. "You're mighty quiet over there." He nudged Larkyn's foot under the table.

"Sorry." Her voice sounded strained.

Gabe tilted his head and tossed a glance toward Sara. Women could decipher other women better than men. Sara's face read, "Not now."

Gabe selected option number two. "I have an announcement to make."

Since everyone seemed to be chewing, he continued. "I am now employed. I accepted a job today as assistant to the head of AVA, which as you know, is the local Atlantic Veterans' Alliance chapter. It's not full time and I'll never get rich, but I'll have a chance to share some of what I've learned from my experiences."

Sara gave him a wide smile, her green eyes sincere. "That's wonderful, Gabe. What will you do?"

Right. "I'll hang out with the vets who come by, get to know their needs, and refer them to resources. The head guy, Manuel Perez, who goes by Pancho, is more into career counseling, and I'll be more about sports. I want to start working out there instead of at the Y, but the equipment is pathetic. Our offices are in a house that needs repair, and we need to build a gym. It's all kind of in the dream phase, but we're having a cycling event in the spring that we hope will make some money."

Nothing from the lady at his left. Had Larkyn even heard him?

"Congrats, bro'." Cisco chipped in with his support. "Just so you know, you have to get your own place when my bride takes over."

"Don't bother him about money." The bride shushed him. "This sounds like a labor of love to me."

Sara understood. She usually did. "Thanks. I didn't realize how much until I met some of the guys. I've been told I'm a natural leader, so I want to make that work from this side of military service."

"Absolutely." Sara's endorsement covered for silence from Larkyn. "I guess you have female vets too?"

Gabe hadn't met any yet, but yeah, there were. He got up to refill his glass. "That's another thing to think about. Anybody else?" He brought the two-liter bottle to the table. Larkyn remained in a trance.

He touched her shoulder as he passed. "Are you all right? You don't seem to be with us."

"I'm sorry." She said again. "It's just ..." She faded out.

"Hey." He squatted down to her level.

She swiveled in her seat and wrapped her arms around his neck, nearly knocking him over.

"Whoa." He grabbed the tabletop. Not quite perfect balance on this leg, but close.

Larkyn let go with an anguished cry. "I'm so sorry. I didn't mean—"

"Will you stop with the sorrys?" Sara patted her arm.

Larkyn wiped at her eyes. "I'm s—. I didn't mean to ruin dinner."

Cisco entered the arena. "I agree. Let's finish this fabulous pizza while it's hot, and then we'll talk. Larkyn, we love you, okay? Now eat something."

Gabe suppressed a laugh. His cousin was anything but subtle, however, his point was well taken. Nobody was bleeding. Whatever had happened could wait a few minutes.

They finished the meal, put the plates in water, and went to the living room. Gabe took a seat on the corduroy couch, and Larkyn sat beside him. Or rather plastered herself to his side.

No one commented on the body language as Larkyn told her woeful tale.

"Where's Faye now?" Sara asked.

"I don't know. I basically told her to leave. She might be driving to Maryland by now."

They sat with that a moment. It hadn't been the kindest response, but Larkyn's frustration was understandable. Armed with only half of the story, how could the law expect Martin to cave?

Cisco leaned with his forearms on his knees. "What happens now?"

Larkyn straightened. "The police will question him. At the office, I suppose. They can request he come to the station, but he doesn't have to. I suspect he'll have a lawyer present as soon as he knows what's going on. He'll refuse to answer questions. If they can't get a warrant, he doesn't have to do anything. They can call him a person of interest, but without new evidence, we're done."

"And Faye knows this?" Sara sounded incredulous.

Larkyn's voice rose. "Even her lawyer advised her to name Martin as the father. Faye has no idea what financial needs Mallory may have in the future. What if she gets sick? What if she wants to know her father? Or go to college? But it's more important to her to keep Martin out of her life."

Sara frowned. "She sure hates the guy."

"She does. Because of the way he treated her about being pregnant, and then because he got them both in trouble by leaving the scene. Not to mention what happened to Matthew." Larkyn sagged, and her voice lost its edge. "But I guess justice matters more to me than it does to Faye. Martin must be caught."

Gabe rubbed his forehead. No wonder Larkyn was angry, but carrying it around for too long would eat away at her heart. When he'd left matters up to God, he'd found peace, but he was pretty sure she wasn't ready to hear that. Instead, he asked, "How did it go at work today?"

She shifted to face him more directly. Her eyes had cleared and affection for her washed through him. How beautiful ...

"I did fine until ... I mean nobody seemed to notice me—" She halted, glanced away for a moment, then resumed, "Until they asked me about my Thanksgiving." Another quick pause. "I happened to slip."

Uh-oh. The proverbial cat inside the bag was making noise.

"I, uh, said something about Gabe. Kate and Georgia were all over it."

"Gabe?" Sara's eyebrows arched.

"All I said was his name."

Cisco's lips curved into a smug smile. "Ohh. You never talk about anyone but Matthew. And suddenly you mention another guy. That's big news. Bigger than Faye."

His cousin was no dummy. How had he seen this coming?

Her blush gave them away. Sara, the astute one, hadn't a clue. She sat with her mouth open.

Cisco smirked at his coup. "Am I right, or am I right?"

Gabe took Larkyn's hand and kissed her fingers before God and present company. "You guys should never have let us go to the movies alone." He grinned at Larkyn, and she smiled back with doe eyes. "We haven't talked about anything yet, but our friendship has, shall we say, advanced to something more."

"Larkyn?" Sara's voice turned into a squeak.

"Gabe's been marvelous. We're definitely more than friends." Larkyn clasped her hands like a child. "Matthew understands."

Oh, well. Gabe pulled back, his smile less open. Matthew had given his blessing, had he? Hopefully, he wouldn't always be getting a vote. Larkyn must've felt his vibe because she clarified.

"Hey, y'all. I know Matthew is gone. Gabe has helped me in practical ways, and he's helped me understand about God." She set her face. "I have a future, and for now I want Gabe in it."

"Yay." Sara beamed. "I love that. You guys are perfect together. Aren't they?" She elbowed her fiancé.

Gabe avoided Cisco's smirk, then changed his mind and owned it. "That's what we plan to find out."

Larkyn flipped her hair back with a teasing grin. "It's not like you didn't push this, Sara."

The word was out, and all was fine. Gabe wanted to kiss her outright, but unlike Cisco, he'd wait for a more private moment. Her qualifier, *for now,* made sense, though Gabe couldn't imagine anyone better for him.

He prayed that if this was right, Larkyn would come to the same conclusion.

CHAPTER TWENTY-NINE

Larkyn drove downtown, dreading the day ahead. With Faye no longer around to spy from inside the case, Larkyn needed *eyes on the situation*, as Gabe put it. With that in mind, she'd gone to work as if nothing was wrong.

After a nervous couple of hours in her office, Trudy sent her a voice message canceling their meeting about Christmas plans.

By eleven, Larkyn couldn't keep still any longer. She took a casual stroll past the Hamiltons' suite of offices hoping to snoop a bit. While standing beside Kate's desk, two men in dark pants and white shirts arrived. They didn't look like clients.

"Raleigh Police Detectives." The taller one spoke and showed his ID. "Here to see Mr. Martin Hamilton."

Larkyn's heart hitched, and apprehension flooded her middle.

"I don't see an appointment." Kate flipped a page and turned it back. Kate's youth and cheerleader freshness seemed hardly a match, but the girl was tough. Larkyn had seen her in action.

The gentleman didn't blink. "We don't have an appointment, Miss, but we're here on police business. I think your boss will want to see us."

Maybe the police came more often than Larkyn knew, this being a law office and all, but she couldn't believe it when Kate seemed unconvinced.

At that moment, Martin's door opened, and he stepped into his private reception area. Kate's head turned. Larkyn swallowed her breath. If only she could disappear. The detectives seized their chance to cross the distance and reintroduce themselves.

Smooth as silk pie, Martin smiled, shook their hands, and invited them in with a nod toward Kate. "No calls."

"Wonder what that's about," Kate spoke without alarm. "Here. These are Trudy's notes about Christmas. She said to give them to you and to proceed as you saw fit."

Larkyn took the paper, glad to have a cover for being there. *Oh, to have ears in that room.* She scanned the page. Decorate the lobby and the conference room. Hire caterers. Select a menu of finger foods and desserts for lunch before closing the office early on December 24.

Three weeks and two days. The world could end by then. Hers probably would. Possibly Trudy's as well.

She needed to get out of here.

But she needed to stay.

"Larkyn?" Kate interrupted the ricochet in her head.

"Hmm? What did you say?"

"I said, it sounds like a fun assignment. Do you need any help?'" Kate peered at her from behind her bangs. "Something isn't right, and don't tell me you're fine. You weren't yourself yesterday, either."

The confession almost spilled, but Larkyn caught herself. No gossip. "I don't know what you mean, Kate. I guess I'm a little tired."

"Is it Gabe? It must be hard to start a new relationship after—you know."

"It's a little weird." Larkyn snatched at yesterday's excuse. "But don't worry about me, okay?"

"Whatever you say." Kate looked unconvinced. "See you at lunch?"

"Sure." Okay, now she needed to leave. No telling when the men would come out, and she was tired of lying to her friend.

Larkyn passed Georgia's office on the way back to her little corner. How deep did these friendships go? Would they stand the pressure of what Larkyn had discovered? Judging by what happened with Faye, no telling. A few moments at Kate's desk had shown her how hard it would be to oppose the lord of the law firm in person. Except God was with her.

Larkyn had the promise she'd quoted to Gabe. *The Lord upholds the righteous.* God knew the truth, and he was bigger than Martin.

At lunch, she tried to act normal. "Thanks for giving me Trudy's instructions," she made an off-hand reference to being at Kate's desk. "The big boss seemed pretty busy this morning."

Kate poured Italian dressing on her salad. "No more than usual."

"Oh. I just mean he had visitors without an appointment. It looked like you weren't going to let them in."

Kate mixed the dressing in with her fork and took a bite.

"*I* was busy this morning." Georgia popped the top on a can of lemon-lime flavored seltzer water with care for her manicured nails. Georgia's nails would probably offend the dress code if such a thing had been put in writing. Kate's nails were regulation length, with shiny, natural polish.

Larkyn probed again. "Where was Trudy, anyway?"

"She came in after you left, just as the detectives were leaving. I told her you'd gotten the list."

"What list?" Georgia finished pouring her drink over ice and tossed the can in recycling.

Not what detectives? Georgia seemed to see nothing unusual in their appearance.

"What happened after that?" Larkyn abandoned subtlety. She had to know.

Kate took a moment to finish chewing. "Nothing. What do you mean?"

Larkyn's lunch tote sat, zippered and untouched. Who could eat? "I mean when the detectives came out. Did they speak to Trudy? Did she and Martin talk?" *Calm. Calm. You're losing it.*

Kate swallowed and narrowed her eyes at Larkyn. Georgia picked up on the shift in mood.

"Okay, stop." Kate put her fork down. She didn't sound angry, but her face wore a serious mask.

Georgia's head swiveled back and forth, one to the other.

Kate addressed Georgia. "I'm concerned about Larkyn. She's acting strange and she won't say what's wrong."

"Really?" Georgia looked her up and down. "What's goin' on with you, girl?"

Nothing wasn't going to cut it anymore. Larkyn searched for guidance. She despised typical office gossip and while this wasn't typical, it *was* gossip. "I can't talk about it here, but I promise I'll explain. Can you trust me?"

She saw respect in their response. Respect was awesome. She might get through this yet.

"Okay." Kate pronounced the verdict. "I can't imagine what is wrong, but we can wait till you're ready, right, Georgia?"

"Mm-hm," Georgia murmured with a sly edge, as if cogs whirred behind those intelligent eyes churning with the same tenacity that made her good at her job.

Let her colleagues presume whatever they wanted. The truth would come out soon.

The rest of the afternoon passed without a ripple in routine. Larkyn was about to catch the elevator down when she heard her name from behind. Trudy.

"Do you have a minute, Larkyn?"

Larkyn hugged her coat and lunch tote against an onslaught of butterflies. "Sure."

They went to Larkyn's little office, the closest place, and Trudy closed the door.

"Let's sit." Trudy took the only seat besides Larkyn's and crossed her legs. The woman might be in her late fifties, but she had an attractive figure and the budget to clothe it well. What did her husband need with a thirty-year-old?

"We had a couple of visitors today," she began, "From the police detective's division." She paused with perfect timing. "They had questions for Martin."

Larkyn didn't move, and she kept her mouth closed. Interrogation 101. Don't volunteer.

"Their questions involved the day your husband ran off the road."

"You mean Matthew?" Larkyn broke her rule, but she couldn't let that go unchallenged. He was a man with a name, not part of a category. And what was this *ran off the road*? As if he did it all by himself.

"Yes, of course." Trudy was almost snippy. "Do you know anything about that?"

Her boss was a skillful questioner. If Larkyn was on the witness stand, she didn't intend to be caught in any lies or contradictions. She'd answer truthfully.

"I may. I ran into Faye Arnold a few days ago. She told me something upsetting."

"Did she tell you that Martin was involved in what happened to Matthew?"

Wow. That was direct. "Yes, she did."

Trudy's tough facade showed cracks. "And you believed her?"

"I did. I do." Larkyn steeled herself to deal with the hurt this had to cause. She might be armored up to stand strong, but this woman had been more comfort when Matthew died than Larkyn's own mother who hadn't even been in the country when the accident happened. When Larkyn was out of work and spending all her hours in the hospital, Trudy had come with a huge basket of fruit and snacks. She'd gone far beyond in the two years since.

"Why?" A simple question from Trudy.

"Why not?" Larkyn didn't say it to be flip. "I mean, Faye wouldn't make it up. There's no reason. Nothing to gain." Except for child support, which she refused to pursue.

"That's the question, isn't it?" Trudy's expression hardened again. "I don't mean to speak against Faye. As far as I knew, she was a good employee. But Martin says she made insinuations. He asked her to leave quietly so as not to cause embarrassment, but he couldn't deal with her ... flirting. He didn't even tell me, because he knew it would upset me."

Had they left the universe and entered another dimension where facts were reversed? "That's not the story I heard. It was the other way around." Her words sounded weak, but the lie had left her off-balance.

Trudy gave her a look of pity. "I'm so sorry you were taken in, my dear. But don't worry. Martin's getting it straightened out."

No. She wanted to scream and beat Trudy with a birth certificate. "Faye is telling the truth. I know it."

Her boss stiffened and uncrossed her legs. She stood. "We need to end this conversation then." She went to the door and opened it to the empty hallway. "I hope you'll come to reason soon, Larkyn. In the meantime, have a good evening."

CHAPTER THIRTY

The next morning, Larkyn turned into the parking deck and wound around to Level B. Her gloved fingers gripped the steering wheel hard as she steered into her parking space, her jaw set against the threat of more tears.

She and Gabe had agreed last night that Larkyn needed to keep working until something definitive happened. The choices appeared to be getting fired, quitting, or a sudden attack of honesty possessing Martin. Why had she been surprised that Trudy believed her husband?

Larkyn slammed the door of her Jeep, the impact resounding off the concrete walls. Her remote chirped and echoed as she walked away.

Upstairs, all appeared normal. The list of instructions for Christmas lay at the top of the pile in her inbox. She left the paper there and booted her computer. Where would she be by Christmas?

"G'Mornin'," Georgia called in passing. Except she didn't pass. She stopped and stuck her head around the corner. "Whoa. Look at you."

What? Too early for spinach in her teeth.

"You." Georgia pointed at her clothing. "Woo-hoo." Her voice carried.

Larkyn curbed the desire to shush her. A strategy sure to backfire. "How are you this morning?"

"Just peachy. But don't tell me you don't know what I'm talking about. The outfit. The makeup. You look great, my dear."

Larkyn let her breath out slowly. She'd jazzed up her boring skirt and sweater with a scarf, contrasting tights, and mid-calf boots. Big deal. The added bracelet should've stayed in her jewelry box. The mascara in the drawer.

"It's Gabe, isn't it? He must be quite a guy." She slid into Larkyn's office and planted herself in the chair.

"What's going on?" Kate poked her head in too. "I was putting my lunch in the fridge and heard you guys."

"Don't you love Larkyn's new look?" Georgia crowed as if she'd discovered penicillin.

Kate gave her an appraising once-over. "I like it. The purple in your scarf brings out your beautiful coloring."

Coloring? Larkyn didn't have coloring. She was washed out and nondescript.

"You should go bolder, Larkyn. It really suits you." Kate pronounced.

Georgia stood. "Yep. We expect more news at lunch."

Kate sent Larkyn a solid thumbs up before they left her alone.

Larkyn opened her billing software, but the screen might as well have been blank. Something had to happen soon, because she couldn't keep pretending.

Patience. Gabe's advice. He carried an inner toughness that matched his powerful physique. A lazy smile crossed her lips as the memory of his leisurely goodnight kiss spread warmth throughout her body. She found nothing fake in his courage or false in his warm caress. She hadn't felt that breathless in a very long time.

Just before lunch, Trudy showed up at her office door and asked for a moment of her time. Larkyn's stomach sank to the tops of her boots, but she kept her chin up and her shoulders back.

"Come with me." No, not a request. A demand.

She trailed her boss past Kate's desk into Martin's office. Kate raised her head. Martin never handled accounting matters. Larkyn's presence was not the norm.

"Take a seat." Martin gestured. He wore a conservative striped tie knotted perfectly under the collar of an immaculate dress shirt, and every styled hair knew its place.

Following orders, she lowered herself to the edge of her chair while Trudy remained standing with crossed arms as she delivered her intro.

"I hope this nonsense with Faye will end here and now, so we can all get back to our jobs."

It seemed wise to keep her mouth shut, so she did.

Martin stared at her. A tactic meant to intimidate. Make her nervous. Make her explain. Larkyn remained still.

The manicured fingers of his left hand drummed on the desk, his gold wedding band tight around the flesh. At the moment of his choosing, he leaned back in his chair. "I understand you're in on this little plot Ms. Arthur concocted."

"I'm not *in on* anything." Larkyn found a backbone from somewhere.

"You deny that you know about her accusations?"

Larkyn met his scrutiny without flinching. "I know what Faye shared with me."

"Which is?"

Whatever game he was playing, she could play too. "It's probably whatever the detectives said."

Martin's eyes narrowed, and Trudy spoke up. "I told her they came yesterday."

"You know slander is against the law." His deep voice was meant to turn her bones to jelly. Not today.

When Larkyn didn't comment, he lunged forward, forearms on his blotter, fingers interlaced. "The police were fishing, little lady. If they had any evidence at all, those detectives would have taken me in. As it is, they left with what they came with. Nothing. Because there is nothing."

Larkyn's heart beat fast but not from fear. All her angst of the past two years focused on the man behind the desk. *How dare he*? Not one word of concern about her loss or what she'd been through. Just bluster and threats and outright lies.

"Do you deny that you forced my husband off the road on the morning of September second, two thousand and twelve?" Who was talking? Larkyn's voice had a life of its own.

For the briefest second, his pupils widened. She'd made contact. Then his hand came down like a gavel.

"You will not sit in my office and accuse me this way. Faye was a shameless gold digger. She tried to entrap me. When it didn't work, she came back to try again. This is your last warning, Ms. Wagner. If she or *anyone else* persists in this preposterous charade, they *will* regret it." He took a breath, his face showing blotches the color of beets. Even Trudy seemed taken aback.

Larkyn held her body erect. She refused to look away.

"We're done here." Martin grabbed some papers and straightened them in an officious display of moving on.

Trudy opened the door and waited for her to exit. "We'd appreciate you not spreading this around, Larkyn. Gossip can be very destructive." Her voice held a hint of sadness, even regret, but not enough to break the ice in her eyes.

Larkyn left, miraculously calm, but after the door closed behind her and she stood alone in the reception area where Kate should be, the floor tilted. With a steadying palm on the corner of Kate's desk, she put one foot in front of the other, beginning the journey to the miserable solace of her office.

She made it as far as the ladies' room.

Lurching through the door, she collapsed against the vanity top and silenced her erupting sobs. Her body quaked until she had to draw a breath. Inhaling a rush of air, she convulsed again until she felt deflated like a flat balloon. With one look at her red-rimmed eyes, she yanked a handful of paper towels from the dispenser and turned on the water to blot her face.

"Here you are." Kate breezed in.

Larkyn didn't turn around, but she was fully visible in the mirror. Kate's easy greeting turned sharp. "What's wrong, Larkyn?" She seemed confused. "We didn't see you in the break room, so I checked your office."

Larkyn lifted a hand and dropped it. Her eyes filled again.

"Oh, no." Kate put an arm around her shoulder which doubled her cries. "Something's happened. You were fine a few minutes ago." Kate hovered. "Do you want to come and eat?"

Larkyn shook her head. She couldn't possibly.

Then the door swung open, and Georgia appeared. "Hey. What're you gals doing? I'm eating by myself out there."

Kate gave Georgia a shrug. "She doesn't want to eat."

Larkyn blew her nose.

Georgia scrutinized the scene. Her bold bracelets jingled as she stuck a fist on her hip. "Listen, Larkyn, we're your friends. Something's been bothering you for days. You're going to hurt our feelings if you don't let us in."

The appeal went straight to Larkyn's heart. She'd never intended to hurt anyone's feelings. Just protect her own. Like she'd always done. Before she had friends to trust.

"I can't talk here," she whispered.

"Downstairs, then. Let's go to the sandwich shop." Georgia was already moving. "I don't mind tossing the rest of my wilted excuse for a salad. Kate?"

"Sure. My leftovers can last another day."

Larkyn smiled. "Are you sure?"

They frowned at her with something akin to insult. "Get your purse, you goofball. We'll meet you at the elevator."

"Go on down ahead of me. We shouldn't be seen together."

The two exchanged a bewildered look as Larkyn shooed them out. After a minute or two, she took the stairs to the lobby. Georgia and Kate stood at the counter of the small coffee shop adjacent to the café where Larkyn joined them. Fortunately, the lunch crowd had dwindled. They weren't likely to be seen.

"Today's Special" was Greek moussaka. Too heavy. But an order of tomato soup and a plain croissant would work.

Trays in hand, the trio surveyed the lobby.

"Let's find someplace secluded." Larkyn's sights roved beyond the fountain and boutique shopping. She spied a vacant table shielded by planters overflowing with potted philodendrons.

Her coworkers followed.

"Why all the cloak and dagger?" Georgia emptied her tray of a BLT with onion rings. Kate stuck a straw in her smoothie.

Larkyn took a deep breath. "I don't know how much I should say," she looked from one to the other. "Something happened over Thanksgiving weekend."

"I knew it." Kate said softly, but at Georgia's *shh*, she covered her mouth.

"I ran into Faye Arthur." She glanced at Kate. "She worked for Martin before you."

"I know." Kate nodded.

No one moved to eat. "I'll try not to drag this out." Larkyn wiped her palms down the skirt of her back-to-normal wardrobe. "She's been living in Maryland. We talked, and she came to my house for dinner. She didn't know about Matthew, so I told her about the accident, and she about flipped. She insisted she'd been there and seen the whole thing happen."

Georgia's eyes bugged, and Kate drew back. Whether they believed her or not, Larkyn steeled herself to finish. "Faye said she was riding with her boss—our boss. They were the ones who forced Matthew to steer onto the shoulder where it was narrow and sandy. We knew from the tracks Matthew lost control and went over the side. We just didn't know why." She shuddered at the terrible moment. "Not on purpose." She'd come to believe this. Completely. "But they didn't stop to see if he was okay."

"You're kidding." Georgia sounded unconvinced.

Larkyn didn't need this. "Of course, I'm not!" she snapped back.

"Go on," Kate said in a quiet voice.

"Faye and I talked. She agreed to report the accident. Yesterday, the police came here to see Martin." She glanced at Kate. "He denies the whole thing, says it's all a lie. They're furious at me for thinking Martin could do this. I wasn't fired, but even so, how I can work here anymore?"

Kate spoke gently, her voice barely audible. "And you believe Faye? One hundred percent?"

Larkyn couldn't reveal in full why she believed. Despite everything, she respected Faye's privacy. She couldn't mention Mallory. "Yes, I do. For a number of reasons."

Kate toyed with her engagement ring. "Did Faye say why she was in the car with Martin?"

Larkyn nodded without explaining. At dawn on a Saturday? The reason was obvious. "What's going to happen with the police?" Georgia changed the subject before Larkyn had to elaborate.

"I'm not sure. Right now it's her word against his."

A second passed. "Wow," they said together.

Larkyn breathed an easy breath for the first time since she'd followed Trudy down the hall. Her friends had summed the matter up, all right. Wow.

Gabe glanced at the flurries through his office window at the AVA. The space contained a scarred wooden desk with a slightly more modern executive swivel chair and a radiator that clanged when the steam came on. Which happened often because today's alternating drizzle and sleet brought plenty of winter air seeping past the ancient paint job covering the window's woodwork. None of this bothered him in the least. What bugged him was their mission lay in a similar state.

He'd seen progress today, however. His calls yielded appointments with a couple of sports equipment dealers who might offer a significant discount to the AVA, as well as a contractor who was willing to look at the cost of preparing a space for the weights and machines once they had them in hand. *If* they had them in hand.

Cycling presented a different challenge. Gabe rode a regular bike. But some of the injured men and women would require expensive custom hand bikes to join the team. Raising money like that could take a while.

The clang of the radiator interrupted his thoughts. Sleet pinged against the windowpane. Gabe cleared his desk and took his empty coffee cup to the kitchen. Jacket in hand, he slapped Pancho's door frame on the way out.

"I'm checkin' out."

"Hey." A holler stopped him. "There's a guy you might like to meet. Served with the Marines in Helmand Province. Wants a buddy to go shooting with."

Gabe grabbed the top of the doorframe with both hands. He hadn't fired a weapon in almost a year. "Sure. Bring him by."

Pancho swiveled in his rolling chair. "Any thoughts about that video?"

"A few." Gabe planned to feature one of their regulars, someone with a hand-bike, and maybe someone like himself, who had a disability but could ride without special equipment. "I'm hoping we can shoot it with a phone, but I'd love to jazz it up with one of those digital cameras that films from the rider's eye-view."

"I like it. Do you know how to put that together? And make it look professional?"

He did not, but he knew someone who might. "My cousin's an IT guy. Should be nothing for him."

"Okay, I'm trusting you." Pancho nodded.

"Thanks. I think it'll be good." Pancho offered nothing more.

Gabe waited. What did he expect? Applause? "Okay. See ya, man."

"Watch the roads." The boss had turned back to his paper.

Gabe clunked down the wooden stairs, working his knee. He could use a run more than anything right now, but with this crappy weather, he could forget the track. Working this job cut into his time at the Y as well.

Hustling into his truck's cab, he got the defroster blowing. While his windshield cleared, he punched up a call to the woman who'd turned his life on its axis. No answer. Where was she?

Gabe pulled out of the lot onto slushy streets crawling with fraidy-cat drivers. At least Larkyn had a Jeep and probably knew how to drive it.

The weather reminded him that though spring seemed a long way off, Cisco's wedding would be here soon. He'd better start making plans to get out of the newlywed's house.

Come on. Park if you can't drive. Gabe growled at a slowpoke inching away from the red light, wipers whipping as if they were fighting a blizzard. *Oh no, you don't.* He gunned the gas and wheeled around before the yahoo on his left could box him in.

A few blocks later he slowed for flashing lights. A tow truck forced him to sit while it maneuvered into traffic pulling a dented four-wheel drive. Unbelievable. What was wrong with these people?

Gabe's right foot jerked with impatience at yet another delay. Why didn't Pancho think him capable of producing a decent video? How long would Cisco rag on him if he was forced to ask for technical help?

The lane cleared, and Gabe edged ahead. Pressure to get out of Cisco's house irked him too. Not that he had to leave right away, but how would Larkyn feel about a place he could afford?

Old arguments with his mom about going to college rose up to taunt him. She'd supported their family by teaching school. His sister had married a dentist. And then irresponsible Cisco became a brilliant computer nerd.

Once upon a time, he'd been proud of who he'd become. Now, even firefighting seemed to be beyond him.

Comparisons were a trap but face facts. The girl he'd fallen for had an accounting degree and highfalutin parents.

Did he honestly expect to live up to her expectations?

CHAPTER THIRTY-ONE

Sara tapped on Gabe's bedroom door. "Gabe?"

He closed his Bible. "Yeah?"

"Cisco and I are going over to see Larkyn. Are you coming with us?"

He expelled the air trapped in his chest. He'd come straight to his room before anyone else got home. Did he have his head screwed on straight, yet?

"She needs us, Gabe."

She probably did. The last they'd talked, she'd been rattled by her boss but ready to return to the lion's den.

"She knows you tried to call before. She and I were on the phone."

He got up from the bed and ran his fingers through his hair. "It'll be tight with three unless we take my truck." He finished the sentence while opening the door.

Sara stepped back. "Good idea. It's probably the safest vehicle."

"How bad *is* the weather out there?" Gabe followed her up the hall, stuffing his arms into his camo jacket.

"Not terrible yet but getting worse. They're predicting all this mix to change to snow as the temperature drops."

"Where's your boy?"

"Right here." Cisco emerged from behind them. "Had to dig out my hat."

They crossed the sidewalk with baby steps. Gabe hadn't tried walking in these conditions, but his muscles adjusted, and the leg did its job. Cisco held Sara's arm as he helped her hike up into the cab.

"What about dinner?" Gabe started the engine.

"We talked about burgers." Sara edged closer to Cisco to stay off the center console.

The short drive took longer than usual, but they arrived without mishap.

Larkyn met them at the door. "Thanks for coming. How was the drive?" Her attention lingered on Gabe.

"Not bad." He gave her a side hug, and she tilted her face, presumably for a kiss. Gabe complied, and his mood improved. He brushed her cheek lightly with his fingertips.

"Come." Larkyn herded them into her great room/living room/den—Gabe never knew what to call the space. Bluish flames licked at some phony gas logs below an elaborate Christmas wreath.

Larkyn caught him looking. "I'm not finished, but it won't be like before. This house used to look like a Christmas store." She laughed, obviously delighted.

Christmas in suburbia. Gabe preferred not to go there. Today's slow slide into doubts about his sudden romance gathered momentum.

"Tell us about what happened today." Sara slipped her shoes off and curled her legs beside her on the sofa.

Cisco made a show of clearing his throat. "Excuse me, but Gabe here had a valid question. What're we doing for dinner?"

Larkyn clasped her hands under her chin. "I have all the fixings for hamburgers if you guys don't mind using the gas grill in this weather. It's new. Our old one got smashed.

Gabe and Cisco exchanged looks, their eyes conveying a silent understanding. Rise to the challenge if they expected food anytime soon. Gabe was less concerned than his cousin who lived from meal to meal, but he'd had a long day, and hunger didn't help.

"No problem." Gabe could handle a grill. "Do you have a lighter?"

"It's got a starter. Just open the gas line and press it."

Right. Gas grills with automatic starters. Did it play "Jingle Bells" too?

The women patted out the beef while the grill heated to four-hundred degrees on its gauge, as per the lady of the house's instructions. Then Gabe and Cisco hovered like frozen amateurs, coercing raw meat into seared, succulent burgers. When they fled back inside carrying their bounty on a large plate, the table was set, the condiments out, buns ready to toast.

Cisco, bless him, took the buns back outside to finish the job. Larkyn pulled a pan of hot beans off the stove and poured them into a bowl. The can in the sink promised traditional homemade Boston baked flavor. Yum.

They took their places around the table, and Larkyn extended her hands to each side. "Please pray for us, Gabe."

The request bit him in his snarky attitude. *Sorry, Lord.* "Uh, thank you for this meal, Father. Thank you for giving us this comfortable shelter from the weather out there. And, um, thank you for being with us. Amen."

After all the preparation, Larkyn picked at her food. Things must not have gone so well at work today. But she gamely joined the conversation which bounced from this to that facilitated by Sara, using the denial/distraction school of problem solving.

Cisco ate and smiled at all the right places. Or so it seemed to Gabe, who still chafed with qualms of inadequacy about his future. How had Cisco overcome his bachelorhood? Had Sara's charms simply swept all his issues away? Those two had their work in common, at least. Advanced degrees and everything.

After dinner, it was time to deal with the reason they were here. Everyone had a cup of coffee, Larkyn's mostly cream, but hey. They moved to the room with the fireplace, and Sara started the show.

"Tell them what happened today."

Larkyn shrugged. "There's not much to say. I got my answer about the police visit. Martin is using the his-word-against-hers defense to its full advantage. He claims Faye came on to *him*, and that he had to put a stop to it by letting her go. He demanded I believe his version of the story and got angry when I asked him point-blank to say whether or not he forced Matthew off the road. Then, he basically threatened me, and Trudy warned me not to gossip."

Bitterness rose in Gabe on her behalf. But he'd worked his tail off to get past what he considered mistreatment by the Defense Department's disability system. When he stopped blaming and refused to be a victim, his life got better. No, he hadn't gone back into combat, but he'd moved on.

"And tell them what you've decided." If Larkyn couldn't speak for herself, Sara was there.

Larkyn's lower lip trembled. "I have to quit my job. Like tomorrow. There's no way I can stay."

The idea of never going back to her office rocked Larkyn to the core. Would there be *nothing* left of who she used to be?

She sought Gabe's eyes, but he was enthralled with his hands.

"What do you think, honey?" Sara patted Cisco's arm beside her.

"I think it stinks. I think Larkyn should sue the guy if the police can't do what's right."

Gabe shifted and his voice sounded impatient. "How's that supposed to work? If there's no evidence, there's no evidence. You can't sue with nothing."

Larkyn knew this, but Gabe didn't have to sound so negative. "Cisco was trying to help," she whispered.

"Give us your opinion then, cousin dearest." Cisco offered a hand as if bowing.

Gabe remained silent for a moment, then pursed his lips and spoke deliberately. "I can understand why you wouldn't want to work there anymore. Going back today was hard, but I imagine you're glad you did since now there's no doubt where everyone stands."

She nodded. Gabe was so calm. He'd seemed a little distant all evening. No, a lot distant, but this was more like him. It would be nice to be sitting together like Cisco and Sara, but he'd taken the rocker, leaving her to pick a seat alone.

"Yes." She twisted her rings, stopped, and stilled her hands. Why did she keep wearing these rings? Was that what was bothering Gabe? She'd put them in her jewelry box now if taking them off would make him happy again.

Gabe hunkered over, elbows on his knees. "I guess the question is, how much do you like your job? I imagine accountants can always find work, so it's not about the money."

Gabe was right. Larkyn could find another job. She'd miss Georgia and Kate, though. With so much upheaval in her life, it would be nice to keep her work friends.

"I'll miss my coworkers, but I can't stand to be in the same room as Martin anymore. Or Trudy, either." So very sad.

Gabe raised up, his tone disapproving. "You're deciding based on hatred for your boss?"

Larkyn winced. "I didn't say that." Gabe's conclusion wasn't fair. She did hate Martin, though. She hated him passionately. She hated his arrogance and his phony reputation.

"What're your other reasons?"

Was Gabe goading her? Larkyn lifted her chin and pressed her lips together. "He's evil. Why do I need more reasons?"

Sara glanced at the man who loved her, who sat beside her on the sofa. Cisco's smirk had disappeared.

Gabe cocked his head. "I don't know, you tell me."

Larkyn's back stiffened. Why was he being so mean?

"Hey. I'm just saying that hatred won't get you where you want to go." Gabe acted as if it were logical. "Martin's a complete jerk—maybe he'll always be a jerk. But you have a choice."

"So, I'll be a jerk if I'm mad at him for killing my husband?" Her volume rose.

"Not what I said." His voice sounded flat.

The pressure rising in Larkyn's head might just take it off. Her temples pounded. She'd never had anyone treat her like this. Well, maybe her mom, but she and her mom had history.

"You don't even know me, Gabe."

"Ahem." Cisco cleared his throat. "Let's tone it down a bit."

Larkyn made an effort. "Explain to me, please, what you *did* say, then." She stood and paced like she had with Faye, her hands in fists. On second thought, that hadn't ended well. She sat back down in her chair.

Gabe sighed. "I simply mean that you have a choice about your attitude because you're *not* a jerk. You can forgive Martin."

At her intake of breath, he pressed. "I'm not saying he's right. He's not. But you can take the higher road. You can turn what he's done over to God and let God deal with him. It's a lot more effective, believe me."

God? Oh, brother. Larkyn liked God a whole lot better than she had before, but forgive Martin? When he wasn't sorry? When he wouldn't even admit he was wrong?

"You listen, Gabe." A scowl took over her face. "I've been reading the Bible, and I've been trusting God to take care of me even though he's never done it before. He answered my prayers when Faye exposed Martin. Now, the only right thing is for him to admit his crime. He should be punished too, but we're not even talking about punishment yet."

She crossed her legs and folded her arms over her chest. No one had a reply? Fine. Maybe they were listening, finally.

"I'm so sorry, Larkyn." Sara's apology irked her.

"Why? It's not your fault." Larkyn's tone jabbed at her friend, and the room became charged with silence.

"Okay." Gabe pushed himself to his feet. "I'm sorry too, Larkyn. I can see I jumped the gun."

He was leaving?

Gabe seemed to address Cisco. "It's been a difficult day. I think it's better to call it quits."

A difficult day was right. But it sounded like he meant his own, not hers. Larkyn's throat constricted when Cisco followed Gabe's lead.

"We appreciate the burgers, Larkyn." He pulled Sara to her feet. Sara stared at the floor. The new floor covered with her beautiful rug.

When Larkyn said nothing else, Sara let Cisco lead her away. She raised her head and met Larkyn's gaze. "Talk to you tomorrow?"

Larkyn swallowed hard. "Sure."

She couldn't look at Gabe, who reached the foyer first. Instead, she observed the unfolding disaster from her place in the living room as they put on their coats and Cisco pulled his silly knit hat down over his hair. In disbelief, she approached the door as they filed out into the night. Snow fell in a steady swirl of feather-like flakes illumined by her porch light. When they shut the door, she moved to the window and peeked from behind the curtains.

Gabe's wipers swept the snow away in two wide arcs on the glass. The truck backed out leaving tracks. He turned in the street and headed away. Two red lights disappeared into the darkness.

CHAPTER THIRTY-TWO

Larkyn raised a mug from her set of Christmas dishes to her lips. The aroma of cinnamon, cloves, and orange rind did little to dispel the gloom in the room or in her heart.

She'd awakened to a scene of crystalline purity spread over the neighborhood. A day made for hot chocolate and baking cookies. Her chest fell as her breath streamed out. So much for dreams.

She moaned with the ache of watching her friends desert her.

The fight wasn't all her fault.

She contemplated the depths of her holiday tea. Why, on one of the worst days of her life, could Gabe not be the littlest bit sympathetic? Instead, he'd spouted on about the evil of hatred—as if she had the problem.

She rocked in her chair as the flames played with the logs in her fireplace. A faint hiss from the gas line replaced the crackle of real burning wood. Fake fire. What else was fake in her life? Gabe? Trudy and Martin, for sure.

Restless, she wandered to the window. The sun had broken through, scattering the storm clouds, leaving a brilliant blue that made her squint. The streets would be clearing as the temperature rose and cars ventured out. Her Jeep would drive just fine.

She had no excuse to stay home. Not that she wanted an excuse. If she made it to the office while things were quiet, it wouldn't take long to clean out her desk and be gone. Easy, peasy. Over and out.

Ha.

She showered quickly and dressed, shoved her feet into boots that allowed for thick socks, donned her coat, and draped a bright wool scarf around her neck.

At already half-past nine, she needed to go. Hiking her purse strap up on her shoulder, she ignored the unmade bed. Worrying about Gabe would have to wait too. One crisis at a time, please.

Was Gabe a crisis? Her vision misted. Yes. He was.

Her four-wheel drive handled the streets with ease. Except for historic blizzards, snow never lasted. This car had been Matthew's gift to Larkyn the second year of their marriage. He probably wanted it as much for his rock climbing as for her, but she loved her Jeep. Today it served her well.

Well before ten o'clock, she entered her office, small box in hand, and got to work. Leave the pens, staples, sticky notes, legal pads, and paper clips. Her personal items amounted to a plastic container of Tic-Tacs, some single-serve almond packets, her coffee cup, and a framed photo from her honeymoon. Not much to show for almost eight years.

Hoping to catch her friends, Larkyn hurried to the break room. Would they miss her? When she came through the door, Kate was putting her lunch in the fridge and Georgia was making coffee.

Both turned.

"Oh, my gosh. Larkyn." Kate rushed to wrap her in a massive hug. So much for wondering whose side Kate was on.

"Thank you." Larkyn smiled as Kate let her go, glad she didn't blubber.

Georgia reached out with a slanted grin. "You're here."

"I am." Larkyn tugged at the hem of her sweater. "But not for long. I just cleaned out my desk. I need to make some entries on the computer so everyone gets their paychecks on time, but as soon as that's done—" She pantomimed chewing her nails. "I've got to talk to Trudy."

Speaking it out loud stirred up a hollow dread that threatened her resolve. It was one thing to think about quitting, quite another to walk down the hall.

Kate fidgeted. "Listen. I don't know if I should say this." She took a breath. "But I want you to know it's not hard for me to believe you and Faye."

Georgia cut a glance at Larkyn before peering closely at Kate.

Larkyn angled her head. "I'm glad to hear that. Do you mind telling me why?"

Kate spoke so low they had to lean in to hear. "There was this time when I think Mr. Hamilton was hinting at something. It made me uncomfortable. I was very happy when I got my ring, and he could see I'm engaged." She finished her confession with a nervous twist of her hands.

Larkyn moved in to hug Kate. Such a thing should never happen. Thankfully, this dear girl had escaped.

"Y'all are freakin' me out." Georgia shivered her shoulders. "I'm glad I have nothing to do with the man."

Bleakness swelled, sweeping over Larkyn like an incoming tide. How much damage could a person do to those around him? She drew a deep breath, hoping courage would materialize. "I'm going to miss you guys ... a lot." Her voice cracked. She steeled herself, biting her lower lip. "Please, let's plan to get together, so it's not goodbye."

Yes. Of course. Absolutely.

Promises. So easy to make, and so easy to forget.

"What're you going to do next? About work." Georgia crossed her arms over the gold chains that hung to her waist.

"I don't know." Larkyn sidestepped the question. "I'll think of something."

"G'morning ladies." Jamal, an immigration lawyer, moved past them to reach the microwave. He riffled through some mail in his hands.

Time's up. Larkyn would make this quick and clean. A surgical cut. And be gone.

Voices and enticing smells met Gabe as he left the bathroom. Sausages? His stomach growled.

He heard voices in the kitchen, but he didn't head that way. Cisco had insisted Sara spend the night, because he didn't trust her Mini on the roads. Gabe knew for a fact that Mini Coopers were great unless the snow was too deep, but he hadn't offered to share that. Cisco probably lacked confidence in the driver, not the car.

He made his bed by the force of habit. Sara had bunked on the sofa, which Gabe admired. If his cousin was willing to save himself for the wedding night after his inglorious past, more power to him. Ah, the wonders of true love.

He sat on the bed, opened his Bible, and stared unseeing at the pages.

Love. Not what he'd been looking for when he came to North Carolina three months ago. His plan had been to stay as long as it took to move on with becoming a Hot Shot. But love had intruded anyway. Not that he claimed to love Larkyn—yet. The question after last night's fiasco required an answer. Was he ready to love any woman at this point in his life?

He paged to a well-worn spot and read silently. "Trust in the Lord with all your heart. Lean not on your own understanding. In all your ways submit to him, and he will make your paths straight."

The verse from Proverbs helped him come to terms with being spared from death instead of Josh. Since Gabe's choice would have been to let Josh survive, it seemed only right to submit to the one in charge of such weighty matters. Whether he understood or not, he chose to trust God.

"Okay, Father. It looks like we're back here again."

God didn't answer in words, but a review of the facts came to mind.

Door to the infantry—closed. Door to firefighting—closed. Door to using his experience with veterans—open. Door to a relationship with Larkyn—open. Until last night at least. Was that door still open? Did he want it to be?

Gabe left the questions pending to track down those heavenly smells. He joined his cousin and Sara laughing over a frying pan.

"Smells good." He announced himself with an attempt at cheer.

"Hey." Sara radiated good humor. "Have you looked outside?"

Gabe peeked outside. Bright sun shone onto a covering of glistening diamond dust.

"MyoPro overreacted to the forecast and announced they'd be closed today. Can you believe we get the day off?" Sara explained why a measly three inches had stopped the economy.

Gabe moved to the cabinet and got a plate. "Strange. I guess New Yorkers take pride in staying open despite the snow."

"If they didn't, winter would be one long vacation." Cisco chuckled. "One egg or two?" His hand hovered over the carton.

"Two, thanks."

"Coffee?" Sara lifted the glass carafe.

"Please." Gabe sank to the seat of a chair and watched his cup fill. He sipped and pined over nothing in particular as Cisco scrambled the eggs and Sara made toast. What a team.

Cisco divided the eggs three ways. Sara put the toast beside the sausages and set them on the table. Gabe said his blessing to himself and filled his plate when the others did.

They ate a few bites before someone addressed the obvious.

"Um, how are you, Gabe?" Sara took the prize.

He grumped, then looked at her. "Would you buy unsettled? Confused?"

"We should have tried to referee." She looked at her future partner in life.

"No, no." Cisco shook his head as he swallowed a bite of toast. "You are not responsible for their relationship, honey. Our courtship wasn't always smooth, if you remember."

Did Cisco say courtship?

Sara grinned. "Remember the time you called me by the wrong name on the phone? Yeah, I'd say we had issues."

Cisco winced. Water under the bridge apparently, because instead of justifying himself, he turned to Gabe, an always convenient target.

"Seriously, man, I think things happen for a reason. There's gotta be something you guys can learn from this."

"You're a counselor now?" Gabe quipped. Then wished he hadn't. His cousin spoke wisdom. "I can tell you I was in a bad mood to start with. I'd been comparing myself to Larkyn's previous lifestyle, knowing I can't provide the same. I feel inadequate. Did you hear her say *our* grill like her husband's still in the house?"

"Oh, Gabe," Sara patted his forearm. "You shouldn't ever feel less than. You're amazing. I know Larkyn doesn't compare you to Matthew or anyone else."

"Sa-ra," Cisco warned. "Gabe feels however he feels. He's come through things we can't even imagine, so let him figure this out for himself. And do not speak for Larkyn. She has to do that for herself."

"I was only trying to encourage him, Cisco."

"I know you were. But don't." Cisco ate on.

Sara's sunny face telegraphed a sudden drop in barometric pressure.

"Hey there, guys." Gabe reached for the coffee pot "Thanks for your confidence, Cisco. I do have to figure this out. And thank you, Sara. Your heart is full of kindness. I appreciate both of you."

"Can I ask a question? Is that allowed?" Sara took a mild dig at Cisco. She would be fine with his cousin. He saw it more and more.

"Shoot."

"Do you like Larkyn? Are you serious about her?"

Gabe exhaled. He could hedge. *What do you mean by serious*? But he had to be honest. "I do like her, Sara. And, yes, I'm as serious as I can be for a guy with no real money coming in. The AVA is great. My heart's in it, for sure, but the salary won't support us, and I can't see a wife supporting me."

Slight dizziness swept through him. "When I hear myself say things like support a wife, I kinda freak. It's only been about six months since I had my Army career all mapped out with no room for women at all. I think I need some time. But then, I look at Larkyn. From the very first day, she was different. I can't imagine finding anyone I could love better than her."

Sara's lips curved in a smile of satisfaction. "That's beautiful."

Gabe pressed his lips together. He wished the real Gabriel DeSantis would please stand up.

CHAPTER THIRTY-THREE

Surgical cuts might be clean, but they weren't painless. Larkyn didn't want to work through a two-week notice, but she wouldn't have to. Clearly, the Hamiltons didn't want her at work any more than she wanted to be there. Which explained why she was at home on a Friday morning looking at a breakfast she'd barely touched.

Her last day had come and gone without a send-off, without good wishes or appreciation. Like Faye, she simply wouldn't show up anymore. Larkyn pushed away from the table. With weary arms, she carried her plate of cold scrambled eggs and congealed grits to the trash and dumped them. The plate clattered into the sink.

Did Gabe honestly think Martin didn't deserve her anger? How ridiculous. Was he insane? If Gabe was right, how could she ever be a Christian? How could anyone? It didn't make sense at all.

She snatched up a pillow from the sofa seat and pounded it with her fist. Despite the trauma of a tree falling on her house, her life had been getting better. For a while.

Her Bible lay closed on the coffee table. When had she opened it last? An answer she didn't like pricked her conscience. If God had all the answers, she should be looking in his book.

A few minutes later, she closed the Bible. Flipping pages of mysterious text wasn't working. *God, what am I supposed to do?*

Wait a minute. Dena and Ted were bound to be home from Charlotte.

She tucked the Bible under her arm and made her way along the sidewalk to the Thompson's front door, where the banner on Dena's wreath urged, *Let Every Heart Prepare Him Room*. Larkyn sized up the challenge and knocked.

"Come in, come in." Ted greeted her like a long-lost daughter, which she might as well have been.

"Thank you, Ted. Is Dena home?"

"She sure is." He shut the door behind her and called. "Dena, Larkyn's here."

"Send her to my sewing room."

"Second door." Ted pointed.

Larkyn gave him a nod of understanding, freeing him to return to the game she could hear on the TV.

The sight of Dena's sewing room stopped her. Bright fabric in shades of every color filled a bookcase. Likewise, a rainbow of spools of thread sat on rows of little pegs. Half the sewing paraphernalia Larkyn didn't recognize, but Dena stood at a normal ironing board, pressing squares of cloth printed with little ducks.

"What do you do with all this?" Larkyn looked up and down.

"I make quilts. See?" Dena indicated a stack of folded coverlets about crib size. "I quilt for missionaries, but this will be for that grandbaby I keep hoping will appear."

Larkyn fingered a bolt of soft flannel cloth.

"I was about to take a break. Would you like some tea?" Dena set her iron aside and turned it off.

"No, thanks." Larkyn didn't want Ted to overhear the conversation. "Can we just stay in here?"

Dena motioned Larkyn to the chair in the corner. "Just move that stuff to the floor."

Larkyn replaced the bags of batting with her bottom as Dena took the seat in front of her sewing machine. "What's on your mind, my dear?"

"I hardly know where to start." Larkyn's shoulders tensed, and her hands waved about as she described the recent events. Had it only been a week since Faye showed up at Henderson's grocery?

Dena pondered before she spoke. Larkyn liked that about her.

"Sometimes finding the truth is painful. How are you doing?"

Did the tears that sprang to her eyes answer? Larkyn lifted her hands in a helpless gesture. "Not good. That's why I came. I'm doing terrible."

Dena looked like she might cry too. "Do you feel like a bowling ball dropped on your already broken heart?"

Larkyn covered her face with her hands and cried for the millionth time. *Yes*. Her heart had been healing. And now look.

"There's more." She choked out. "I had a fight with Gabe. Nobody's speaking to me. I'll probably never have any friends again."

"I'm so sorry." Dena patted her knee.

Wasn't she going to tell Larkyn her thoughts were ridiculous? Apparently, not.

"Gabe said I shouldn't hate Martin. Can you believe it?"

Dena stayed calm, her eyes gentle. "Why do you think he would say such a thing?"

Larkyn squinted, trying to come up with a reason. "He admitted Martin is bad, but said I had a choice. He said I didn't have to hate him because I could turn him over to God."

"Hmm."

When Dena didn't exactly jump aboard in agreement, Larkyn chugged ahead. "You don't agree with Gabe, do you? I know you love God, but what if he let Ted get killed and left you all alone? Then he didn't even let you get mad about it?"

Dena pondered again, her wrinkles drawn down in sorrowful lines. "Can I tell you what I've learned about God?"

"That's why I came." Larkyn nodded.

"God doesn't get angry with our emotions. He hates sin because it keeps us from him, the one with love and comfort, but he's not angry at us or how we feel. Your anger is natural and appropriate, but if you don't find a way to let it go, anger will lead to bitterness. Once you harden your heart with bitterness, you shut off God's love. You'll end up feeling like you're on your own again, like before. Sin lies waiting, Larkyn. Ready to eat you up and ruin your life."

Larkyn contemplated Dena's collection of fabrics and the plain, nondescript carpet covering the floor. Her life after Matthew had been the carpet, worn and beaten down, a colorless dirty beige. Bleh. But in the last couple of months, she'd begun to see colors. Splashes of fun brought laughter back. The Bible called it joy, and Gabe was at the center. He had made the difference.

"Oh, Dena." She covered her face again. "What do I do?"

"I see you brought your Bible. May I see it?"

Larkyn handed her the lovely purple book. If Dena could show Larkyn the solution, she'd be a genius.

Dena turned the pages as if she knew exactly where she was going.

"Before you read that," Larkyn cut in, "I have to say something. I get that it's bad for me to be hard and bitter, but what about Martin? He's guilty, and he's lying about it. That has to be worse than holding a grudge. Especially when I'm right and he's wrong. Don't you think he's the problem, not me?"

Dena tilted her head as she listened, her hands placed palms down on the open pages. "You trusted God once. Your heart was soft, and you gave it to him. Are you taking that back?"

"No." She didn't want to take her heart back from God, but he ought to *do* something. "What about justice, Dena? Surely, God cares about justice."

"He does care but think a minute. Did he give you justice when you came to him for help? Or did he give you mercy?"

Larkyn frowned. "Mercy, I suppose."

Dena raised a brow.

"But Dena," she leaned in hard to make her point. "Martin shouldn't get mercy. What he's doing is evil. God *hates* evil." Right? Of course he does.

"Honey." Dena's voice stayed gentle. The woman was unflappable—like some saint. And she was kind. Maybe *too* kind?

"It's hard to take in, but Jesus bore Martin's punishment the same as he did yours, mine, and everyone's."

Larkyn frowned. She narrowed her eyes. This was so unfair.

Despite her rejection, Dena continued. "God knew that sin had to be removed if the world was to ever be saved and go back to the way he designed it. The only effective way to deal with sin was death. Yet if all the sinners *died*, who would be left?"

Dena peered at Larkyn. "How do you think God could deal with sin without destroying the human race?" She didn't wait for an answer. "He took the form of a man and died *for* us. Jesus was that man, God's son. Because Jesus was exposed to everything we are in the world but never sinned, he was qualified to step in front of God, the judge, and say, 'punish me instead of them.' Everyone who *accepts* what Jesus did for them walks free.

"But—"

Dena interrupted this time. "I think I know what you're going to say, so let me finish. It's up to Martin to humble himself and receive forgiveness. If he persists in lying, he can't do that, and he'll never be free. You may not see him suffer, but I promise you he will suffer and lose out on the good things he could have had. God wants to save everyone, but he gives us all a choice. Be thankful you chose to accept God's forgiveness, child. If Martin doesn't come to the truth, he will lose everything."

Tightness cinched Larkyn's chest trapping her so she couldn't squirm free. She'd tasted anger and resentment most of her life—against her parents, against the hit and run driver, against God himself. After discovering God's goodness, though, she didn't want to eat that old garbage again.

Dena patted the book in her lap. "Do you know that famous verse that says, 'For God so loved the world that he gave his only Son, that whoever believes in him will not perish but have eternal life'?"

Larkyn remembered, but with her throat closed, her answer stuck.

"Further down here," Dena found her place, "in John 3, verses nineteen and twenty, it says, 'And this is the judgment: the light has come into the world, and people loved the darkness rather than the light because their works were evil. For everyone who does wicked things hates the light and does not come to the light, lest his works should be exposed.'" Her head came up and she looked into Larkyn's soul. "Does that sound like someone we know?"

A light tap on the inside of the open door caused their heads to turn. Ted stood bearing a loaded tray. "You gals have been holed up in here a while. I thought you might like a little something to wet your whistles."

"That's very nice of you, dear." Dena stood and pushed more clutter aside.

Ted set the tray down and scrutinized his handiwork. "There ya go."

From the tags on the tea bags, Larkyn saw he'd selected Lemon Zinger.

"How's the game?" Dena took a cup first.

"It's a recording of last Sunday's. The Panthers are going down, I'm afraid."

"Well, thank you for the tea." Dena gently excused him.

"You bet. I could bring some of those pumpkin bars you made?"

"This will be fine," Dena smiled. "Maybe, we'll come out and have some when we're finished here."

"Sure." Ted hesitated, but when Dena didn't invite him to stay and hang out, he took a step back. "Okay, then." He left.

Poor Ted.

Dena took a sip. "I guess my whistle was drier than I thought." She chuckled. "Do you like lemon?"

"I do. It's refreshing." Larkyn swallowed. Zinger seemed to fit their conversation.

"Now, where were we?" Dena picked up the Bible.

After hearing Dena, Martin's behavior horrified Larkyn in a whole new way. "You were talking about people not wanting the light. It's scary."

"Yes. Do you see how backward they have it? Children fear the *darkness*, not the light. They know turning on the light is good."

How true. What happened to the change them? Sin, of course.

Light dawned in the midst of Larkyn's muddle. God had his long-term plan for justice, unlike her own. If she wanted to walk in faith, she had to trust and wait.

"Is there no way I can hope for the truth to come out, here and now?" she wheedled. "How does it look to go forward? I'm not sure how to let my anger go."

"For one thing," Dena's pale eyes sparkled, "you can straighten things out with that fine young man of yours." Her smile imparted hope. "And you can pray. Pray that the truth will be exposed, somehow. And pray that Martin will *see* the light and choose to come out of the darkness he's in."

Dena's faith lit a candle. The message was not at all what Larkyn had come to hear, but the flame in some mysterious way was better than her ideas. She'd seen the phrase, *peace that passes understanding*. Maybe forgiveness and trust were keys to that peace.

Gabe stretched and massaged his forehead. He pulled his phone out and checked the screen. No calls, no texts, no emails but it was nearly six o'clock. After his hearty breakfast with Sara and Cisco, he'd come on down to the AVA. He tried not to call it the office since that smacked of what he'd sworn he would never have—a desk job.

But who was he kidding?

The thing that made this job different was the people. Gabe dealt with people, not paperwork, and he could get into that. He liked seeing the courage and the grit which showed itself in the way these warriors tackled life, playing the hand they'd been dealt. But Gabe hadn't seen any people this Friday after the storm. Pancho had shown up for a little while before departing for parts unknown.

At six-fifteen, he admitted he had no reason to stick around except avoidance of the empty evening ahead. Besides, his stomach was getting cranky. Theoretically, he should be able to end this impasse with Larkyn, but his position hadn't changed. Maybe he and Larkyn were just totally different people. His head said it was better to find out now, but his heavy heart didn't like it.

Gabe locked up and hauled his butt to his trusty truck. The door still squeaked when he opened it, but the engine cranked right up even in the cold.

At the first stoplight, his phone came to life. Sara.

"Hey." He snatched it up from the passenger seat as the light turned green. "I'm driving."

"Are you coming home?"

"Yes." He eased into the intersection, keeping his distance from the other moving objects on the road.

"Would you like to go see some Christmas lights?"

Was this a trick question? "Let's talk about it when I get there. 'Bout fifteen minutes." He dropped his cell into the cupholder and got both hands on the wheel. *Christmas lights?*

Whatever.

CHAPTER THIRTY-FOUR

"Hi, my friend." Sara's voice came through the speaker on Larkyn's cell as she pawed through the pantry for something chocolate. Several hours after talking to Dena, sadness had crept back in with the setting sun. God expected her to forgive Martin. Could she ever do that? Could Gabe forgive her if she didn't?

"Sara? Hi." Larkyn hoped the disappointment in her newly grieving heart couldn't be heard. Pitiful.

"Are you busy?"

"Not really. Just crying about the wreck I've made of my life." Larkyn joked.

"Well, forget that," Sara chirped. "I just got home from work. We're gonna drive down to Benson and take in the Christmas lights. You should come with."

Not a word about Wednesday? Sara loved questions and loved Larkyn's answers even more. A couple of questions of her own came to mind, but she rejected them. It was Gabe she needed to talk to.

"Larkyn? Did you hear me?"

"Where is this coming from, Sara? Our last evening ended badly."

"Cisco and I wanted to see the lights—or I wanted to see the lights and coerced him into taking me." She rephrased with a lighthearted scoff. "You love this time of year. I was sure you'd want to come along."

"Because I made a mess of things, and now I'm alone again."

Audible groan. "Stop being dramatic. You guys had your first fight. It's normal."

"You think so?" Larkyn chewed a nail. After her long talk with Dena, she understood Gabe's point better, but why had he been so harsh? "Gabe's never treated me that way before."

Sara seemed to weigh her words with uncharacteristic care. "Cisco has warned me to let you guys work this out yourselves because you need to." She hesitated. "Do you know how jealous I was over the women he dated before me? I accused him of treating me like a groupie, and he accused me of being childish. It was epic."

"You never told me that."

"You'd lost your husband, Larkyn. I had a new boyfriend. And it didn't feel right to add to your troubles with mine."

Larkyn sank to the closest stool. She didn't deserve Sara. And probably not Gabe.

Sara read her brain waves. "Whatever it is you're thinking, stop. I didn't tell you so you'd get down on yourself. Every serious relationship has conflicts. If not, how can you get beyond the superficial?"

Hm. She and Matthew hadn't fought, but their relationship hadn't been superficial. Was it special? Would they have run into problems later on?

Larkyn clenched her teeth as realization struck. If her active, athletic husband had been paralyzed, life would have been drastically different for them. Matthew would have been miserable. Could death have been merciful in some terrible way?

"Sara?" Larkyn cringed at her sobering thought. "I've got to deal with this fight. What do you think I should do?"

"Come with us. Look at the Christmas lights. We'll listen to carols, go to the candy store, maybe ride the carousel."

"What about Gabe? Did you ask him? What did he say?"

"I invited him, but he was driving home and couldn't talk. I didn't mention you."

"What if he doesn't want to go?" Could she handle his rejection?

"You'll never know unless you try." Sara's logic was flawless.

Larkyn closed her eyes. She couldn't go back to living in the shadows after enjoying the light. "Okay, I'll try. I can focus on Christmas if Gabe won't go."

"You'll come?" Sara's voice hiked half an octave.

"Yes, but I need to change out of my sulking clothes. Have you had dinner?"

"No. We'll figure that out too. Go ahead and change. I'll stop by and pick you up on my way to Cisco's."

Gabe crunched with care on the last remnants of snow as he traversed the sidewalk from his truck to Cisco's front door leaving the frigid air outside. Not that thirty degrees was cold. He must be getting soft.

"Did you hear from Sara?" Cisco met him on the way to his room.

"Yeah, I did. Something about Christmas lights."

Cisco followed him into the bedroom. "That's right. There's this farm south of here. Sara wants to go, and she wants you to come too."

She did, huh? Well, good for her. But what else did he have planned? Not one thing. A little distraction might be good.

"I'll be a lot better company if I get something to eat. What's the plan for that?" Gabe ran his hands through his hair and considered his two-day growth of beard.

Cisco gave him a broad smile. "Did you think any plan I'm involved in would leave out food? Come on. You look fine. Sara will be here soon."

Cisco left him to wash his face and hands in the bathroom sink. Forget Sara, he needed a shave. Did he dare hope for a way to bridge his differences with Larkyn? And what were those, exactly?

She hadn't been able to see his point about forgiving Martin. Okay. He contemplated his face in the mirror as the razor removed his stubble in swipes, then paused to rinse the blade. How long had it taken him to work through what happened to Josh?

Ouch. He angled his jaw for a look at the nick the razor had taken from his chin. Not too bad, he blotted it with a tissue. Right. Three or four months to forgive himself?

Uhh ... more like five or six.

He splashed his face with water and inspected it for shave cream. He owed her an apology if it wasn't too late to make amends. At least if she hated him, it wouldn't be because he didn't try. With his towel still in hand, Gabe headed up the hall.

Sara stood in the foyer. She'd brought Larkyn.

Gabe halted. Moment of truth.

"Gabe." Sara cried with excitement, and Larkyn whirled to face him.

They froze for a moment, eyes locked, each assessing the threat level. Gabe dropped his towel and moved to close the distance with no idea of what to do or say when he got to her.

Larkyn stepped out and met him. With a whimpering cry, she fell into his arms.

Gabe had seen such scenes in movies but never expected to be in one. He clutched her to his chest, and the tension of the last two days drained instantly.

His eyes filled with tears at her shuddering sobs. "Oh, sweetheart."

Gabe might have questions about the future, but if she would only stay right here, they could take them a day at a time, the way the Lord instructed.

Cisco kept from making cracks, and Sara only squealed a little as their hug dragged on. Gabe nudged her back far enough to see her tear-stained face. He moved his mouth closer and hesitated as if asking for her permission. Her blue-green eyes melted into a morning sea—and he dove in for a swim.

CHAPTER THIRTY-FIVE

Larkyn covered her bowl of oatmeal with whole milk. Instead of delving into the yummy creation topped with pecans, shredded coconut, and dried cranberries, she sat with chin in hand, smiling like the Mona Lisa. A yawn escaped.

Surely no one in last night's parade of vehicles snaking its way through thirty acres of magical lights could have enjoyed them more than she had. Cisco's cramped backseat fit perfectly, keeping her in the shelter of Gabe's arm. Relieved to be free of her anger, every sight and sound washed her soul with the thrill of being there at all—with friends, with Gabe, and with Cisco's Christmas soundtrack. She'd sprung forward, at least, a hundred times to peer out the window and sink back to Gabe's cozy embrace exhaling peace with every ooh and ah.

She sang the "Drummer Boy" tune under her breath and surveyed the unpacked bins of Christmas decorations she'd recovered from the garage. How different her living space looked now with more modern furniture and floors. Her photo gallery was gone, but she'd been able to save a few special frames with their contents and scattered them about the house.

She ought to unpack these bins, but where would she put so many decorations? The house would resemble a holiday explosion rather than a tasteful display of what the season meant to her now.

Her oatmeal had gone cold, but the flavors hadn't suffered a bit. Instead of reheating, she finished it off with hearty bites and smiled some more.

The night had ended with hot cider at the candy store, where Gabe told her about his video. Matthew's GoPro camera would be perfect. She offered to let him use it.

Oh gosh. He'd be here any minute. Dashing to the sink to rinse her bowl, she scurried to her room. Time to get out of her jammies.

A quick face wash would have to do. Low ponytail, a dab of gloss, flannel shirt, skinny jeans. Where were her shoes? She got it together in time to answer the doorbell with a breathless, "Hi!"

Gabe stepped inside the foyer and took her hands in his. "Good morning." He kissed her knuckles, and his brows went up.

She met his softly questioning eyes. "I took the rings off last night. The ceremony said till death do us part. I know it took me too long to see, but I'm no longer married to Matthew."

Gabe captured her gaze until she lost her bearings in the magnetic pull of his eyes. His arms pulled her close, and his lips covered her mouth with a kiss that pushed her imagination to new levels.

"Does this mean I can court you, in my cousin's words?" He spoke into her hair.

Grateful for a moment to collect herself, she giggled. "Cisco said that?"

"Does it?" His arms stayed firmly around her.

"Yes." She breathed. "Call it anything you like, but yes."

His jubilant smile captured her heart with promises she thought were dead forever.

"Okay." She fanned herself with her hand. "Let's move on to what you came for."

"I have." He wiggled his brows.

"Seriously, Gabe."

"I am," he deadpanned.

"Oh, come on. Let's get on with this." She took hold of his arm and pulled him down the hall.

"Wait. I was kidding." He resisted, but his grin was out of control.

"Gabriel—what's your middle name—DeSantis." Larkyn did her best to sound commanding though her burning cheeks betrayed her. "The GoPro camera is down here in the office."

"Whew." He swiped his brow. "For a minute, I thought you were going to put me in a compromising situation."

"You." She swatted at him. "Do you want to borrow the camera or not?"

"Yes, I do." He straightened his face. "Lead on."

She opened the door to the room with the desk, the bookshelves, the computer monitor, and placed her hands on her hips. The GoPro had to be here somewhere since she hadn't run across it anywhere else.

Opening and closing desk drawers, she found nothing. Perhaps somewhere in the bookcase?

"What's this?" Gabe pointed to a box tucked between old textbooks.

"Oh, thank goodness." She pulled it out, wiped the dust off, and handed it over. "That model is certainly dated by now. I'm sure you could get a better one."

Gabe turned the box in his hands. "We don't have funds for a better one, sweetie. This will do just fine." He handed it back and watched over her shoulder as she opened the container and lifted the inside packaging.

She raised her gaze to him. "I'm sorry. I don't understand." She puzzled over the empty box. "It's not here."

Gabe glanced around the room. "Did he always keep it in the box?"

"As far as I know. He was very organized. I can't think of anywhere else to look."

Gabe hesitated as he spoke. "It might be crazy, but could he have been wearing it the day of the accident?"

Larkyn plopped onto the desk chair at her elbow. Could he?

"I didn't see him leave. He said goodbye, but I was half-asleep."

She bowed her head in thought. *What if he did?* "I don't know, Gabe. The rescuers recovered his bike and his helmet, and one shoe. I have them all. The helmet's all banged up."

Gabe walked to the window. "Is there any other place we could look?"

Larkyn grasped for ideas. "If it was elsewhere in the house, I think I'd have seen it, especially with all the work going on. Unless he loaned it to someone, which I don't think he ever did." Larkyn paused. "I'm sorry, Gabe. What'll you do?" Her hopes deflated.

"What're you talking about?" He strode from the window toward her. "I'll figure out something for me. Don't you think the more important question is what do *we* do now?"

We? "You don't mean we should try to find the camera in that ditch?"

"That's exactly what I mean." Halfway to the door, he stopped. "Don't you agree?"

She'd never seen Gabe so fired up. Charging hard into battle he must have been fierce. She hated to disappoint him.

"It's been two years. There are vines and weeds in the ravine. It'll be muddy."

Gabe gave her a baffled look. "Are you suggesting we wait for the mud to dry out? Come on! This is huge. How can you stand not knowing what that camera might have on it?"

A tingle ran up her arms. It might be a wild goose chase, but how could she ignore this hope, however slim?

"We'll need boots." Larkyn sprinted down the hall. "Do you have boots? Of course, you do. Mine are in the closet."

He laughed when she emerged with her polka dot rain boots in hand. "Excellent. We'll stop by Cisco's for mine."

According to Larkyn, she hadn't traveled this road since she'd brought her parents to the site of the accident after the funeral. Gabe drove slowly as they looked for a curve that would've kept Matthew out of sight as Martin rounded the corner into the glaring sunrise. Where was it?

"Slow down." Larkyn craned to see out the windshield as she scoured the roadside for landmarks. The city had worked on the shoulder.

"It doesn't look the same at all." She grumped.

"Keep looking." Gabe remained undeterred though Larkyn appeared to strain between fear and hope. Being here had to be hard, but this was worth trying.

Amazed, he'd watched her faith stretch to agree with releasing her boss to God and praying to transfer her need for revenge to him. Did she realize that no one could say how God would act, or what he would do, or when? Her hope seemed guarded and plagued with doubt, but he didn't fault her for that anymore.

Gabe slowed the truck further as they approached a spot where the road disappeared around a bend. He pulled to the side and braked with two wheels off the pavement. "It looks like they tried to shore this up with gravel, but it's narrow. What do you think?" His hand rested on the gear shift, engine idling.

Larkyn scrutinized the ravine. "I think we should look. Is it safe to park here?"

"No. Let me pull around the curve, and we'll walk back." Gabe rolled to a place where cars coming from behind could see them and got as far to the right as possible. "You'll have to get out on my side."

Larkyn inched over the console to exit from the driver's door. They trekked along the shoulder to the place where the curve obscured their vision in both directions.

Gabe's head wagged in wonderment. "Of all the chances."

Larkyn squeezed his hand. "Just like what happened to you and Josh. Split seconds between life and death."

He accepted her assessment. "It's why I have to believe that God is good. Otherwise, the randomness would be pointless. Depressing."

"I've lived with pointless all my life." She shuddered. "I'm trying to believe, but what if we don't find it?"

He placed his hands on her shoulders and closed his eyes. They needed help, for sure. "Lord, if Matthew's camera is in this ravine, lead us to it. If it's not, please show us what to do. We ask for the truth to be revealed. Thank you, in Jesus's name."

Her rigid muscles relaxed a bit under his touch, but the set of her jaw remained. "All right." He yanked his head to the right. "Let's go."

Gabe began the descent by sidestepping, his natural leg leading, arms wide for balance. Larkyn followed his tracks. Thick, tangled kudzu vines barren of leaves covered the ground. Winter had culled the weeds as well.

Rocks lined what might become a creek bed with enough runoff saving them from miring in the mud.

They spread out, parting the vegetation as they kicked at it here and there. The gully smelled rich with decay.

"They only recovered one shoe," Larkyn offered randomly.

A few moments later, she added "I don't see anything, do you?"

When Gabe pulled vines away to expose a boulder, she froze. Was this the rock Matthew's head landed on? If so, they were close. Creepy bumps prickled his arms at what the discovery would mean.

He searched around the boulder and beyond for another twenty yards. "It's wet down here, but I don't see any pools of melted snow." He pointed beyond where he'd parked the truck. "The ravine slants that way. Slightly downhill. If this floods with a lot of rainfall, the camera could've been carried downstream."

Larkyn expelled a breath. "Then we'll never find it."

"I'm sorry." Gabe picked his way in the direction of where they'd started.

"Are we giving up?"

What could he say?

She placed a hand on her forehead. "I wanted to believe we'd find the evidence down here."

Gabe hated to admit defeat, but they couldn't cover every square inch of this ravine. He contemplated the steep climb to the road. "Let's see if we can get out of here. Then we'll re-group."

She didn't say the words, but he heard the logical question, regroup ... how? There had to be something.

Larkyn scurried up the incline while he trailed behind, reduced to grasping at protruding rocks and branches. He topped the bank on his feet and not his knees. Hallelujah.

He started the truck with Larkyn brooding beside him and eased back onto the road. "We'll follow this downstream and see if anything pops."

The Lord had a plan. Surely.

They exited the woods and their view widened. The road passed over a culvert before winding its way toward busier parts of town. Gabe checked his mirrors and pulled up next to a road sign. "Did you see that?"

"What?" She peered over her shoulder at the view behind.

"There's a metal drainpipe going under the road."

"So?"

"Come on."

Larkyn gave him a look that said *whatever* and followed Gabe back to his sighting. He judged the duct to be a good three feet high. A screen for catching debris covered the entrance.

"I suppose it's worth a try." Larkyn's hands jammed in her pockets. "It's our last chance."

Gabe didn't like negative predictions, but this one probably summed it up.

"I'll go down." She offered, peering over the edge at a steeper slope than the earlier one.

"Take it easy." He grimaced but had to let her go. It rankled that if he got down, he might not be able to climb back out.

Larkyn slid down the gravelly slope created by road crews to handle the water flow from the ravine. Reaching the bottom on her rear, she stood and took stock.

From Gabe's vantage point, the corrugated pipe looked old enough to have been there a while. If the camera was there, it had made a long journey downstream.

"Be careful," he called, imagining sharp and rusty things, not to mention nasty trash. Hopefully, nothing dead.

He couldn't see her below him, but grunts and cries of disgust rose. He almost laughed, but it wasn't funny.

"See anything?"

"No. Not yet. It's gooey down here."

Gooey? Better not think about that.

"Oh." Her voice changed. "Oh, Gabe." A squeal. "Ew, gross."

Larkyn emerged into view, her right hand raised, delight and disgust on her face. "I found it. It's nasty, but I think I got it."

CHAPTER THIRTY-SIX

The sheriff's department and the Raleigh PD had been quite interested in Matthew's ruined GoPro. Since Gabe in his wisdom insisted, they left the camera exactly as they found it and carried it to the authorities sealed in a half-gallon Ziploc bag. That had been Saturday. Today was Tuesday, and her nerves couldn't take much more.

Having nowhere to go and nothing to do while Gabe and the rest of the adult world continued to work didn't help. Thankfully Sara had suggested they all get together for take-out tonight.

Larkyn tossed the paper with its stupid want ads on the floor. Did anybody advertise that way anymore? She should get on a job search website, and put her résumé in. After she wrote a résumé.

Listing her one employer. Who hated her guts.

Right.

The résumé could wait.

Her phone signaled an incoming text from somewhere to her left. Ah—the barstool where she'd left it. Skittering across the floor in her sock feet she snatched it up. *Calm down.* The police wouldn't send a text.

GABE: Heard we're having Chinese. What's your favorite?

Oh, Gabe. What a sweetheart.

Larkyn: Anything.

She added a big smiley face. Gabe made everything better. Was it bad to feel that way?
His words came back.

Gabe: Tell Sara what you want. I'll go along with you.

Really?

Larkyn: You may be sorry.

She chuckled at herself.

Gabe: Never.

He upped her smiley with a fat red heart.
Oh, my. She was falling. Fast.

Gabe hadn't arrived when Cisco opened the door for Larkyn. Aromas of soy sauce, garlic, and ginger ignited her appetite. Chinese food always did that.

"Sara's on her way, and I think Gabe had to stop for gas." Her host's smug smile combined with his typical humor. "I think you've bewitched my cousin. I've never known him to be so smitten."

Larkyn lay her coat over the sofa back. She'd stayed in what she'd worn all day—black yoga pants and a cream fleece pullover that felt like a cozy blanket.

Her cheeks warmed, but she kept her voice from sounding like a schoolgirl. "How did the two of you grow up to be so different?" She tagged along to the kitchen where the smells intensified.

Two large fold-together containers and a white bag waited on the table along with a pile of packets—hot mustard and sweet and sour sauce. Plates and chopsticks lay ready.

"I think Gabe looked at me and decided to be the opposite." Cisco leaned against the counter in a rare display of seriousness.

Larkyn raised her eyebrows. "Well, you're both pretty terrific, but I have to say, I'm smitten myself. I feel like I almost lost him there last week."

"Oh, he was miserable." Cisco's eyes held a gleam. "He tried to hide it, but the guy could hardly carry on a conversation."

"Hello. I'm here." Sara shut the front door and came around the corner. "Oh, that smells good. I'm starving."

"Just waiting on Gabe." Cisco kissed her hello and gazed into her eyes. "Did I ever tell you how beautiful you are?"

Sara melted against him. "Let me think ..."

Larkyn averted her eyes. These guys needed to get married soon. She cleared her throat to no avail.

Gabe appeared through the back door in his leather jacket and jeans. "Break it up." He nudged his cousin on his way to Larkyn. He cupped her face in his hands and touched his lips to hers. "How ya doin'?"

Larkyn nestled under his chin and slid her arms around his waist inside his jacket. Flannel. Mm. If this was smitten, she liked it.

"I'm doing okay. It's weird being home all day, but I've had a chance to read some things that Dena gave me. God's brought us this far. I just know he's going to answer my prayers."

Gabe didn't comment, but he held her extra close.

"You mean the GoPro?" Sara opened the boxes. "Thanks, honey. This looks yummy."

What else could she mean? Larkyn was too hungry to put up with chopsticks tonight, but she'd wait for Gabe to pray. "The police have had it four days already."

Everyone passed the boxes. Oh, boy. Shrimp fried rice and Kung Pao Chicken. Larkyn extracted an eggroll from the bag.

"Father, we thank you for this food." Gabe's fingers tightened on hers. "And we trust you have our lives in your hands. Amen."

"What do you think they're going to find?" Sara brushed stray strands of hair away from her face and repositioned the headband controlling her riot of curls.

Larkyn scooped a mound of fragrant, sticky rice, heavy with shrimp bits and veggies onto her fork, and answered Sara. "Whatever Matthew saw when the car went by." The implication struck her. Could she bear to watch?

Gabe stepped in to her rescue. "Best case would be something that identifies Martin Hamilton. To give the police hard evidence."

"Busted." Cisco bit off the end of his eggroll.

"We hope." Larkyn stared at her fork still poised above her plate.

As the bite finally made it into her mouth, her phone vibrated on the tabletop. Unfamiliar number, but local area code. Normally, she'd let it go to voice mail, but not this time.

"Excuse me." She pushed her chair back while chewing, swallowed hurriedly and spoke as she moved away. "Hello?"

"Mrs. Wagner? This is Sgt. Booker from the Detectives Division."

Larkyn's knuckles blanched as she squeezed her cell phone and sent a furtive glance toward the table. She fought the quiver in her voice. "Yes, this is she."

"I apologize for calling this late, but the item you turned in wasn't brought to my attention until yesterday. I'd like to speak to you about what we found if it's convenient."

"Yes, it's very convenient." She cringed at sounding like an idiot. But who cared?

"As you know, the camera has been exposed to the elements for quite a while, but we were able to clean it up. The housing is made to be waterproof, and it turns out that the memory card inside was undamaged."

Larkyn's heart fought to get out of her chest. Blood pulsed in her neck as she held her breath. The world narrowed to the voice in her ear.

"We recovered several images, ma'am. The ones relevant to our investigation show what looks to be the passenger side of a black SUV."

Oh my gosh, she knew it. Martin drove a black Tahoe. She laid her free hand on her chest.

"The images are blurred, but our technicians were able to enhance them enough to pull up a woman's profile visible through the passenger window. She turns her head just as the camera veers away, but we captured a view of her face. We'd like you to take a look and see if you can identify the woman."

"Yes, of course, I can." Larkyn already knew who it was. She reached to the door frame for balance. "Thank you, thank you. This is what we were hoping for. Do you want me to come now?"

"Tomorrow would be better. I called because it's been a few days. I figured you'd be waiting."

"Oh, I have been," she gushed. "Mr. Booker? Are you one of the detectives who visited Martin Hamilton about this accident?"

"I am."

"I worked for him. Did you know that?"

"No, ma'am. You worked for Mr. Hamilton? The accused?"

"Yes. I was so disappointed when you didn't have enough to arrest him. I'm friends with the witness who came forward, Faye Arthur."

"I see. Then there's a good chance you'd recognize her if you saw her in these photographs?"

"Oh, yes. I'm sure I would. Can you see the driver?"

"No. Just the passenger," he said matter-of-factly. "See you tomorrow around nine?"

"Yes. Okay. I'll see you then." The call disappeared from her screen.

She returned to her friends. Their eyes were trained on her face.

"I heard a lot of yes's." Gabe ventured in a cautious tone.

Larkyn pursed her lips, struggling with the news. "They want me to identify a picture of Faye, but you can't see the driver. I guess it's something ..." her voice trailed off.

Sara's eyes gleamed. "Come on, silly. It verifies her story. It proves she was telling the truth and makes it harder for your boss to blow it off. Now if she would just tell them she was pregnant and produce the little offspring," she lifted her hands in conclusion, "you'd have a slam-dunk case."

Larkyn's lips drew down, taking her hope with them, "That's not about to happen."

Gabe spun his pen on the table as Pancho called for progress reports from members of the Memorial Day committee, the tag they'd given themselves. With

Matthew's GoPro in the hands of law enforcement for the foreseeable future, he needed other options for the video.

"Are we keeping you from something?" Pancho interrupted Gabe's musings with the business at hand.

Gabe covered the pen with his hand like he'd been caught by his second-grade teacher. "No, sir. Just thinking about how to get around a snag in my procurement of a camera."

"I'm not your superior officer, DeSantis. No need to address me as sir. We won't be saluting either." Pancho grinned, and the others chuckled.

"Sorry. Guess I'm a little distracted. Won't happen again, si—." Reflex produced the required answer and almost another *sir*.

"You know we're all friends here, right?" Pancho nodded to the others. "What's the status, or snag as you put it?"

Gabe weighed his explanation before proceeding. He'd gone with Larkyn to make the positive ID of the photo, and in the process, they'd learned that the video's date and time stamp substantiated Faye's claim. If they could associate the lawyer with the car, they'd have him nailed.

"I was set to borrow a camera from a friend, but it turned up missing. Turns out that the camera card contains evidence of a crime, so I won't be able to use it."

"The camera or the card?" Pancho lounged in his seat.

"Both. I mean it's being held by the police."

"Whoa, what kinda friend is this, Gabe?" Pancho hooted with the others.

"I plead the fifth." He tried to keep his face straight, but his lips wouldn't cooperate. Oh, well. If he was providing entertainment for the day, he might as well do it up right.

Raul frowned. "You're seriously not going to tell us?"

Gabe felt an incoming call from the region of his jeans pocket. Larkyn's name lit the screen.

"Excuse me." He stood and let himself enjoy a taunting smile. "My friend."

He walked back to his little office and closed the door in defense against rumors. The ones he'd invited just now.

"Hey, sweetheart."

"Gabe. Guess what?" Her voice tingled with excitement.

"Martin confessed." He deadpanned.

"No." Scorn tinged the word. "But his secretary, Kate called me. She's one of the women I eat lunch with. My friend. Anyway, she called to tell me she happened to see a printout of a travel itinerary including plane reservations to Baltimore in the name of Trudy Hamilton."

His antenna rose. "That's where Faye lives."

"Yes! Why would she be going there, Gabe? I think she's going because she has doubts about her husband." Her sentences picked up speed. "I'm sure she's going to question Faye herself."

"Maybe." He cautioned. "Did Kate say when she's going?"

"Friday," Larkyn stated. Her tone left no room for this to be coincidence.

He ought to get back to the committee, but his thoughts weren't on the meeting. "All right, say the police went to see Martin on Wednesday with the photo, and his wife buys tickets that day or the next, it's possible. Seems awful fast."

Larkyn slowed down, but barely. "I know, but what else could it be? We have no clients in Baltimore. Maybe she had doubts already?"

That made sense, but his natural brakes responded. Gabe divided events he faced two ways—things he could do something about and things he couldn't. His model avoided a lot of fruitless worry and empty effort. "So, what does this mean to you? What do you want to do about it?"

Larkyn's silence told him she hadn't gotten that far. He gave her time.

"It tells me not to give up yet. Maybe God is working after all."

After all? He let it go. "I agree with that. What's next?"

"If we wait for Trudy to come back, Kate won't see her again until Monday at the earliest. I can't sit around that long, Gabe."

"I'm not sure you have a choice, honey." He hated to bear the bad news. Besides, seeing the trip plans was a fluke. Kate might never hear anything about what happened on the trip.

"No. Wait, Gabe. What if I apologize to Faye? Do you think she'll speak to *me*?

Hm. An apology was a great idea. "I like it. Whether you get cooperation or not."

"I know." She sounded resigned. "This forgiveness stuff is hard."

Wetness in his eyes and a desire to smother her with kisses caught him by surprise. Larkyn's beauty did that to him often but being drawn to her growing faith? He'd never expected to feel this way about a woman, never imagined such a thing. "Ah, listen. I'm in a meeting about the bike race, so I need to get back, but thanks for calling with the news. I'll pray for Faye and Trudy, and for the truth."

"Thank you." The hope in her voice rebounded. "This isn't over yet, Gabe. I know it."

She let him go with surprising ease. He stared at the instrument in his hand.

No, not by a long shot, he agreed, thinking of more than the hit and run. God had blindsided him, sure enough, and he hadn't seen it coming.

The words had come close to slipping out. *I love you.*

He'd say them soon. Wouldn't be able to help it. And there'd be no going back.

CHAPTER THIRTY-SEVEN

Larkyn's kitchen door swung open, admitting a draft of chilly air.

"Keep coming." Gabe back-stepped in.

Who was he talking to? Larkyn turned the heat down under her pot and left the wooden spoon on the spoon rest. Fragrant boughs of a Frasier fir passed through the doorway with Ted bringing up the rear.

"Howdy, Larkyn. You got yourself a real nice one here. Where do you want it?"

He and Gabe paused while she hurried to lead the parade. "It's always been there by the fireplace." She showed them the spot stopping to turn on the gas logs before getting out of their way.

"Okay, Gabe." Ted lowered his end with the stand attached. "We got it."

Larkyn's iPod surrounded them with carolers singing "It's Beginning to Look a Lot Like Christmas" as Gabe guided the top part upward, and the tree settled in its traditional place. Gabe stepped back, inviting her approval.

She checked the shape from different angles and asked them to rotate it a few degrees. "Perfect. Thank you, guys." She clasped her hands together under her chin. "I love it."

"Y'all have fun, then." Ted winked at Gabe and started back to the kitchen door.

"Wait. I've made my special hot chocolate." Larkyn scooted after him and rummaged for the thermos she and Matthew—*Stop*. Previous campfires at Jordan Lake weren't allowed to occupy her thoughts today. Uhh ... and how about that box of highly explosive sentiment sitting near the tree? Her old anniversary ornaments, vacation mementos, and silly inside jokes belonged back in the closet, ASAP.

Larkyn tipped the saucepan to fill the thermos with steaming milk and melted Dove bars seasoned with cinnamon and vanilla. "Take this to Dena. You guys can drink it now or later." She screwed on the cap and handed it over. "Tell her it's for all the tea and zucchini bread and everything else I've eaten at your house."

"Much grass," Ted quipped in butchered Spanish as he left with the gift in hand.

The door closed as Larkyn raised her sights to Gabe.

His arms were crossed, hips resting against her countertop, dark hair just long enough to fall across his forehead. *Mercy.*

"And now for you." She'd made the cocoa for him.

"And now for me, what?" He tilted his head and raised one brow, holding eye contact longer than rational thought could bear. What had she been about to do?

Turning her body in self-defense, she faced the cabinet and forced her limbs to work. Two more mugs. Easy does it. Don't spill.

She managed to veil the tremor that threatened to reveal her thumping heart. "There's a tin for you on the coffee table." She spoke with her back turned. "Let's take these drinks to the living room."

Instead of doing her bidding, his arms encircled her from behind, trapping her between the newly polished granite and his body. He snugged up his embrace and found her neck just below her earlobe with his lips.

"And now me, what?" he said again, his voice low and husky.

"Hot chocolate," she whispered, barely able to breathe. "Cookies."

He held her a moment more, then loosened his arms a little. "Cookies?"

The reprieve gave her strength. Did he know how his presence affected her? Somehow, he'd put on the brakes. What might she have done if he hadn't?

She nodded vigorously. "I made them for you."

He gave her one last squeeze. "Okay. Let's go check 'em out."

With a hot, filled mug in each hand, she kept her eyes off Gabe as she led the way and placed the mugs on napkins festooned with holly.

"What have we here?" Gabe reached for the tin and pried the top off.

"It's your reward for serving above and beyond the call of duty." She grinned at the patience he'd shown as they shopped for her Christmas tree.

"All these are mine?" He selected a green frosted tree with sprinkles and took a delicate bite as if it were a work of art.

"Absolutely. Every last one." Her breathing found normal again. She could handle this side of Gabe.

"I'll have to hide them," he said with a snicker as he lost his reverence and polished it off. "Delicious." He spoke through crumbs.

She used to make them every year. No need to say why she'd stopped or why this year was different.

Gabe strung the lights while she unwrapped ornaments on the floor and wondered what Trudy was up to on her trip. If she did meet Faye, would it make any difference? Would Faye even talk to Martin's wife?

When Gabe had covered the tree with multicolored lights in sparkling jewel tones, he eased to the floor to join her.

"What's this?" He held up a painted sand dollar from the forbidden box. The gold inscription read *Our First Christmas.*

"Oh, Gabe, don't look at those. I shouldn't have gotten them out and there are plenty of other ornaments."

His Adam's apple bobbed, and his voice came out thick. "I'm sorry you lost him."

The comment struck her like a punch to the chest. Grief? Joy? She buried her head in his shoulder.

His arms came around her back and he stroked her hair. When she lifted her face, his eyes were glassy.

"No, Gabe, no." Losing Matthew would always be a painful part of her past. She took his cheeks between her palms and placed a kiss on his lips. "I don't understand ... I can't imagine ... but what if I'd never known *you*?"

"Come here." He pulled her against him again. "It's good we don't have to understand, sweetheart, 'cause I can't imagine trading this for a freezing night in a foxhole."

"At least I know I'm better than *that*." A laugh bubbled up in her throat.

But Gabe tilted her chin to face him. His brown eyes seemed to melt. "Seriously, what I mean to say is ... I've fallen in love with you. I love you so much that I'd give you up if you could have Matthew back."

Her mouth parted but nothing came out. Thank goodness people didn't have to make such choices. Only God.

She searched for his heart in his rich brown eyes. "I love that you love me, Gabe. It feels crazy that this could happen, but I love you too."

Nat King Cole crooned about roasting chestnuts as she nestled up under his arm. "We'll never know what would have happened if Matthew and Josh were alive. It's a miracle, but I'm okay with that."

He kissed the top of her head and laid his cheek on her hair. "Thoughts like that are too much for my brain. It's one of the reasons I'm glad I know a God who's in charge of it all. And who is always good."

The hour was late when Gabe got back to his cousin's. The Honda's hood felt warm and the Mini wasn't around. No offense to Sara, but good. He could use a man-to-man talk. He entered the house, expecting to find Cisco up.

"Anybody home?" He called into the quiet.

"Here." A muffled voice.

"Where?" Gabe didn't move.

"The attic, man. Let me out."

The attic? Gabe didn't know they even had an attic. But there, a cord hung down at the end of the hall back by the master bedroom. "What're you doing up there, bro?"

"Does it matter? Just pull the steps down." Cisco sounded a little testy.

"Hang on." Gabe took the tin of cookies Larkyn had made and stuck them in his dresser drawer. He returned to the hall, grabbed the cord, and pulled. Pulled harder.

"How did you get stuck up there?" He yanked again.

"Don't even ask."

Was Cisco kidding? Situations like this could not go without an explanation. "Seriously, bud, how in the world?"

"Just get the stupid door open." Definitely testy now.

"I'm trying." Gabe pulled with steady pressure. Straight down, then left, then right. "Why don't you push from up there as I pull. There's got to be a catch of some sort."

"But if it lets go, I'll fall."

Gabe heard shuffling above as his cousin presumably got in position. Then came metallic screeching.

Cisco puffed. "Wait." Pounding and more noises. "Pull again."

Gabe pulled and the steps groaned. A sudden pop and the door in the ceiling opened a crack. With another easy tug, half of the ladder came down into place, and Gabe unfolded the bottom.

Cisco backed down the stairs. "That was close."

The two returned the stairs to the upward position and walked up the hall together. Having the same idea, they entered the kitchen, grabbed two drinks from the fridge, and popped the tops.

Gabe took a swig. "You gonna tell me or not?"

"Where ya been?" Cisco countered with another question.

"We bought a Christmas tree. I helped Larkyn put it up." Gabe had nothing to hide. Except some cookies. And the part about looking at every tree in the lot at least twice to compare size, shape, and softness of the needles. He'd watched Larkyn bond with the tree as the seller bound it for transport. He'd understood then how fully she gave her heart to the things she loved.

That was the moment he went over the cliff.

Cisco intruded on his thoughts. "Gettin' in mighty deep, don't ya think?"

Gabe rotated his can on the table. He took another swallow and set it down. "Maybe."

"Don't get me wrong. I'm glad for you both." Cisco raised his chin, sincerity in his eyes.

The comment nudged Gabe to proceed. Who else knew him as well as his cousin? Lounging in the wooden dining chair, one arm slung over the back, he approached the subject with caution. "How did you know that Sara was the one? That you wanted to change your life for her?"

Cisco hooted. "You mean quit carousing?" His expression sobered. "Don't take this wrong, okay, but it was Larkyn and Matt's marriage. We worked together, and I watched him. He always seemed happy and satisfied. Not like me at all. I realized I was jealous and asked him what the deal was."

Gabe shifted and sat forward.

"Matt told me that his commitment didn't tie him down, it set him free. I began to see what he meant. And, honestly, man, I envy you with Larkyn. I wish Sara was my only one, not just the last one."

Did Gabe know his cousin at all? He blinked and shook his head as if to clear it. "Can't say I saw that coming."

Cisco laughed. "I guess the time was right for both of us, because Sara's forgiven me. We've put the past behind us."

Gabe pondered as he stared at his hands. "It's taken me by surprise, y'know? I had my plans." Since his cousin had been so candid, he took a breath. "It seems I've fallen in love, but I'm afraid I could make a serious mistake with Larkyn if I'm not careful. About the commitment thing. How do I know it'll work for life? What if one of us isn't ready?"

"You're the guy with the faith, man. Do what you always do."

"Yeah." Gabe pressed his lips in a rueful smile. "I need to pray about a lot of things."

"You'll find a way." Cisco raised his can as if for a toast. "To second chances."

Gabe raised his own and the aluminum clinked. "To second chances."

CHAPTER THIRTY-EIGHT

Monday morning Larkyn pounced for her phone when she saw the name lighting the screen. Kate Sherwood.

"Kate?"

"Hi. I have the news you were interested in."

Her friend's vague sentence alerted her to play along. "That's great. Can you talk?"

"Not really. It's been a busy Monday. People in and out all the time, but the trip I mentioned went fine and everybody's back."

"Can you confirm the destination?" The conversation continued in code. Was all this necessary? Surely the phones weren't tapped.

Kate whispered. "Yes. I saw a hotel receipt. Does that help you?"

"If it was near Baltimore. Is that all you know?"

"Try Westminster—Oops, Mia's here. I need to go." Kate hung up.

Mia. Family law. Could it be about Mallory? Larkyn sank to the bed she'd been making. Kate had done her part. Now Larkyn *had* to call Faye. Hopefully, she would talk.

Larkyn's hands shook as she scrolled backward to find the number attached to the text Faye had sent her the day they met at the grocery. Before keying it in, she bowed her head.

"God, please forgive me for acting hateful to Faye. And help me tell her how sorry I am in a way she will believe me."

Amen.

"Hello?" A wary voice answered.

Larkyn squeezed her eyes shut. "Faye, it's Larkyn. I called to say I'm sorry. I wasn't very understanding."

Larkyn bit her lip as she waited through the silence.

"Hey." Pause. "Look, I'm sorry, too—excuse me." Faye paused again. "Mom, can you take Mallory?"

Larkyn's tension eased a little. Faye hadn't hung up.

"It's okay, honey. Mamaw's going to get you some juice."

Larkyn listened to the noisy exchange while Mallory decided if juice was worth leaving her mother.

Faye again. "I'm going to my room." Another pause. "Okay, that's better. I didn't want Mallory to hear us. Children pick up more than we think."

How like the Faye Larkyn knew—straightforward and always on the ball. Larkyn had to smile.

"Thanks for talking to me." She breathed her relief. "I hope you guys are doing well."

"We're fine. I hope you are too."

"I'm okay." Time to get on with it, she urged herself. "It's just that I found out Trudy made a visit to Westminster over the weekend and, well, I wondered if she went to see you."

"As a matter of fact, she did." Faye sounded amused. "It seems that my talk with the police wasn't useless after all."

Larkyn deserved that. "I'm sorry I got so mad at you. It took a lot of courage to do what you did. And now you've gotten Trudy to show up at your house. Was it horrible?"

"No, thank goodness. And she didn't come to the house. I was shocked when she called and asked to meet me. She didn't seem to know about Mallory, so I agreed. I thought maybe if I found out what she wanted it might help you."

"Thank you, Faye." Larkyn meant it. Totally. "Trudy and Martin claim you were fired for trying to seduce him. It made me sick. I quit my job. I was afraid that was the end of it."

"What a snake." Faye snorted. She seemed remarkably immune to the slander.

"You were brave to face her." Larkyn quivered, imagining the scene. "I wonder why if Trudy believed him, did she go to see you?"

"Trudy Hamilton is a clever woman, Larkyn. She came because she was suspicious. When the police got that picture of me and questioned Martin a second time, she dug a little deeper. She checked some financial reports as well as her husband's accounts and credit card bills. There were charges for hotels and meals while she was with her sister in Wilmington. Even a jewelry receipt. Mr. Unfaithful didn't cover his tracks."

Stupid or arrogant? "Wow. How fortunate. For us anyway."

"I suppose." Faye's sigh telegraphed her weariness with the whole mess. "Trudy came to question me in person, and I guess she found me credible enough, because she went on to ask if there was more to the story than the photograph."

Larkyn gulped in air. "What does that mean? Why would she ask that?" More importantly, what did Faye say?

"I don't know," Faye answered. "She looked me in the eye, and I just couldn't lie. It's one thing not to volunteer that I was pregnant, but another to lie to the woman's face when she asked a direct question. I told her there was more."

Larkyn pressed the phone to her ear, every muscle tensed. Her friend's flair for the dramatic could be forgiven.

"I made her promise not to tell anyone else. She'll use it to confront her husband, and nothing more. She promised not to take the story any further."

"And you believed her?" How could Faye trust a promise like that? She had more faith than Larkyn did.

"She was pretty angry. She told me she'd make him take a DNA test if he didn't admit what happened. I didn't try to stop her."

Wait. The test that Larkyn wanted to force? "I don't understand. You were completely against this. Now you're fine?"

"I'm not fine. I told Trudy how I feel about Mallory ever knowing her father. She cried, Larkyn. I felt sorry for her. She wanted to see a picture, but I refused. I didn't want her to get all maternal, even though there's no relation to her. I said I can accept a legal acknowledgment of his paternity, but I don't want his money, and I don't want my daughter to know him unless she asks, and only when she's over twenty-one."

Larkyn expelled the air she'd been holding in. "Wow, Faye. I hardly know what to say."

"I understand, believe me. If there *is* to be a test, they'll need a sample from Mallory. It's too much for me right now."

"I'm sorry." Larkyn rubbed her forehead with her fingers. How had life gotten so twisted? She had one other troubling issue. "Um, I have a confession." Larkyn bit down hard and plunged ahead. "I told my closest friends. Not anyone connected to H&H, but three other people know a child is involved."

Faye laughed, but she didn't sound happy. "Isn't that pathetic? I adore my daughter, but I'm pretending she doesn't exist. This is so wrong."

Once again, Larkyn had no answer. But words came. "*I* know she exists and that she's adorable. I'd love to meet her someday." Wouldn't that be something? Maybe in the land of happy endings. "I appreciate you talking to me, more than you know."

Faye's voice softened. "You're welcome. I haven't forgotten that I started all this." She added. "You can call me anytime."

They said goodbye and hung up. Larkyn stared at the empty screen. Who would have thought that hope would appear out of nowhere?

CHAPTER THIRTY-NINE

Dressed in his best ratty sweats, Gabe reclined on his bed, hands clasped behind his head. To say he had doubts was overkill, but even after his talk with Cisco, he didn't have peace.

Facts. He'd done his first tour in Afghanistan at the age of twenty-five. He'd been the old man in boot camp, old for his infantry platoon, old for a first deployment, but none of that bothered Gabe. The wait to join up matured him, revealing natural leadership skills duly noted by those in charge. Those skills placed his Army career on the fast track with nothing but success ahead.

Until the blast.

Gabe rolled to his side and sat up.

His injuries had sidelined him, putting his life on hold for almost a year. After living in North Carolina for only three months, it seemed that God had placed him on another fast track. Not to fighting fires but to a relationship with a woman. A relationship bound for domestic life.

He might as well say it—marriage.

His head in both hands, he bent over his knees. Marriage was as terrifying as war in its own way. He'd never even gone steady.

Hold it right there. Since when had he let fear call the shots?

Gabe stood abruptly and snagged the keys to his truck from the dresser top. The view on the road to Jordan Lake looked different now that the leaves were off the trees. Barns and homes previously hidden by the foliage were visible through bare branches. The December day had warmed into the sixties, leaving no trace of the snowstorm. The weather here made no sense. Summer lasted well into fall when it got a little chilly. Snow came out of nowhere, then it felt spring-like in less than a week. Come on.

He walked onto the dock and sat down. Water sloshed lazily against the pilings keeping a quiet, gentle rhythm below his dangling legs. The smell of dank wood and fish rose in the balmy air.

Gabe faced most decisions with a list of pros and cons. His pros had to do with Larkyn, the intriguing woman he'd been drawn to before thoughts of a relationship with anyone made any sense. In just a couple of months, he'd seen her character emerge. How, pressed by revelations of her boss's crime, she'd listened to the woman next door, received Christ, and surrendered the outcome to God.

The two of them shared a foundation that hadn't been there before. Faith. Essential for the long haul.

If they stayed together.

Married.

And had children.

His heartbeat stepped up as if he'd been climbing stairs.

What would it be like to live with Larkyn? Wake up beside her each day?

A piercing call from above drew his eyes to a hawk. The majestic bird soared free and easy as it circled, floating on air currents invisible to Gabe. Even Cisco, the one who defied the rules, saw love and marriage as freedom from what he'd thought was the good life before.

Gabe hated to admit that his uncertainly boiled down to money. He hated that fear could be a factor at all. If he could face bullets and bombs, what was this about?

His faithless father emerged from the shadows. The one who'd abandoned him, his mom, and his sister for the lie of gambling which led to drink. His dad thought a lucky streak at the tables would solve his problems, maybe give him respect, but Gabe knew better. By God's grace, he was not that man.

The practical question of a job had been answered by Pancho and the AVA. As he'd said before, no one would get rich working for a nonprofit, but Gabe was resourceful and God, his Father, even more so. He wouldn't lead Gabe into something God couldn't handle.

The weathered old boards creaked as Gabe got himself upright and stood on the dock. He could see nothing to stop him from following his heart.

Father, turn me aside if a future with Larkyn is not your will. But if you want to bless us in marriage, then open the way. Show her it's your plan.

His moves now in God's hands, Gabe headed home. The next step would be tricky.

With time on her hands, Larkyn finally got around to having Dena over to her house. They'd done a quick tour and were ready to sit for a minute.

"It's taken me too long to do this, but thanks for coming." She turned off the kettle and filled a plate with the last of her homemade cookies.

Dena rubbed her temples. "I'm trying to finish another quilt in time for Christmas, but I'm glad you called. My eyes needed a rest. I think I need new glasses."

The scent of peppermint rose with the steam as Larkyn poured.

Dena sampled a gingerbread man. "How are you doing with that young man of yours?"

Larkyn dunked her teabag. "We made up. He helped me buy my Christmas tree and put the lights on it."

"Mm. It's a very handsome tree." Dena chewed. In a moment, she spoke again. "Did you get far in the Book of John?"

"I read it all. I'm reading lots of things now. I can't believe how easy it is to understand."

Dena's smile grew wider. "It depends on which translation you read. The Bible I gave you reads more like we talk today."

Larkyn nibbled a cookie and stared at the tree.

"I can tell there's something on your mind, sweetie. Why don't you tell me what it is." Dena's pale eyes missed nothing, new glasses or not.

Where to begin? "You remember why I was angry before? What brought on the fight with Gabe?"

Dena nodded. "He spoke about forgiving."

Larkyn scrunched her nose. Indeed. She'd been so offended. "There have been developments. After Gabe and I made up, we found Matthew's camera. Did I tell you about the camera?"

Dena puckered her brow. "No, but keep going."

"Okay. We realized Matthew might have had a camera on his helmet, and we found it." Larkyn clapped her hands together. "We took it to the police, who captured a picture of the woman my boss was with when the accident happened. When the police went to see him a second time, he made up more lies. I had quit my job before that, but it turns out his wife had questions. She looked into their finances and found evidence of the affair. I don't know how much I can say without breaking a confidence, but the result is his wife knows the truth, and she's going to confront him."

Dena's wide eyes held a twinkle. "Wow. I'd say God's been at work, wouldn't you?"

Larkyn blinked. She hadn't thought God worked that way.

"Honey, there are no coincidences when God's involved. Don't you remember what we talked about? You turned your boss over to God. Then you forgave Gabe. Those were two important steps of obedience."

Tears pooled in Larkyn's eyes. "I can't believe all this happened because I had faith."

Dena's soft pink cheeks rounded with her smile. Larkyn snatched a tissue from the box on the counter and dabbed at her eyes. "God's been helping me do this, hasn't he?"

"Yes, he has." Dena's smile grew wider. "He's always for us even if we don't get the result we expect or the timing we want."

"I think Gabe was trying to tell me that." Larkyn sipped tea that had gone lukewarm. "It seems I've fallen in love with him. It's a little scary."

Dena clapped a hand over her heart. "You and that handsome soldier? My lands, what a blessing."

Larkyn's face warmed as her smile spread out of control. "God will help us together, right?"

Dena laughed. "If you two put God at the center, you'll be fine, even through the rough spots." She peeked into her empty cup and moved to stand. "I hate to rush but I need to get back to quilting. This good news has spurred me on." She fanned herself in jest.

Larkyn cocked her head. "Maybe I'm just a worrywart, but good things make me nervous too."

"Good or bad, God is with you, honey. Just talk to him and remember to read his Word. Trust will grow."

Trust had grown already. Had it started with the tree or Gabe? Larkyn shook her head at the miracle of it all.

CHAPTER FORTY

Larkyn could hardly wait to see Gabe's face when he saw the gift she was getting him for Christmas. Past the big-screen TVs, each one displaying the same program in scintillating color, she found the department for smaller electronics. Like a safari hunter, she sighted the photography section and zeroed in. Not thirty-five-millimeter, not point and shoot, she searched for her target—wearable action video cameras.

"May I help you, miss?" Doug's name tag was pinned to the company's bright blue vest, which he wore over a perma-press, button-up shirt with black pants and Converse sneakers. Add the trendy, spiked hair, and she'd found just the person she needed. A nerd of the highest caliber.

"Do you have GoPro cameras or something similar?" She sounded intelligent, right?

Doug's eyes brightened. "This way. I love those things. I've had three. Anything you want in particular?"

"Just something a person on a bicycle could use to make a video." She wasn't an aficionado. Hopefully, Doug didn't hold it against her.

"We have the HERO3+ and the just-released HERO4. Black or silver?" Her guide spoke over his shoulder as he led her to a locked case.

What would Gabe like? "Black, I guess. Does it matter?" She queried as only the naive might do.

Doug began with size and weight, then picked up speed with frames per second, battery life, resolution, Bluetooth, and WiFi connectivity. She lost track with all the choices.

"Newer models are coming out all the time. HERO5, scheduled for release soon, will have an app called GoProQuik so users can share and edit more easily." He barely took a breath before continuing. "You'll need a helmet mount. What about frame mounts? Then you could use two cameras."

Her budget wasn't unlimited, but Larkyn wanted Gabe to have everything he needed. With the camera she'd promised tied up in police custody, providing another one was the least she could do.

"Doug?" Larkyn cast the lists of features aside since she didn't understand them anyway. "I need your help. Can we put together the basics for producing a good quality video without bankrupting me?"

All Doug's whitened teeth showed. "You bet. I know exactly what you need."

Half-an-hour later, a satisfied and excited Larkyn sauntered out of the store carrying a bulging plastic bag. Christmas shoppers jammed the parking lot, coming and going at a steady pace. Counting her blessings that this deed was done, she tucked the parcel on the floor of the back seat and geared up for fighting the traffic.

Her cell phone chirped. Without looking at the screen, she answered. "Hello."

"Larkyn, this is Trudy Hamilton. I'm glad I caught you."

Whoa. Larkyn's eyes closed as bees swarmed her stomach. A one-word prayer popped into her head. *Help.*

"Larkyn? Are you there?"

It was almost five p.m. The end of a normal workday. "I am."

"I know you're upset. I don't blame you." Trudy's voice sounded curiously vulnerable. "Would you give me a chance to explain some things?"

The bees buzzed off. Trudy wasn't her boss anymore. She was just a woman with an unfaithful husband. A person Larkyn was glad not to be. "I'm listening." She used a moderated tone. Open. Not eager, not hostile.

"Are you free to meet me for coffee? I'd like to talk in person."

Did she want to? She had a choice. But news from the source could not be ignored. "Okay, I can do that. Where would you like to meet?"

"Madeline's?"

No, thank you. She wasn't about to ruin Madeline's with this unpleasant business. "What about Caribou Coffee? I just finished shopping nearby."

Trudy agreed. Larkyn had fifteen minutes to prepare herself.

Larkyn arrived first. Glad to have a moment to absorb the choices on the menu board, she scanned the seasonal beverages. Peppermint mocha, Cinnamon-Eggnog Latte, nope. Save those for a happy occasion. A plain Americano with room for cream suited the seriousness of this meeting.

A few minutes later, Trudy entered, obviously just from work. Her fitted gray skirt and jacket set off by a sapphire blouse and silver earrings set her apart from the rest of the clientele. Larkyn's black denims and trusty fleece pullover blended well.

"Thank you for meeting me." Trudy pulled her wallet from her handbag and spoke decisively. "A medium-sized dark roast, please."

Larkyn's repertoire for awkward situations didn't give her much to work with, but the barista announced her drink so she claimed it from the counter and said, "I'll go grab us a table."

A stop for some half-and-half and a generous sprinkling of cinnamon sugar followed by a sweep of the room revealed no vacant tables, but two plump armchairs in the alcove would be even better.

From her comfy chair, Larkyn observed Trudy's approach. Her former boss fussed with the business of sitting down and placing her cup in a suitable spot before she seemed able to look at Larkyn. If the woman was nervous, it had to be a first. Eventually, Trudy forced a smile and addressed the reason for the meeting.

"I went to see Faye Arthur last weekend and found out she was telling the truth."

Okay. Right to the point. Larkyn kept her face impassive. No one needed to know she was already aware of the trip.

"The question," Trudy continued with a return of confidence in her voice, "is what are we going to do now?"

Larkyn held her tongue from blurting the obvious, though her teeth pinched her lower lip. *Uh, confess, maybe?*

Trudy dropped her gaze again. "Did you know that Faye had a child?"

Larkyn swallowed hot coffee. "She told me, yes."

Trudy's expression revealed her surprise. Suspicion laced the questions she fired back. "When? How did you know all this?"

Larkyn unloaded the explanations she'd never had the chance to share. "I ran into Faye by accident. She came to my house. We were catching up on our lives since she'd left H&H."

"And she just so happened to tell you about this thing that happened on the road?" Trudy's lips pressed in a line.

"No." Larkyn drew the syllable out, her temper in check, but barely. "Faye wasn't out to say anything to anyone, but she asked where Matthew was. She didn't even know he'd died." Did Trudy see there was no *plot*? "When I told her how it happened, she realized she'd been at the scene. Everything fit." Larkyn scowled. "I thought this was a friendly meeting."

Trudy looked taken aback. "Yes, it is. I'm not accusing you or Faye. I just wondered how you became involved."

Oh, really? Larkyn had learned a thing or two in the past couple of months. "I became *involved* by accident as I said. We made the connection in the course of our conversation." She clipped her sentences off in quick succession. "I expected Faye to report her role in the hit and run. I also wanted her to tell the police she was pregnant. But she refused to take a chance that Martin would find out about his child and want to become involved. Searching for the camera was happenstance as well."

Dena's words popped into her head. *No coincidences with God.* "If you want to know who's behind all this, I think it's God."

Trudy looked stricken. Larkyn's boldness surprised even her. After a moment, during which the pounding of Larkyn's heart subsided, Trudy nodded slowly.

"This is helpful. I've been struggling with my response to what I've found." She held the disposable cup in both hands as if to warm them. "I've heard enough to convince me Faye told the truth, and I've made a decision. If Martin won't own up to his actions, he needs an ultimatum."

Was this where the paternity test came in? Poor Faye. Or maybe not. Not if God was in charge.

Trudy wilted with a heartbreaking slump to her proud shoulders. "Either Martin confesses about what happened, or I will dissolve our partnership in the firm and file for divorce."

Larkyn crossed her arms and squeezed, caught between her elation and Trudy's obvious pain. She shouldn't be happy. Trudy's wounds were fresh and painful.

Her former friend and mentor pulled a tissue from her bag. "It might be the only language he'll understand."

Trudy dabbed at her eyes. "I'm sorry you had to endure all this, my dear." With an ironic laugh, she added, "To think we became friends because of Matthew's death. Now I find out—" She swallowed as a tear spilled down her cheek.

Larkyn wasn't completely immune to mercy. She touched the arm of her adversary. "I'm sorry too, Trudy. You're a victim in this as well."

"I don't feel like a victim. I feel like I'm partly to blame for not confronting my husband long ago with the missing pieces in our marriage." She blew quietly into her tissue and patted her cheeks with a delicate touch to preserve her make-up. "Instead, I turned to my relationship with my sister and her family, to my job, and to you, actually. I let Martin do as he pleased. I settled for a successful business partnership without a personal one."

Larkyn's shock at Trudy's honesty gave way to the weight of the truth. Infidelity, a child conceived. A man's death. People divorced for less. Didn't it serve him right? "How could he work with me right there and never say a word?"

Trudy gave her a half-hearted shrug. "You might also ask how he could sleep in the same bed with me while carrying on with someone in the office. Our whole life was a lie."

How devastating. But no more than Larkyn's wreckage. She turned the conversation abruptly. "Faye was so afraid he'd want to exercise his rights with Mallory."

"I wouldn't worry about that." Grief came back into Trudy's voice and sadness to her eyes. "He won't. I promised Faye I wouldn't bother them either. I have no claim to the child."

Her last simple statement seemed to be the hardest. But no wonder. She'd given up having a family for the business. Then her husband fathered a child. She probably longed for a grandchild at this stage, but Mallory didn't belong to her and never would.

Trudy tucked the knot of used tissue into her empty cup and reached for her bag. "Depending on the charges, Martin will be disciplined by the North Carolina Bar. The firm will be under my control, assuming it survives. I'd be glad to have you back."

Thankfully, Larkyn was sitting down. Her face must have shown everything passing through. Dismay, gratitude for the truth, confusion by the offer.

"Just keep that thought for later." Trudy gave her a little pat and pushed herself to her feet.

Larkyn watched Trudy's back as she crossed the coffee shop and exited through the door. The woman had strength, but it seemed that Trudy had both shrunk then grown since she first strode in.

CHAPTER FORTY-ONE

Larkyn's reaction to Gabe's proposal was pretty much what he'd expected.

"You what?" Her turquoise eyes turned stony, though they never lost their beauty in the midst of those lovely lashes.

"I want to meet your parents." He reiterated calmly as if speaking to a person with hearing loss.

"No. That's a bad idea, Gabe." Catching the determination in his expression, she added. "You don't know them."

He grinned. "And that's the point, right?" Two points for team DeSantis.

She eyed him as if he'd suggested jumping off a cliff together. "You don't want to know them, believe me."

Okay, so this was harder than expected. "Why wouldn't I? They brought you into the world, didn't they?"

Was that red in her cheeks good or bad? In light of her increasing hyperventilation, he couldn't tell.

"Gabe. I mean it. My parents are snobs. I don't want them to insult you. Besides, I'm always depressed after being with them."

"Sweetheart." He pulled out all the stops, bringing her into his arms despite the troublesome gear shift. "It's important to me, okay? I'd like you to meet my family too."

The fight in her shoulders receded as she molded to the curvature of his side.

"How about this weekend?" He pressed the advantage. "We'll go wherever you want to after. Dinner, shopping. You name it."

"Bribery?" She pushed away, back to her own space again. "You want to meet them that bad?"

"Yes," he'd said with conviction.

Two days later, December the twentieth, here they were, headed to Chapel Hill for the moment she dreaded. He tuned the radio to the Christmas song station to ease the stress emanating from the passenger seat. Great. A little "Holly, Jolly, Christmas." Just what the occasion called for.

When Gabe turned into the neighborhood, some of his nonchalance hit a speed bump. Serious wealth and status exuded from every gated entry. An award-winning architect and a history professor. What had he gotten into?

"That one." Larkyn sat forward like a setter on point as Gabe steered onto the brick-paved drive and climbed to the Georgian mansion she'd described as a museum. The lawn was perfect, as were the trees and bushes. This was home?

Gabe parked outside the separate three-car garage that hosted gabled windows above. An apartment for the chauffeur? Surely not, but his heart hadn't pounded this way since he'd first tried to walk using parallel bars.

"You ready?" He took her hand and squeezed. "Remember all you've overcome. Can't be worse than facing that boss of yours."

She gave him a shaky smile. "I learned to turn them off, before. Now it feels like we're here for their approval. Why do we have to do this, Gabe?"

He straightened his shoulders and spine. Stood tall in his khaki slacks and gray sweater. "You, we, are not inferior, sweetie. We came to honor your parents for their position and for what they did in raising you. We're not begging for acceptance. There has to be something good in them because you turned out amazing."

He overcame her dragging feet with an arm around her waist but halted before they mounted the steps to the porch. Tilting her face up with his finger to look at him, he repeated. "You're so much stronger than the little child that lived here, darling. Believe me?"

Her eyes gleamed with pooling tears, but she nodded.

"Father God," the words leaped to Gabe's tongue. "Remind Larkyn that she belongs to you now. She has nothing to fear with you in her heart."

Larkyn beamed a tremulous smile and accepted the seal of his kiss.

It didn't feel right to ring the doorbell, but it didn't feel right to barge in either. Fortunately, her mother opened the door before she had to decide.

"Welcome." Evelyn Baxter chirped in a voice that conveyed the same.

Larkyn ducked her head, then brought her gaze to her mother's piercing green eyes. The jab she expected didn't come.

"Hello, Mom. This is Gabriel DeSantis. Gabe, my mother, Evelyn Baxter."

So formal. Larkyn took a breath. Gabe looked fabulous. Even his shoes were shined.

Evelyn offered her slender, bejeweled hand extending from the sleeve of her undoubtedly cashmere sweater. "Pleased to meet you, Gabriel."

"Gabe is fine." He shook her hand with a nod that hinted at a bow and dropped his arm to his side. His stance evoked the image of a soldier standing at ease before his commander, dress uniform and all.

Her mother seemed a bit taken for the moment until her father stepped up.

"Good evening, Gabe. I'm Peter. A pleasure to meet you."

"Sir." They went through the shaking ritual, and Gabe maintained his bearing, respectful, but not stiff, while Larkyn looked on, her heart aflutter, observing this from the wings.

"Come in." Her mother retook control and ushered them to the den where the traditional tree stood in all its artificial glory amid the leather furniture and bound volumes of her father's favorite tomes of the past. This was where she'd hidden under the tree as a child, staring up into the branches and lights, absorbing their magic with wonder. "Have a seat. Would you like some mulled cider or coffee?"

"Come on, Evelyn." Her father pshawed. "How about a Scotch, young man?"

Larkyn glanced at Gabe. They'd never drunk liquor together. Maybe he liked it.

"Cider's fine. How about you, Larkyn?" He surreptitiously squeezed her fingers from his place beside her.

"Sure, Mom. Cider sounds good."

Her mother left, and the room felt emptier. Larkyn had never realized how large her mother's presence loomed, even greater than her dad's.

Gabe squinted over his shoulder at the bookshelves. "I see you have books on the history of war. Have you read Anthony Beevor's *Stalingrad*?"

Her father beelined to a place on his shelves and pulled a copy. "Right here." He extended the copy to Gabe who rose to meet him. "Groundbreaking book. Marvelous. How did you hear of it?"

"I read it for a college class before I enlisted." Gabe kept it simple.

Larkyn observed with awe a side beneath the easygoing guy. An extremely literate soldier she hadn't yet encountered.

When her mother returned with a tray, the men were in discussion. "Leave the boy alone, Peter." She admonished her husband.

"Not a boy, I'd say," her father countered. "This young man's an Army combat veteran. Infantry to be exact."

Larkyn exchanged a glance with Gabe, her brows lifted, along with the corner of her mouth. "Way to go," she mouthed discretely, as even Evelyn ceased fussing over the refreshments. Some sort of horrendous fruit cake.

The men rejoined them as her mother served, and Gabe sat close to Larkyn. They took the red cocktail napkins handed to them. *Happy Holidays from the Baxters*.

"Thank you for introducing us to your young man, Lorna. It's nice to know what's going on in your life."

Larkyn choked on her cider, immediately covering her mouth with her napkin. When she could swallow, she reset the cup in its saucer. No one seemed to have noticed. Whew.

"Tell me where the two of you met, Gabriel, dear."

Peter rolled his eyes at his wife but didn't correct her again.

"Yes, ma'am," Gabe said, cool as could be. "We met at an engagement party for some mutual friends. The groom is my cousin. I've been living with him since my discharge."

Her mother listened and opened her mouth with a follow-up when Larkyn jumped in. "Gabe didn't plan to leave the Army, but he got injured during his second tour in Afghanistan. He was awarded a Purple Heart."

At least Peter acted impressed. "Thank you, Gabe, for your service. I'm proud to make your acquaintance and delighted our daughter brought you to meet us."

"He asked me to, Dad." She said, eager to show them Gabe's character. "He insisted."

Evelyn couldn't seem to help herself. "What sort of injury did you receive?"

Really, Mom? Larkyn took the lead before Gabe could make some humble disclaimer. "He lost his leg. A bomb blew it off above his knee."

From this blunt announcement, the conversation roved. From the upcoming end of the NATO coalition and its replacement, Operation Resolute Support, to the rules of engagement forced upon soldiers like Gabe, and finally politics—a minefield he advanced through intact though Larkyn's jaws ached with the pressure endured by her molars.

Later, on the drive home in the truck, they enjoyed a laugh.

"I hope that was worth it." She faced him as far as her seatbelt would allow.

"Hey, they're not so bad. I could get along with your dad." Gabe glanced in his mirrors as they merged onto Interstate 40. Then he flashed a wicked grin. "I have to ask you something, though, before our relationship goes any further."

Uh-oh. He was kidding, right? Larkyn braced just in case.

"Why did your mom call you Lorna?"

She slapped at his leg before her hands flew to her face. "You monster. I was hoping that would slip by."

"Come on. You hafta tell me." He gave her a look designed to melt her heart. Which wasn't all that hard after his brilliant performance for her parents. Except it wasn't a performance. It was real. And dazzling.

"It's my legal name. Lorna Kaye Baxter. Satisfied?" She huffed and crossed her arms.

Gabe snickered. He could be a lot like Cisco. She ought to tell him that.

"I'm sorry." He smothered his grin much too late to be effective.

"I can tell," she scoffed. "It's just like my mom to embarrass me."

Gabe's face lost its humor. He shot her another glance. "You think that's why she did it?"

"Why else would she?"

"It depends." He steered past a lumbering flatbed loaded with pipes. "Where did Lorna come from?"

Larkyn shrugged. "A list of the world's worst baby names?" Silence. He didn't believe her? "If you really want to know, I think it might have come from a great-aunt on my father's side."

"Well, there ya go." Gabe gloated. "It's a family name. Plenty of weird ones running around. Did you know Cisco's full name is Francisco Apollo?"

Larkyn's pout collapsed with a squeak. "Really? D'you think Sara knows?"

"She does. But don't say anything. He's very sensitive."

Larkyn chuckled. "Thank you, Gabe. You're right about everything. That's one thing I can forgive my mom for, I guess."

"Only the one?"

She groaned. "This forgiveness thing is getting out of hand, don't you think?"

"Hey, I didn't make the rules. I just know obeying them brings about good."

Why was he always right?

CHAPTER FORTY-TWO

Gabe and Larkyn merged with the stream of people scuttling through the blustery wind and entered an immense modern structure. Its soaring windows cast a bright welcome to the crowds on Christmas Eve. According to Pancho, Discipleship Church served the community in multiple ways, from their food pantry to healing ministry, from pregnancy support to housing the homeless, *and* literacy classes.

Whew. With so much outreach to the community, did they have time to be still before the Lord?

Not up to him to judge, Gabe knew. His AVA friends had been urging him to come and see for himself. Fair enough. He'd come.

When they crossed the threshold and paused inside, Larkyn's gloved fingers let go of his hand as she attempted to restore order to her hairstyle. Gabe loved the soft feathery hair she complained about at times. Who cared if it flew in every direction? Having escaped the wind, it fell into place as she raked her fingers through from underneath. Tonight, she had one side clipped in a black barrette with sparkly, diamond-y things that exposed small, black-pearl earrings dangling from her earlobes.

"You're beautiful." His whisper earned him a nervous smile.

"This church is beautiful," she whispered back. "Look at the greenery."

How could he miss it? Lavish garlands of cedar and magnolia leaves draped the entrance. Huge wreaths adorned each pair of doors leading to the sanctuary, and candles jutted up from clusters of holly on every windowsill.

Observing the crowd, he steered Larkyn with his hand on the small of her back. "Let's find a seat while we can."

A young usher of about fifteen, judging by her braces, handed them a program. "Merry Christmas," she recited with a smile.

"Merry Christmas," Larkyn replied as they moved on.

She took an audible breath at the sight of the imposing auditorium housing rows and rows of theater seats on two levels. Impressive. The stage was dimly lit at the moment, but chairs and a few large instruments rested to one side. Two large screens hung left and right for the benefit of those in the back. Guess it didn't matter where they sat, but the front seemed better so it wouldn't feel like watching on TV.

Gabe led them down the gentle, carpeted incline past rows where most of the seats had been staked out with Bibles and programs. Not impressive. But eventually, he sighted a vacant pair. The couple seated next to them smiled hello and went back to their conversation. Larkyn shrugged out of her coat, leaving the red scarf to hang around her neck. Gabe's jacket had stayed in the truck, since his bulky pullover sweater alone would bring on a sweat.

They people-watched as the rows filled with regular folks, old and young, fancy and casual, in animated chatter or silently hunting a seat.

Larkyn edged closer and spoke from behind her hand. "I pictured something more like *Little House on the Prairie.* Pretty silly."

"We could find a little church, sweetheart." Gabe laid his arm across the back of her seat as if she belonged to him. A pleasing tremor coursed through him. Once he'd stopped second-guessing himself, his whole spirit, soul, and body urged him to move ahead.

"I didn't mean that." She smiled up at him, then allowed herself to resettle in the shelter of his arm. "I'm nervous, I guess."

Gabe squeezed her gently. "This is new for me too." He hadn't been to a church since meeting Jesus, but he and Cisco had been forced to attend Midnight Mass every Christmas Eve growing up. The gold had been beautiful. Lots of gold and marble.

Larkyn nudged him. Musicians in formal wear filed in from the side and filled empty seats on the platform. Two violinists. A fellow to play the bass. Horns, percussion, piano, cello, followed by guitars and keyboards.

"Honey, look." Larkyn had been reading her program. "We're singing these carols along with the Nativity story."

Gabe read. "O Come, O Come Immanuel," "Silent Night," "Hark the Herald Angels Sing," and "Joy to the World." The songs punctuated Scripture readings from the Old and New Testaments. After that, the pastor would speak, and the service would end with "O Holy Night."

The orchestra tuned up, and Gabe's heartbeat quickened. The conductor turned to face the audience and spoke a welcome. The lights dimmed. A young boy came to the lectern and read. "For unto us a Child is born. Unto us a Son is given. And the government will be upon his shoulder. And his name will be called Wonderful, Counselor, Mighty God, Everlasting Father, Prince of Peace." Everyone stood to sing.

Maybe it was the haunting minor key of the first carol or the sweeping power of the instruments together, but

Gabe's throat closed with a lump that barely let him croak the words. He'd been in a church for Christmas most of his life, but tonight was vastly different.

He'd had his share of disappointments, but until exploding metal tore into his body, he hadn't experienced the reality of Jesus. Another miracle stood beside him.

Larkyn had a death grip on his forearm. The hand that shared the program with him trembled. Did anyone else feel the hope and power in the words they were singing?

"Rejoice! Rejoice! Immanuel shall come to thee, O Israel."

The Messiah had come. Their lives were redeemed from tragic loss, and Gabe couldn't wait to begin the future.

Where was Gabe going? He'd turned the wrong way. Before Larkyn could ask, he answered.

"I'm taking you to a nice restaurant for dinner. I promised that once, and we never went."

"It's okay, honey. Everything's so expensive."

"Call it a Christmas present then." The glance he cut her way brooked no argument. "We're dressed up nice. It's Christmas Eve. Let me do this, please."

"If you put it that way." She gave him a flirty smile. "I'd love a romantic dinner for Christmas. I didn't bring your present, though. It's under my tree."

Gabe lifted his brows with a suggestive smile. "I'd love to come over in the morning. With Cisco gone to see Sara's parents, I'll be on my lonesome."

"We can't have that now, can we?" Larkyn grinned. A leisurely brunch had been her plan followed by watching him open his gift. "It just so happens that a sausage, egg, and hashbrown casserole is doing its thing in my fridge this very moment.”

Satisfied that tomorrow morning was settled, Larkyn watched for signs of a fancy restaurant. In the country? A few more miles down the quiet highway, Gabe signaled his turn, and they passed through an open gate. The tires crunched along a gravel drive bounded on both sides by a split rail fence festooned with little white lights. What was this place? The drive ended at the parking lot, where more lights strung overhead created a magical aura.

Gabe opened the door for Larkyn and took her hand. They climbed two steps to the covered porch of a rustic building decked with garlands of pine tied with red ribbon bows. Inside they were greeted and shown to their table in a cozy, private corner near a cheerfully crackling fire.

“This is so nice.” Larkyn crossed her ankles under her chair and whispered. “How did you find it?”

“Let’s just say someone suggested it for special occasions.” Across the white linen tablecloth, the light cast a warm glow on his handsome features. Gabe’s eyes sparkled. How did she belong here with him?

They dined on steaks, grilled shrimp, and mushroom risotto with asparagus on the side. Yet Larkyn’s thoughts were scattered. So many firsts this Christmas Eve.

“What did you think of the church?” She tentatively broached the subject that had her preoccupied.

“It was good.” Gabe trimmed the tail from one of his shrimp before dipping it in butter. “It’s hard to mess up Christmas Eve.”

At her silence, he continued. “Okay, yes. I liked it. Found myself thinking about the ways I’ve been blessed this year.”

“I know.” She leaned forward. “Me too. The pastor reminded me that we celebrate the birth of a baby, but the baby grew up to die for us. Dena and I talked about this, but it seems more real tonight."

Gabe swallowed and took a sip of water. Since he seemed content to listen, she finished her thought.

"It's sad, but his death was the only way we could return to God. He adopts us, Gabe. We're like his family. And with the life of Jesus in us, we can change the world."

Gabe stopped eating and focused on her face. "Why do you think the world hasn't changed that much?"

Larkyn narrowed her eyes. "Is that a trick question?"

"What? No. I mean it."

She leaned forward, both elbows on the table. "Satan didn't give up, Gabe. He fights to keep what he can. Dena says that a lot of Christians don't realize the war we're in. We have good lives. We're comfortable ..." Her voice trailed off. She was a perfect example of being content with Matthew as her crutch. She had no use for God and blamed him for letting Matthew be hurt. But it wasn't God. It was a series of evil choices that created the situation.

Gabe took one of her hands in his. "I can't believe we're having this conversation. Do you know how much *you've* changed?"

"Before you get too impressed," she wrinkled her nose. "I like being forgiven, but as you know, I'm not as keen to forgive."

The waiter appeared and reached in to refill their glasses. "How're you folks doing?"

"Great." Gabe gave him a mysterious nod, then smiled at Larkyn with a tad of mischief. "I wonder how Cisco's doing with Sara's family. His future mother-in-law has booked them for a couple's shower given by her cronies."

She had to laugh at Cisco's pain. Men could be so uncivilized. On the other hand, they were brave and did things she never wanted to touch. Like killing roaches.

When their plates were removed, the waiter presented slices of Buche de Noel, a lovely dessert made of chocolate cake rolled up with cream filling and frosted to resemble a yule log. Each piece sported an edible holly leaf and red berries. Next to Larkyn's portion, the waiter placed a small, foil-wrapped box topped with a shiny bow.

"What's this?" She sat back.

"It's the rest of your present."

Oh, dear. Was this what it looked like? Maybe not—but he'd asked to meet her parents. She wasn't ready. Or was she? Was there a way to be sure?

The thoughts zinging through her mind had to show on her face.

Gabe spoke with sudden gentleness. "It's safe to open it, sweetheart."

She unclenched her hands that had fled to her lap and took the shiny box. Fumbling with the bow, her fingers gained some coordination as she loosened the perfect folds in the wrap and peeled it away.

Breathe, she admonished herself as she removed the lid and lifted the cotton batting.

Oh!

On the bed of cotton underneath lay a gold band without a stone. With a pounding in her chest, she gingerly lifted it from its nest and gazed at the intricate whorls and tiny scrolls of exquisite silver filigree.

Gabe took the ice-cold fingers of her left hand and warmed them against his cheek. He pressed them to his lips and cleared his throat. She dared to meet his gaze.

"This was my mother's ring. She stopped wearing it when my father left our family, but she kept it. When I was home for Thanksgiving, she gave it to me for the special woman she was sure would come into my life." He squeezed her hand. "I'd spoken of you so I'm not sure if she saw the future or just knew there would come a day."

Larkyn soaked up every word. Never had she imagined she would be in this place again.

"I'm not asking you to decide if you're not ready. But I love you, Larkyn. I'm asking you to marry me. I'll be here until you know for sure."

Giddy relief made her head swim. It wasn't that she didn't love Gabe, didn't know how fantastic it would be to marry him. She just couldn't latch on like a dependent child the way she'd done before.

Expectancy filled his face, as his tender brown eyes drew her in.

She wasn't the same as she'd been before. She had God now. It wasn't all up to her to do it right.

Gabe believed. He trusted and he was willing to wait. Was that her answer?

Her smile stretched so wide it hurt. "Dear Gabe. I love you, and I would love to wear this precious ring." Her throat closed as her eyes filled with tears. "I don't need to wait." Her head bobbed, and the words broke free. "Yes! Yes, I will marry you."

Gabe tried to reach her for a kiss, but the seating didn't help. He left his chair and pulled her to her feet, taking her in his arms. "I didn't plan this very well," he murmured as the rest of the patrons clapped for what came after.

"You did it perfectly," she said, beaming through joyful tears.

CHAPTER FORTY-THREE

Gabe kept glancing at Larkyn. In silence, she stared out the window into the dark, stopped to look at her ring, then stared some more. She'd placed it on her left hand as an engagement ring, though it lacked a proper diamond. What was going on in that beautiful head? Second thoughts? After a mile or two, she angled toward him in her seat.

"Gabe? Are you in a hurry?"

Relieved that she was talking, he answered quickly. "Nothing waiting for me, sweetheart, except an empty house. What do you have in mind?"

"I want to go to Trudy's house, but it's in the other direction."

Gabe slowed the truck, looking for a place to turn. "I can take you there, no problem. Do you want to call first? What if she's not there?"

"I'm almost certain she *won't* be there. I'm hoping Martin will." The tremor in her voice suggested otherwise.

He pulled into the empty lot of an auto parts store closed for Christmas Eve and braked. "Whoa, you want to see Martin Hamilton?"

Without raising her head she nodded. "Yes."

Gabe let the engine idle, his left wrist across the top of the steering wheel. "Do you mind explaining why?"

"Oh." She looked directly at him now. "You don't get it? Don't you remember the fight we had? You said I should take the high road and not get bitter, but I was too angry. All I could do was hate him."

Oh, yeah. The fight. He'd just about blown his chance at a relationship with Larkyn that night. "I remember."

"I went to Dena's the next day, and she showed me in the Bible how Martin's in the darkness and what would happen if he didn't come into the light. She helped me see how I could turn him over to God." Larkyn gave a little shrug. "And then we found the camera."

Gabe blew out his breath. "I guess I owe a lot to Dena." His own words had created a mess. Someone wiser had cleaned it up.

She offered him a tender smile. "The service tonight convinced me. I need to remember why Jesus came."

She looked directly at him, and resolve filled her next words. "What Trudy said about divorcing him if he didn't come clean? It made me happy. Like I'd won—and he would lose." She lifted her palms, empty. "Trudy's probably in Wilmington with her sister's family and Martin is all alone. He's trapped right now. If Trudy carries out her threat of the paternity test, Faye's story can be used in court. He'll likely become a convicted felon, divorced, and lose his license to practice law." Her eyes glistened. "Don't you see how terrible that is?"

They sat in the darkness of the cab. Most people had settled in by now. They saw very few lights from passing cars. Gabe took her hand. He softened his tone.

"Sure, it's awful, but he brought it on himself." Compassion was admirable, but it didn't change the fact that her boss had broken the law and someone died. "Actions have consequences."

"I know they do." She squeezed his fingers. "But Jesus bore all our consequences."

Gabe took a deep breath. Far be it from him to argue with the grace of God, especially after the stand he'd taken before. But grace didn't abolish punishment by legitimate authorities there for the good of society.

"A person can be forgiven, but they're still accountable, honey."

Larkyn sighed. "I know he's accountable and should be, but he still needs peace with God."

Gabe had no answer. She was right. She understood more than he imagined. "I love you, Larkyn. I truly do."

Her aquamarine eyes glossed over. A weak smile emerged. "If you turn around here, we need to go back to the second stoplight."

Gabe came with her to the door. Surely Martin wouldn't kick her off the porch with him there. Lights from the sprawling, contemporary house sitting on the golf course shined through closed plantation shutters. Larkyn had been here several times in the early weeks after the funeral when Trudy decided to be her friend. Tonight, she clutched Gabe's hand for strength as they waited for someone to answer.

Larkyn flinched when the door swung open. She sucked in a breath at the sight of her boss. Uncombed hair. A sloppily tied maroon smoking jacket revealed his white undershirt. He wore dark slacks and leather slippers. His hand held a glass of brown liquid.

His eyes grew wide, and his lips turned down as his gaze traveled from one visitor to the other. "What are you doing here?"

Father God, I need you now. Larkyn opened her lips with an inadequate answer. "May I talk to you, please?"

"You and who else?" Martin slurred his words a little. Someone else might not notice, but Larkyn knew his office voice.

She raised her hand to indicate Gabe. "This is Gabe DeSantis. He's here as my friend. I know it's Christmas Eve, but I only need a minute."

Martin leaned on the door frame and stared at Larkyn through slitted eyes. He appeared to vacillate between slamming the door and letting them in. *Father, I came. You sent me.*

"Christmas Eve, bah." His rendition of Scrooge hit close to the real thing. "Come in and get it over with."

Gabe held the storm door for Larkyn who stepped over the threshold first. Martin turned his back on them as he crossed the wide foyer into the spacious living room. An enormous tree stood before a wall of windows, its light reflecting off the glass. An uncapped bottle of Glenlivet stood on the coffee table and the muted big-screen TV flickered with a mindless commercial.

He dropped into his leather recliner without offering them a seat.

"Pour yourself a drink," he scoffed and gestured toward glasses on a tray across the room.

Larkyn chose a position on the leather sofa. Gabe stood guard near the bookcase, the three of them forming a triangle. His stance displayed the military bearing she'd observed with her father. His man-to-man posture, she supposed, thankful he'd agreed to support her on this awkward errand.

She cleared her throat. Water would be nice, but she didn't dare ask. "We've been to church—"

"Spare me, please." Martin interrupted with another huff of derision.

"No," Larkyn stated, from where she didn't know. "I will say what I came to say."

"Whatever." The silky sleeve of his jacket fell back as he flicked his wrist.

Haltingly, she began the speech she'd rehearsed to herself in the truck. "Christmas is about Christ coming to forgive mankind." Ignoring his eye roll, she forced herself to continue. "Tonight, I was impressed that all the bad things I've done no longer stand between me and God. I came to share that good news with you so you can know God loves you too."

"'Cause I'm such a lousy sinner?" Sarcasm and scotch made a noxious blend. But at least he'd listened.

Larkyn drew a breath. "We're all lousy sinners, Mr. Hamilton. You're no one special." The ad-lib came just as God had promised. No reply? She took it as her cue to continue. "I know the trouble you're in right now. I know that your lies are about to be exposed, and the truth will be clear to everyone."

He raised the glass to his lips and swallowed.

"What if you could be forgiven and have peace?"

"What if you got out of my house?"

How strange. The sting from the viper didn't hurt so much. It spurred her on. "I could leave. But I wonder if you want me to."

"Why would I want you to stay?" He sneered at her. "You and your pathetic religion. Just like my wife."

Larkyn looked with curious calm at this man she'd feared and loathed. He hated Trudy's faith? Had everything started there? How tragic that this deplorable man couldn't see how blessed he was. To the point that he'd let everything he'd built be trashed.

She glanced at Gabe who had to be silently praying. How else did she have the courage to say what she was about to? "I will leave, but first I have to tell you about meeting Gabe on the ground at the side of a road. I knocked him off his bike. With my car."

She paused to catch Martin's reaction but didn't see one.

"Thank goodness he was okay," she breathed, "but everything happened so fast. I felt sick. Horrible. Guilty. I couldn't believe I'd been so careless." Sharing it brought astonishing freedom. Her burden cast aside, she kept her face quiet as she waited for him to acknowledge her confession. Inside her heart was thumping. If he would only listen.

Seemingly tired of remaining silent, Martin kept his sarcastic edge. "Oh, what a sweet little story. Is that what I'm supposed to say?"

Larkyn didn't have a clue what would happen when she'd knocked on her boss's door. Not a display of drunkenness, for sure. The lawyer she knew could have shredded her if he'd been sober. Instead, they found the man behind the facade, the one Dena had described. Martin looked lonely and tortured by the state of his life. He'd probably been this way a long time or he wouldn't have gone after Faye in the first place.

"No." Larkyn shook her head, wondering if anything at all would come of this. "I wanted to say I forgive you. I understand how the accident happened. You never *meant* to hit anyone. I understand." She hoped he could appreciate the truth of her words. "What I don't understand is how you left my husband without calling for help. You broke the law to cover your affair. You kept up the lie for two years, knowing I was down the hall. Knowing your wife was my friend. But even that can be forgiven by God, the ultimate judge. He loves you, Mr. Hamilton. I hope you'll receive what he offers. I hope your soul will have the peace I've found. I'm not pathetic. I'm blessed and gloriously happy. I have God and this awesome man, Gabe, to love me. What do you have? What will be left when all this comes out?"

Martin's complexion had taken on a grayish hue. The flesh under his bloodshot eyes hung in dark folds. No longer the sharp executive, he looked like a defeated old man.

Larkyn glanced at Gabe again and lifted one shoulder a little. She was finished. *Time to go?*

Gabe's firm, masculine voice spoke for the first time. "Everyone has something they regret, sir. I hope you'll think about what Larkyn said. You're gonna have to face what you did, but how you face it will make a difference."

They left him staring at nothing—or possibly something in his heart. When they got to the edge of the room, Larkyn took her parting shot.

"I truly mean this, Martin. Have a Merry Christmas."

No explosion followed as they walked across the entry hall. Quietly, they let themselves out and pulled the door shut behind them.

CHAPTER FORTY-FOUR

MyoPro's New Year's Eve party had grown into quite the event since the last one Larkyn had attended. Employees, suppliers, doctors, PTs, and OTs, anyone associated with their prosthetics it seemed, had come to the Brighton Ballroom to celebrate. Out with the old, and in with the new. How perfect.

"Oh my gosh," Larkyn laughed at the gymnastic ability of a couple jitterbugging to "Rock Around the Clock." How could anyone dance like that after gorging on prime rib and crab legs?

"Yeah, just don't get any ideas." Cisco pretended to cover Sara's eyes.

"A girl can dream." Sara pushed his hand away and shimmied her shoulders, bare under the narrow straps of her black sequined dress.

"Come on then, my princess." Cisco stood in his rented tux. "Give me a slow song and I'll make your dreams come true."

A warm flush crept up Larkyn's neck. Now that she and Gabe were engaged, her imagination had become unruly. Cisco's suggestive comment had her reaching for her tea glass.

The object of her fantasies lounged in his chair, nursing a Pelligrino with lime, the tails of his bow tie hanging loose. Their gazes met, and his slow smile sent a thrill along her spine.

"How about you, Lorna Kay, my love? Any dreams behind those mysterious eyes?"

Her eyes were mysterious? Had to be the heavy shadow and mascara Sara had insisted this glamorous occasion required.

"Every single one has come true." She melted with his loving use of her hated given name. "Even some I didn't know I had."

"Ah." He reached for her hand and stroked the ring on her finger with his thumb. "The best kind of dreams can be the ones we didn't consider." He caressed her fingertips with a lingering kiss. "Never, ever did I imagine this. But I wouldn't want to be anywhere else."

She batted her mysterious lashes. "Let's keep it to Larkyn in public, shall we?"

Gabe's chuckle morphed into a cough as his face turned a shade of purple.

"Are you all right?" Larkyn leaned toward him, grinning.

"Yes." He nodded and took a sip from his glass. "I suppose I had that coming."

"You did. But I forgive you." Her heart sang with joy at their private joke. He loved her, and she loved him.

The band leader announced a new song, and Gabe turned serious. "I hear a slow one coming. Shall we see how I do on the dance floor?"

"Absolutely." Larkyn slipped her feet back into her strappy new shoes and straightened the sparkly netting over her wine-red skirt. Gabe's hand felt warm on her skin where the back of the dress took a plunge.

He turned her into a proper dance pose, and she could almost hear him count the beat before beginning. But the mechanics faded as the music swelled and swept them away on a cloud of smooth vocals from Elvis.

Fools rush in? No problem at all. She was delighted to be the most glorious kind of a fool over whatever the future might bring with Gabe.

They swayed, making easy progress under a canopy of silver and gold streamers and white balloons. Could anything be better than this?

As the last notes faded, Sara and Cisco sidled alongside. The ever-vigilant Cisco spoke from the side of his mouth. "There's been a surge for the dessert buffet. Ya wanna grab something before the good stuff's gone?"

Larkyn clutched Gabe's arm in exaggerated alarm. "Wow, we better hurry."

Sara giggled. "I wouldn't want to miss a single fat gram."

"Maybe we should check out the chocolate cake." Gabe gave her a heart-stopping wink. "I seem to remember that slab we had on our first date was pretty popular."

That disastrous date? The cake had been the highlight. But no, not really. Gabe had been a trooper even then. "All I did was talk about Matthew. How could you ever stand to see me again?"

They moseyed in the direction of the desserts. "If you recall, I had issues myself. I was glad we could talk about something real."

Hm. Yes, he'd been blaming himself for Josh's death. "Okay, so maybe we're even." Larkyn smiled up at his handsome face. Gabe in a tux was almost more than a girl could handle.

"Even about what?" Cisco caught the end of their conversation as they wound up in front of the cakes.

"Speaking of getting even." Sara joined them, a plate of tiramisu already in her hand. "I saw a story about the solving of a certain hit and run. A suspect confessed. I wonder who that could be."

Larkyn nodded as she selected a slice of double-chocolate layer cake as Gabe had predicted. "The detective called me. Martin's lawyers have negotiated a plea bargain. He gets weekends in jail, suspension of his license to practice law for a year, plus a bunch of community service. Trudy offered to give me my job back."

"You wouldn't do that, would you?" Sara adjusted her shape-hugging sequins before taking her seat.

Larkyn shrugged. "I told Gabe that hunting for a job feels about as fun as bungee jumping, but you're right. Even with Martin gone, I can't go back to that."

"I'm glad to hear that." Sara surveyed the room. "Did you see any coffee?"

"I'll get it. You too, Larkyn?" Gabe set his German Chocolate beside her plate.

"Yes, thank you. I like it—"

"With cream. We all know." Gabe grinned as he waved off her instructions and headed away.

Sara dabbed a bit of dessert from the corner of her mouth with her pinkie. "I hear Gabe loved his camera. He's excited to make his video."

"And I love my ring." Larkyn displayed it for her friend to admire.

Sara laughed. "You've shown it to me at least three times."

"I have? Oh, well." Larkyn turned her hand to catch how the light glistened on the polished gold and silver. "How did your mom's shower go?"

Sara grinned and leaned close on one elbow as Cisco delved into dessert. "It was fun. She invited couples who've been friends of theirs for years. The men gave gifts and advice to Cisco, and the women to me. It was hilarious but also sweet."

Larkyn leaned closer too. "I can hardly believe in four months you'll be Mrs. Francisco Amato."

"I know." Sara glowed. "My mom is so excited for me. Jean will be in touch soon about planning a bridesmaids' shower."

Gabe returned with the coffees. Larkyn lifted hers to her lips and swallowed the creamy warmth. Her fiancé didn't realize what could happen now that he'd put *her* mom in the picture, but the situation had changed. Together they would work to make sure this wedding was a happy family occasion.

At three minutes till midnight, a soulful version of "As Time Goes By" began to play. Everyone gathered on the dance floor.

The buzz of anticipation built as the time to ring in the new year approached. Sara bounced on her toes and clung to Cisco's arm.

Gabe took Larkyn's hands and faced her straight-on. His gaze searched out the thoughts behind her eyes. She didn't look away as the crowd began the countdown.

Ten, nine …

A year that had begun in such sadness was ending with miraculous hope.

Seven, six, five …

Gabe pulled her closer, keeping both hands captive in his. Her eyes drifted closed for a moment as she floated between heaven and earth.

Three, two, one …

Shouts rang out. The band struck up the familiar tune, and a few sang along. "Should old acquaintance be forgot …" Confetti sprinkled their heads and a cascade of balloons rained down.

It all disappeared in a dizzy swirl as Gabe softly brushed his lips to hers. When she opened her eyes, they spoke the language of her heart. *More … Please.*

He clutched her in a full embrace, wrecking her with a kiss that left her barely able to stand. When she caught her breath, Larkyn encircled his neck with her arms. "Wow. Happy New Year to you too, my love."

Gabe enfolded her again, lifting her feet from the ground. "Happy, happy New Year, sweetheart—always."

The End

ABOUT THE AUTHOR

Caroline Powers has always found it easier to process life through writing, a practice standing her in good stead through years of personal emotional healing and ministry to others. When the nudge to put her wisdom and insight into a novel became undeniable, learning to write fiction began.

Improving with the help of books, conferences, and peer critiques she completed several drafts of her novel and watched the plot evolve. *A Future and a Hope* was selected as a finalist in the Genesis Contest (Contemporary Romance category) for unpublished authors in 2022.

Caroline is a native of Denver, Colorado, but moved many times in the course of her early life. Her home for the last forty-five years has been in the Piedmont Triad of North Carolina with her husband, Dan. The two of them visit family frequently in Albuquerque/Placitas, New Mexico, and Houston, Texas. She loves sopapillas, chili rellenos, Texas brisket, and dark chocolate in any form. Caroline is a member of American Christian Fiction Writers and Word Weavers, International.

You can find her blog at carolinepowersauthor.com

www.ingramcontent.com/pod-product-compliance
Lightning Source LLC
Chambersburg PA
CBHW040802010826
48981CB00028B/75